E. & M.A. RADFORD
MURDER ISN'T CRICKET

EDWIN ISAAC RADFORD (1891-1973) and MONA AUGUSTA RADFORD (1894-1990) were married in 1939. Edwin worked as a journalist, holding many editorial roles on Fleet Street in London, while Mona was a popular leading lady in musical-comedy and revues until her retirement from the stage.

The couple turned to crime fiction when they were both in their early fifties. Edwin described their collaborative formula as: "She kills them off, and I find out how she done it." Their primary series detective was Harry Manson who they introduced in 1944.

The Radfords spent their final years living in Worthing on the English South Coast. Dean Street Press have republished three of their classic mysteries: *Murder Jigsaw, Murder Isn't Cricket* and *Who Killed Dick Whittington?*

E. & M.A. Radford Mysteries
Available from Dean Street Press

Murder Jigsaw

Murder Isn't Cricket

Who Killed Dick Whittington?

E. & M.A. RADFORD

MURDER ISN'T CRICKET

With an introduction by Nigel Moss

DEAN STREET PRESS

Published by Dean Street Press 2019

Copyright © 1946 E. & M.A. Radford

Introduction Copyright © 2019 Nigel Moss

All Rights Reserved

First published in 1946 by Andrew Melrose

Cover by DSP

ISBN 978 1 912574 73 5

www.deanstreetpress.co.uk

INTRODUCTION

DOCTOR HARRY MANSON is a neglected figure, unjustly so, amongst Golden Age crime fiction detectives. The fictional creation of husband and wife authors Edwin and Mona Radford, who wrote as E. & M.A. Radford, Manson was their leading series detective featuring in 35 of 38 mystery novels published between 1944 and 1972. A Chief Detective-Inspector of Scotland Yard and Head of its Crime Research Laboratory, Manson was also a leading authority on medical jurisprudence. Arguably the Radfords' best work is to be found in their early Doctor Manson series novels which have remained out of print since first publication. Commendably, Dean Street Press has now made available three novels from that early period – *Murder Jigsaw* (1944), *Murder Isn't Cricket* (1946), and *Who Killed Dick Whittington?* (1947) – titles selected for their strong plots, clever detection and evocative settings. They are examples of Manson at his finest, portraying the appealing combination of powerful intellect and reasoning and creative scientific methods of investigation, while never losing awareness and sensitivity concerning the human predicaments encountered.

The Radfords sought to create in Doctor Manson a leading scientific police detective, and an investigator in the same mould as R. Austin Freeman's Dr John Thorndyke. Edwin Radford was a keen admirer of the popular Dr Thorndyke novels and short stories. T.J. Binyon in *Murder Will Out* (1989), a study of the detective in fiction, maintains that the Radfords were protesting against the idea that in Golden Age crime fiction science is always the preserve of the amateur detective, and they wanted to be different. In the preface to the first Manson novel *Inspector Manson's Success* (1944), they announced: "We have had the audacity – for which we make no apology – to present here the Almost Incredible: a detective story in which the scientific deduction by a police officer uncovers the crime and the criminal entirely without the aid, ladies and gentlemen, of any outside assistance!" The emphasis is on Manson as both policeman and scientist.

The first two Manson novels, *Inspector Manson's Success* and *Murder Jigsaw* (both 1944), contain introductory prefaces which acquaint the reader with Doctor Manson in some detail. He is a man of many talents and qualifications: aged in his early 50s and a Cambridge MA (both attributes shared by Edwin Radford at the time), Manson is a Doctor of Science, a Doctor of Laws and author of several standard works on medical jurisprudence (of which he is a Professor) and criminal pathology. He is slightly over 6 feet in height, although he does not look it owing to the stoop of his shoulders, habitual in a scholar and scientist. His physiology displays interesting features and characteristics: a long face, with a broad and abnormally high forehead; grey eyes wide set, though lying deep in their sockets, which "have a habit of just passing over a person on introduction; but when that person chances to turn in the direction of the Inspector, he is disconcerted to find that the eyes have returned to his face and are seemingly engaged on long and careful scrutiny. There is left the impression that one's face is being photographed on the Inspector's mind." Manson's hands are often the first thing a stranger will notice. "The long delicate fingers are exceedingly restless – twisting and turning on anything which lies handy to them. While he stands, chatting, they are liable to stray to a waistcoat pocket and emerge with a tiny magnifying glass, or a micrometer rule, to occupy their energy."

During his long career at Scotland Yard, Manson rises from Chief Detective-Inspector to the rank of Commander; always retaining his dual role of a senior police investigating officer as well as Head of the Forensic Research Laboratory. Manson is ably assisted by his Yard colleagues – Sergeant Merry, a science graduate and Deputy Lab Head; and by two CID officers, Superintendent Jones ('the Fat Man of the Yard') and Inspector Kenway. Jones is weighty and ponderous, given to grunts and short staccato sentences, and with a habit of lapsing into American 'tec slang in moments of stress; but a stolid, determined detective and reliable fact searcher. He often serves as a humorous foil to Manson and the Assistant Commissioner. By contrast, Kenway is volatile and imaginative. Together, Jones and Kenway make a powerful combination and an effective resource for the Doctor. In later books, Inspector Holroyd features as Manson's regular assistant. Holroyd is the lead detective in the non-series title *The Six Men* (1958), a novelisation of the earlier British detective film of the same name, directed by Michael Laws and released in 1951, and based on an original story idea by the Radfords. Their only other non-series detective, Superintendent Carmichael, appeared in just two novels: *Look in at Murder* (1956, with Manson) and *Married to Murder* (1959). None of the Radford books was ever published in the USA.

The first eight novels, all Manson series, were published by Andrew Melrose between 1944 to 1950. The early titles were slim volumes produced in accordance with authorised War Economy Standards. Many featured a distinctive motif on the front cover of the dust wrapper – a small white circle showing Manson's head superimposed against that of Sherlock Holmes (in black silhouette), with the title 'a Manson Mystery'. In these early novels, the Radfords made much of their practice of providing readers with all the facts and clues to give them a fair opportunity of solving the riddle of deduction. They interspersed the investigations with 'Challenges to the Reader', tropes closely associated with leading Golden Age crime authors John Dickson Carr and Ellery Queen. In *Murder Isn't Cricket* they claimed: "We have never, at any time, 'pulled anything out of the bag' at the last minute – a fact upon which three distinguished reviewers of books have most kindly commented and have commended." Favourable critical reviews of their early titles were received from Ralph Straus (*Sunday Times*) and George W. Bishop (*Daily Telegraph*), as well as novelist Elizabeth Bowen. The Radfords were held in sufficiently high regard by Sutherland Scott, writing in his *Blood in their Ink* (1953), a study of the modern mystery novel, to be afforded special mention alongside such distinguished Golden Age authors as Miles Burton, Richard Hull, Milward Kennedy and Vernon Loder.

After 1950 there was a gap of five years before the Radfords' next book. Mona's mother died in 1953; she had been living with them at the time. Starting in 1956, with a new publisher John Long (like Melrose, another Hutchinson company), the Radfords released two Manson titles in successive years. In 1958 they moved to the publisher Robert Hale, a prominent supplier to the public libraries. They began with two non-series titles *The Six Men* (1958) and *Married to Murder* (1959), before returning to Manson with *Death of a Frightened Editor* (1959). Thereafter, Manson was to feature in all but one of their remaining 25 crime novels, all published by Hale. Curiously, a revised and abridged version of the third Manson series novel *Crime Pays No Dividends* (1945) was later released under the new title *Death of a Peculiar Rabbit* (1969).

During the late 1950s and early 1960s the Radfords continued to write well-conceived and cleverly plotted murder mysteries that remain worth seeking out today. Notable examples are the atmospheric *Death on the Broads* (1957) set on the Norfolk Broads, and *Death of a Frightened Editor* (1959) involving the poisoning of an odious London newspaper gossip columnist aboard the London-to-Brighton Pullman Express (a familiar train journey for Edwin Radford, who had worked in Fleet Street while living in Brighton). *Death and the Professor* (1961), the only non-Manson series book released after 1959, is an unusual exception. It features Marcus Stubbs, Professor of Logic and the Dilettantes' Club, a small private dining circle in Soho which meets regularly to discuss informally unsolved cases. Conveniently, but improbably, the Assistant Commissioner of Scotland Yard is among its members. The book comprises a series of stories, often involving locked room murders or other 'impossible' crimes, solved by the logic and reasoning of Professor Stubbs following discussions around the dining table. There are similarities with Roger Sheringham's Crimes Circle in Anthony Berkeley's *The Poisoned Chocolates Case* (1937). The idea of a private dining club as a forum for mystery solving was later revived by the American author Isaac Asimov in *Tales of the Black Widowers* (1974).

Edwin Isaac Radford (1891-1973) and Mona Augusta Radford (1894-1990) were married in Aldershot in 1939. Born in West Bromwich, Edwin had spent his working life entirely in journalism, latterly in London's Fleet Street where he held various editorial roles, culminating as Arts Editor-in-Chief and Columnist for the *Daily Mirror* in 1937. Mona was the daughter of Irish poet and actor James Clarence Mangan and his actress wife Lily Johnson. Under the name 'Mona Magnet' she had performed on stage since childhood, touring with her mother, and later was for many years a popular leading lady in musical-comedy and revues until her retirement from the stage. She also authored numerous short plays and sketches for the stage, in addition to writing verse, particularly for children.

An article in *Books & Bookmen* magazine in 1959 recounts how Edwin and Mona, already in their early 50s, became detective fiction writers by accident. During one of Edwin's periodic attacks of lumbago, Mona trudged through snow and slush from their village home to a library for Dr Thorndyke detective stories by R. Austin Freeman, of which he was an avid reader. Unfortunately, Edwin had already read the three books with which she returned! Incensed at his grumbles, Mona retaliated with "Well for heaven's sake, why don't you write one instead of always reading them?" – and placed a writing pad and pencil on his bed. Within a month, Edwin had written six lengthy short stories, and with Mona's help in revising the MS, submitted them to a leading publisher. The recommendation came back that each of the stories had the potential to make an excellent full-length novel. The first short story was duly turned into a novel, which was promptly accepted for publication. Subsequently, their practice was to work together on writing novels – first in longhand, then typed and read through by each of them, and revised as necessary. The completed books were read through again by both, side by side, and final revisions made. The plot was usually developed by Mona and added to by Edwin during the writing. According to Edwin, the formula was: "She kills them off, and I find out how she done it."

As husband-and-wife novelists, the Radfords were in the company of other Golden Age crime writing couples – G.D.H. (Douglas) and Margaret Cole in the UK, and Gwen Bristow and husband Bruce Manning as well as Richard and Frances Lockridge in the USA. Their crime novels proved popular on the Continent and were published in translation in many European languages. However, the US market eluded them. Aside from crime fiction, the Radfords collaborated on authoring a wide range of other works, most notably *Crowther's Encyclopaedia of Phrases and Origins*, *Encyclopaedia of Superstitions* (a standard work on folklore), and a *Dictionary of Allusions*. Edwin was a Fellow of the Royal Society of Arts, and a member of both the Authors' Club and the Savage Club.

The Radfords proved to be an enduring writing team, working into their 80s. Both were also enthusiastic amateur artists in oils and water colours. They travelled extensively, and invariably spent the winter months writing in the warmer climes of Southern Europe. An article by Edwin in John Creasey's *Mystery Bedside Book* (1960) recounts his involvement in the late 1920s with an English society periodical for the winter set on the French Riviera, where he had socialised with such famous writers as Baroness Orczy, William Le Queux and E. Phillips Oppenheim. He recollects Oppenheim dictating up to three novels at once! The Radfords spent their final years living in Worthing on the English South Coast.

Murder Isn't Cricket

The fourth Doctor Manson series title *Murder Isn't Cricket* (1946) opens with an evocative setting of that most English of sporting pastimes: a cricket match between two village teams played on the village green. The rival Surrey villages of Thames Pagnall and Maplecot had just played out a closely fought draw in their annual cricket match. The teams had returned to the pavilion, and the village green had emptied of all spectators, bar one. A dead man was found sitting in a deck chair on the boundary line. He had been shot as the match was played. The man was a stranger to the village. There was no obvious clue to his identity or that of his killer. Nobody had seen or heard the shot fired. The local police are baffled, and call in Scotland Yard.

Chief Detective-Inspector Harry Manson leads on the case, supported by his regular CID colleagues Superintendent Jones and Inspector Kenway, and with scientific assistance from Sergeant Merry, his deputy in the Forensics Research Laboratory. By careful investigation and methodical reasoning, Manson deduces who the dead man was, why he was killed, how it was done, and who the murderer. His logical deductions and the methods used closely mirror those of Sherlock Holmes. At times Manson uses scientific verification, aided by his famous 'box of tricks' containing equipment from the Laboratory. The calculation of the correct angle from which the fatal shot was fired takes account of sun and shadow and involves measurements using a micrometer - reminiscent of methods of investigation featured in John Rhode's *Shot at Dawn* (1934) and Vernon Loder's *Death of an Editor* (1931). Manson's careful analysis of the evidence, and systematic elimination of each suspect during the denouement, display his masterful ratiocination, all explained with measured clarity. The result is heralded as "another feather in the cap of science". The Radfords encourage the reader to share in Manson's thought processes and deductions, and try to solve the mystery for themselves, by providing all clues necessary to arrive at the identity of the murderer. Their 'Challenge to the Reader' posits seven vital points and clues which arose during the investigation. Helpfully, these are listed, post denouement, in a final chapter ('L'Envoi') for those readers who did not succeed in deciphering them. The novel is an enjoyable and satisfying Golden Age example of a well-developed, closely integrated plot, featuring clever scientific investigation methods; it has evocative settings, dramatic interest and a surprising denouement. From its beginning with the murder of an apparent stranger during a village cricket match in Surrey, the story-line expands to encompass illicit drug dealings stretching from Melbourne in Australia to Wapping in London's East End Docks.

The first edition of *Murder Isn't Cricket*, published in 1946 by Andrew Melrose for the Crime Book Society, has an attractive green and yellow dust wrapper featuring a human skull in profile to a cricket batsman playing a drive; the spine shows the skull atop a set of cricket stumps. The book attracted favourable critical reviews. The *Western Morning News* felt that it showed the Radfords reasserting their claim for "a front-rank place among contemporary writers of crime fiction . . . There is no flagging in the technique of either the authors or of the Doctor and a long series of brilliant stories of detection".

The important influence of cricket in English social life and culture is reflected in its frequent appearances in Golden Age crime fiction. T.S. Stribling in *Clues of the Caribbees* (1929) wrote of "the Anglo-Saxon values" inherent in the game. It provides an attractive backdrop, particularly in stories set in villages or schools, for example Josephine Bell's *Death at Half-Term* (1939) and Clifford Witting's *A Bullet for Rhino* (1950). An enjoyable cricket mystery with a village setting is Barbara Worsley-Gough's *Alibi Innings* (1954), cleverly plotted and with colourful characters, involving the murder of the local squire's wife during the annual cricket match between the squire's eleven and the village side. Worsley-Gough attempts to convey the escapist appeal of cricket to the English: "(Cricket) seemed to compress the universe and all time past, present, and to come, into the compass of an afternoon, one field, and the activities of eleven men in white." She describes the setting as ". . . a charmed space, an isolated piece of England with the vast, loud, dangerous world outside shut off for an hour or longer." In the same year as *Murder Isn't Cricket*, Nancy Spain released *Death Before Wicket* (1946); appropriately she had played at national level for the England women's cricket team. Cricket may not only be used to provide background, it can contribute directly to the plot, as in *Murder Must Advertise* (1933) by Dorothy L. Sayers, where the ability of a murder suspect to throw down the wicket from deep field is essential to the mystery. In Nicholas Blake's *A Question of Proof* (1935), a thrilling close finish to a school match enables the killer both to stab the unpopular Headmaster and ingeniously dispose of the weapon while everyone is concentrating on the cricket. Even the cricket bat may be used as a murder weapon, as in *Murder at School* (1931) by Glen Trevor (better known as James Hilton), and *The Skeleton in the Clock* (1948) by Carter Dickson (aka John Dickson Carr). Cricket has often been the sport of English writers and detectives. Sir Arthur Conan Doyle, J.S. Fletcher, Lord Gorell, J.C. Masterman and Henry Wade were all proficient cricketers. Wade's police detective, Inspector Poole, played in the Seniors' Match at Oxford. Other prominent cricketing characters in crime fiction include Sayers' Lord Peter Wimsey, Hornung's A.J. Raffles and Sapper's Ronald Standish.

Nigel Moss

CHAPTER ONE
THE MAN ON THE GREEN

OLD GEORGE CROMBIE hobbled madly on his bent and ancient pins across the main road which runs through Thames Pagnall, in the county of Surrey, and disappeared inside the 'Green Man'. And those villagers who were pursuing their lawful occasions in the vicinity rubbed astonished eyes at the sight; because nobody had seen old George progressing himself at such a pace since the day the village crier had announced that, as a celebration for the relief of Mafeking, the then landlord of the 'Green Man' was keeping open and free house for the night.

Inside, old George, still going strong, passed the saloon, and made his way to the top of the passage which gave access to the Big Room. He pushed open the door and poked his head round.

"Hi!" he gasped.

Thirty heads jerked up from the long table, and sixty pieces of cutlery were halted in surprise. The apparition looked over the double line of white flannels and vari-coloured blazers, and sought and found the eyes of Major ffolkes.

"Ef you'll excuse oi, Squire, an' ef it's all the same to you, there be a dead man a'sittin' hisself large as life on the pitch," he announced.

Out of the stunned, momentary silence the voice of the major boomed.

"W-w-what did you say, Crombie?" he demanded.

"Dead gent, I sez," insisted old George.

"Dead man?"

"Aye."

"On *our* pitch?"

"'S'right, Squire."

"God bless my soul!" The major replaced the piece of fried ham dangling from his fork back on the plate, and stared stupefied at the bearer of tidings. "God bless my soul!" he repeated. "On our pitch."

Not even the boys of the village were allowed on that pitch; the dogs were chased off; cows from their experience had taught their calves to skirt round it in their goings and comings from the meadows; and now a dead man had planted himself there.

The major pushed back his chair. The remaining twenty-nine of the company did the same.

Together they surged out of the hostelry, across the road, and on to the village cricket green. It was six o'clock.

* * * * *

Throughout the afternoon the village green had grilled in leisurely and measured exertion 'neath the heat from the deep blue dome of a cloudless sky. To be exact, the entire compactness of the village of Thames Pagnall had grilled; for the thermometer which hoary Tom Hardcastle had installed, with a wind and rain gauge, on a suitable prospect of his ancient cottage, in dark and glowering mistrust of the official prognostications and post-nates of the meteorological department of the Air Ministry, had registered a temperature of 81 in whatever shade it had been able to find.

On the green, temper had conspired with temperature to heat to the acme of human endurance the concourse of people which had splotched a kaleidoscope of colour on its verdant sweep.

It was the annual match between the cricket elevens of Thames Pagnall and Maplecot.

But perhaps you should know something of the match, the better to be able to comprehend how it came about that Eliseus Leland could be murdered in full view of a thousand people, and not one of them raise the alarm, because nobody saw the deed, or its perpetrator.

Very well. The story goes back to somewhere about the year 1598. In that year of her Majesty Elizabeth's reign, one John Denwick of Guldeford, one of her Majesty's coroners, deposed on oath, concerning a piece of ground in Guildford, that he,

"being at the age of fyfty and nyne years, or thereabouts, hath knowne a parcell of lande for the space of fyfty yeares or more, and saith, being a scholar in the free schools of gulde-

ford, hee and several of his fellowes did runne and play there at creckett, and other places."

Now, one of the other places where the game of cricket was played in those spacious days was the parcel of land adjacent to the palace of Hampton Court; which came, later, to the name of Thames Pagnall. From those days to the present the game of cricket has been played on that land. Trees grew up round it; houses gave shelter to generations of dwellers; by their Tudor roofs you may tell them today. And the parcel of land became the cricket green in the centre of the residences.

Then, in the year 1800, or thereabouts, a young upstart settlement levelled up a piece of land in a riverside village some three miles away put up two sets of wickets and proclaimed itself the Maplecot Cricket Club. It also challenged Thames Pagnall to a match. Three hundred years of cricket condescended to allow the upstart on its sacred pitch. From 1800 to the present day, which is 144 years, Thames Pagnall had played Maplecot at cricket. Fifty games had been drawn by now and each side had won 47. This match, then, was a needle game.

The village had turned out for the game, anticipating a good time being had by all. For there had been a mort of trouble at the last match—after the Pagnall captain had been given last man out with a matter of no more than three runs wanted to win, and him with his eye well in and the bowlers dead tired. He swore on his oath, in the presence and before the face of the vicar, that the ball which the umpire said was l.b.w. singed the hairs of his sidewhiskers on the left hand side.

So, for the match on this present day, independent umpires had been on the field. Two solid months had been spent in arriving at the decision, and the identity, of the umpires. Such sinister influence as young Bill Oates, the plumber, putting a washer on the tap of Mrs. Sellars, had him ruled out by the Maplecot team, since Mrs. Sellars son, Alfred, was the slow bowler for Thames Pagnall. This deadly thrust was countered with a riposte by Pagnall against Farmer Bowen, who had as a milk customer the mother of the Maplecot wicket-keeper! The problem was at last solved by a subscription among the two teams which provided the services of two umpires from a club twenty miles away, for a guinea apiece, tea and two pints of beer.

When lunch was taken, Maplecot had lost nine wickets for the respectable tally of 170 runs (last man 9). Ten minutes of the resumption was sufficient to dispose of the tenth wicket. The scoreboard had then clicked up 175. In their respective tents the two sides debated the prospects.

The second over of the Thames Pagnall innings saw the awaited trouble break out. A tall, burly figure took the ball. He sent down the first of his over, and the crowd jumped as one man. The second ball shook the bails.

A shout broke from the Thames Pagnall side of the field. "Who's he? He ain't a Maplecot man. Take him off."

The Pagnall captain, who had been watching the bowling very carefully from the other crease, approached his *vis-à-vis*. "Isn't that Charlton, the Lancashire fast bowler?" he asked.

Maplecot's skipper grinned. "Sure," he said. "What's wrong with that? He's working in Maplecot now, and eligible. Lodging there, too."

"Since when?"

"Since yesterday."

The Pagnall fears were justified. Two wickets fell to the County man in that over for five runs. Four wickets were down for fifty; and then the squire stalked to the wicket to partner the blacksmith. They put on another fifty before the blacksmith, unsighted by a Maplecot lout walking in front of the screen, let a fast one into his wicket. Ominous mutterings broke out; and a suggestion that the visitor—who doubtless had been wandering backwards and forwards across the screen since the Pagnall innings had opened—should be lynched there and then was favourably received. With 160 on the board, only two wickets remained.

But so, too, did the squire.

He put two balls into the visitors' tent, knocking up the score to 172—and then played forward too late. One man left. Three runs to tie. A snatched single sent hearts into mouths. Another . . . and a wildly returned ball brought an overthrow single.

Level scores.

In a silence which could be felt, the bowler walked to the start of his run, steadied himself, broke into a loping trot and hurled his thunderbolt.

"Owzat?" came a yell.

The 145th game had ended in a draw.

The players slipped on their blazers, and made their way to the 'Green Man' for the high tea which always concluded the year's gala day. The crowd wandered off to their own respective tea-tables, and within a few minutes the green was empty.

Except for George Crombie.

George was greensman, groundsman and general aide-de-camp to the club. He had been so for the last fifty years. And when the last ball had been bowled, and the stumps drawn, and the spectators departed, old George began his work. Trundling a handcart, he skirted the boundary line, collecting, collapsing, and piling on the handcart the deck-chairs, folding stools and collapsible forms upon which the club 'fans' had disported themselves in comfort during the match. These were subsequently wheeled to the shed at the back of Crombie's house, which was the official store-room of the Thames Pagnall Cricket Club.

He had circled some two-thirds of the boundary when he arrived at a chair set a little apart from the others. It was also different from the others; a spectator was still sitting in it. He lay back in the canvas, oblivious to the whistling of Crombie as he approached.

George eyed him. . . . "'Sleep," he communed. "Sun . . . makes some folks want to sleep . . . makes me missus sleep. . . . Bet he dunno match's over. . . . Strange gennelman, too."

Considering the matter from all angles, George decided that, since he had to return that way, he would let the sleeper dream on. He rumbled past him, collected the remainder of the chairs and, some ten minutes later, was back again. The man was still oblivious to the world.

Old George cleared his throat. "Sorry, sir. I'll have to take the chair now," he said.

There was no response; he repeated his warning, more loudly.

Still no reply.

"Dang it! Can't leave chair here all night," said George to himself. He tapped the man on the shoulder. . . . He tapped again . . . He pushed him.

It was at this point that George, developing a somewhat retarded anxiety, saw the figure of Mr. Alfred Bosanquet approaching him over the green. Mr. Bosanquet was one of George's props of existence. He occupied the large bungalow which faced the green on its longest side, commanding a cross-view of the wicket. He was one of the principal supporters of the club, a fact which was recognized by the score-board attendant, who, whenever there was a change in the score, elaborately turned to the board in the direction of Mr. Bosanquet's residence, so that he and his friends, viewing the game from their armchairs spaced out on the front lawn, might be kept *au fait* with the progress of the match.

George Crombie was the Bosanquets' odd man about the place, drawing two hours' pay for one hour of real labour. It was therefore with considerable relief that he now saw his employer approaching him and his problem man.

"George! Those fowl have broken out again," he announced. "You'd better come over and patch up the run." He broke off. "What's the matter?" he asked, sharply.

"Gennelman here . . . can't make him hear me," Crombie explained. "He ain't moved, though I shook him."

"Perhaps he's fainted with the heat and the excitement. Let me see him." Mr. Bosanquet stepped up to the chair and bent over the man. He slipped a hand inside his waistcoat.

"By jove, he's dead!" he announced.

"Dead?" echoed George. "Go on!"

"Quite dead. Here, you go off to the pub and tell the squire and the others. I'll stop here with the body. It mustn't be touched, you know. Get a move on, man. Tell the squire to come at once."

Major ffolkes reached the scene at the head of the thirty cricketers and attendants. "What's this story Crombie has got hold of about a man being dead, Bosanquet?" he asked.

"Oh, fellow's dead all right, Major," was the reply. "His heart isn't beating, anyhow. I felt for that."

"What is it? Heat stroke, do you think?"

"Don't know. But I shouldn't touch him, if I were you. Better get the local cop and a doctor."

"Constable's coming now—with half the village," volunteered one of the flannelled figures.

"That's that blasted Crombie, I suppose, bellowing the news round the place. They'll be trampsing all over the pitch now."

Police-Constable Lambert, of the Surrey Constabulary, saluted the squire, and jerked a finger at the figure in the chair.

"This him?" he asked.

The squire nodded.

"Doctor's coming. I've telephoned Inspector. He's coming, too."

CHAPTER TWO
COMINGS AND GOINGS

DETECTIVE-INSPECTOR CARRUTHERS stopped his car at the edge of the green, where it had a footbridge across the dyke on to the road. He walked to meet his constable, and acknowledged the eager salute of a man who had a body to dispose of.

He eyed the multitude.

"All these people the man's relatives?" he asked, sarcastically.

"No, Inspector. Gent's a stranger."

"Then clear 'em off. All the lot of 'em. Right off the green.

"And don't walk over that pitch—none of you!" roared Major ffolkes, who had seen two wars, and counted death as merely a necessary incident. "Put the standards and ropes round it, you fellows," he appealed to the cricketers.

The inspector walked up to the chair and, standing in front of it, inspected the occupant. The man was lying back in the canvas sling of the chair, slouching rather than sitting. His hat, a grey trilby, was tilted over his eyes, hiding his face from passers-by. It was resting at a comical angle, as though it had fallen, or been jerked forward.

"Anybody touched him?" the inspector asked.

A chorus of "Noes" answered the question.

He stooped over and lifted the hat clear. The hair beneath was a full crop of iron-grey, the face of ruddy complexion, burnt a little by the sun—and recently, for the colour was still a brick red instead of the brown which is the hall-mark of the sun-bronzed man. He wore a brown suit of jacket, waistcoat and trousers, through which ran a thin red stripe. Brown glacé shoes completed the outfit.

"Looks as if he's had a heat stroke, Inspector," suggested Major ffolkes. "It's been mighty hot out here this afternoon, and we've had an exciting time."

The inspector nodded, non-committally. "Well, we shall soon know," he commented. "Here's the doctor."

"Heat stroke be damned!" the police-surgeon announced. "Man's been used to heat. Look at him." He felt the skin of the face. "Warm," he said. "It'd be cold if it was heat stroke." He lifted up one of the eyelids and inspected the pupil beneath. "Natural condition." He studied the position of the figure. "Position's all wrong. Fellow's lying easy. He'd be contorted through trying to get up. Stroke would shock him awkwardly. Whatever he died of it wasn't heat. If you've finished with him, Inspector, we'd better have him on the grass."

Major ffolkes and the constable lifted the figure from the chair and laid him face upwards on the turf. The doctor unbuttoned the waistcoat, loosened the collar and tie, and opened the shirt. His fingers probed and felt and his knuckles tapped—without result. Nothing, either, did he glean from an inspection of the mouth.

"Turn him over," he said at length.

And a second later . . .

"Why, the man's been shot!" he ejaculated.

"Shot?" The inspector jumped.

"Through the back." The doctor pulled down the coat from the shoulders and inspected the wound. "Looks as if it went into the heart," he said. Must have hit a bone in front, somewhere, or it would have come out. Better get him to the mortuary. I can't do anything about him here."

"Just a minute, Doctor." The inspector turned to the men standing round. "Any of you got a camera handy?" he asked.

Mr. Bosanquet nodded. "I've got a cine camera with half a roll of films in it, if that's any use," he volunteered.

"It would do even better than an ordinary camera, if you can spare the use of it, sir," was the reply.

Bosanquet left at a run in the direction of his house.

"Now, Constable, if you'll give me a hand we will put this chap back in the chair, as near as possible as we found him. I want a photograph." They settled the figure, and the inspector, standing back, passed an eye over him. "I think he was a little lower down," he insisted. Mr. Bosanquet was back before the officer was satisfied with the position of the replaced corpse.

"Would you like me to handle the camera, Inspector? I probably know more about a cine camera than you do, and they are a bit tricky." Mr. Bosanquet made the suggestion hesitatingly.

"I was going to ask you if you would be good enough to do so," was the reply. "I want pictures from the front, the back, and from each side. Then one showing the position of the chair against the road past the green—long-distance focus there."

"I'll take a five-second run of each angle, Inspector. That should provide you with a dozen pictures of each pose."

"Right, sir. That will do excellently. You, Lambert"—he called to the constable—"you go back in my car and bring the ambulance, and Sergeant Wharton." He turned to the doctor. "I'd like a post-mortem as soon as possible, Doctor," he said. "And let the attendant have the clothes to keep for me, will you? As little touched as possible. Tell him to put them in my room. If you can give me some idea of the time of death I'd be glad."

"Um. . . . Bit of a job, Inspector. . . . Out here in the broiling sun. Let me see. It's half past six. . . . Um . . . cooling . . . temperature when I took it was 94 . . . normal, 98.4. . . . Say not less than two hours and not more than three . . . that means between four-thirty and five-thirty o'clock. Can't say nearer than that, Inspector. They'll be the outside hours."

With the body speeding to the mortuary, Inspector Carruthers turned his attention to the more serious issues. Hitherto, he had asked no questions since, at the outset, the dead man had presented no more problem than being a dead man. But the discovery of the shot-wound altered the situation. An unnatural death was a suspicious death. The inspector began his inquisition. "Who found him?" he asked.

"Old George," the major replied. "Crombie, tell the inspector what you told us."

George detailed his movements from the beginning of his round of the chairs and forms, ending up with his shaking of the still figure. "See anybody on the green at the time?" asked the inspector.

"No. . . . Only Mr. Bosanquet."

"That's me, Inspector." Mr. Bosanquet stepped forward. "I came across the green to speak to Crombie. He's my handy man about the place, and I wanted him to do a job."

"Right. I'll have a word with you later. What time did this match finish?"

"Just turned five-thirty." It was Major ffolkes who replied.

The inspector considered the point. Half past five was the very latest time of death, according to the doctor. "That means that the man was killed while the match was in progress," he said. "Did you hear a shot?"

The major shook an emphatic head. "Never heard a sound. But then, we were having a pretty hectic time. We dashed near lost the match, you know."

The inspector looked at him pretty hard, and seemed about to say something. He changed his mind.

"*Anybody* hear a shot?" He looked round; but was greeted with negative shakes of heads.

"Did anybody see the man before Crombie found him? Anybody, for instance, see him take the chair?"

Again heads were shaken. "There were a thousand or more people here, Inspector. It isn't to be expected that any single person would be noticed," the major suggested.

"I see. Well, perhaps you'll be able to tell me more when we know who the man is, and what he is. I'll know that as soon as I have gone through his pockets. And I'm going to do that now.

The sergeant, here, will take your names and addresses, and either he or I will be coming along to have another talk with you presently. Oh, there's one thing more." He turned to Crombie. "Did you touch this chair when you tried to wake the man?"

"No, Inspector. Never put me hand on it."

"Did you, Mr. Bosanquet? I gather that you were the one to feel his heart and pronounce him dead. Did you put your hand on any part of the chair?"

Mr. Bosanquet screwed his face into a contortion of thought. "I couldn't be sure, Inspector," he said. "I didn't take any particular notice, if you understand me. I *may* have put my hand on the back of it to steady myself."

"Ah, well, we'll soon know." He wrapped a handkerchief round a stave of the chair, and, carrying it to his car, placed it carefully on the back seat. He squirmed into the driver's seat and drove off.

The green at Thames Pagnall resumed its usual appearance of somnolescence.

The inspector had surmised that there was likely to be little difficulty in arriving at the name and address of the dead man. It was an assumption that, in nine cases out of ten, would have been correct. Most men walking abroad carry in their pockets, or on their clothes, some intimation of their identity; addressed envelopes of delivered letters, bills, visiting cards. The man who had found death on the cricket green had none of these things.

Inspector Carruthers, arriving at his office, found his sergeant staring, in unpleasant surprise, at the articles which he had taken from the clothes and had now arranged on the table. They were few. A silver watch, a fountain-pen, a pocket handkerchief; eight shillings in silver and twopence in coppers, a loose ten-shilling note, which had been with a bunch of keys and a pocket-knife in the left-hand trousers pocket. A small diary was retrieved from a top waistcoat pocket, and a letter from the right-hand inside pocket of the jacket. The sole remaining possessions of the man were a pipe and tobacco-pouch half full of tobacco, a one-ounce packet of tobacco, and a box of matches.

It was to the letter that Inspector Carruthers first turned his attention. A double sheet of notepaper, of the cream-laid variety, the writing on it occupied only half of the top sheet. It read:

Dear Mr. L.,

Why, of course. We shall be delighted to see you. Come along for the week-end.

Yours sincerely,
Kathleen Smith.

It was not until he had read this brief invitation that the inspector noticed one small, but exceedingly important, omission; there was no address. The top right-hand corner of the sheet, where usually a correspondent writes his or her address, had been neatly cut out.

The inspector regarded the mutilated corner with a frown. "Now, what the dickens has happened to that bit?" he asked himself. He turned to the clothes again, and searched hopefully through the pockets, especially the waistcoat top-pockets, in which the mere male has a proclivity for pushing bits and pieces of paper which he considers at the moment desirable to keep. But the sergeant's earlier search had been thorough; no scrap revealed itself.

As he pondered over this problem his eyes caught sight of the miniature diary. "Of course," he communed with himself. "Probably stuck it in there opposite the date." He opened the diary, and thumbed over the pages to June 21—the current date—and from there proceeded to search backwards. But no missing fragment of paper was attached, nor did any entry appear in the pages signifying that he had an invitation date. Patiently, the inspector began his search again, this time among the pages in advance of June 21. Still he found no square slip or address entered under any date.

With this possible pointer to the dead man's identity faded out, Carruthers settled down to examine in detail the entries in the diary. They extended from the third day in April to a date a day or so before that of his death—in fact, to June 18. Previous to the April date the pages were as virgin white as when they had left the printer. Inspector Carruthers waded through them. They appeared to be a record—and not too complimentary a one—of a tour of the countryside which the man had made. In April he had apparently been traversing, or 'hiking', through Yorkshire. An entry on April 12 read.

"B told me that I'd find the Yorkshire moors as adventurous as I should like. Too right he was. Lost in the fog all the day, and then found that I had walked back to where I started from."

From Yorkshire he appeared to have wandered into Nottingham. There were the initials 'S.F.'; there was a reference to R.H.'s grave, and then to a castle. *"There's history there, if you like,"* the diary said.

Under June 11 was the comment:

"Cardinals knew a thing or two in those days—H.C."

On June 12 was the note: *"Kingston—King's Stone"*, then followed: *"H.C again. Fair bonza."*

On the following day, June 13, the diary recorded:

"Saw S.F. today. Strange. Must look into it. May be interesting."

From June 14 to 18 the pages were blank. On the 19th was the comment: *"Very busy remembering. Got stuck up. Wrote to HQS."*

That was the last entry in the diary, except for the 21st—the day of his death. Written immediately underneath that date was the reminder: *"T.P. Saturday."*

The inspector closed the book, replaced it on the table. "Doesn't seem much to help in there," he muttered to himself.

Further deliberations were interrupted by the entrance of Sergeant Wharton. He crossed to the table and looked down on the exhibits. "Anything there, sir?" he asked.

Inspector Carruthers grimaced. "Nothing that I can see is of any use to us," he replied. "You can look through them presently and see what you think. But I'm no forrader. And you?"

Sergeant Wharton scratched a puzzled head. "Yes—and no," he dissembled.

"What do you mean, yes and no?"

"Well, firstly, I can get no tags on who he is. Nobody seems to have noticed him. And that's a damned funny thing when you come to think about it. You know Thames Pagnall, sir. Everybody knows everybody else and what they're doing. They pretty well know what everybody is going to do. If little Elsie goes for a walk with young Tommy down Lovers' Lane at seven o'clock at night, all the gossiping old women know about it next morning. How the devil it gets round in the time beats me. See what I mean? Here's a bloke walks into the village and sits on their precious green. Yet nobody sees the fellow at all until he's a corpse.

"Now, F starts off with the fellows of the Maplecot team. Thought perhaps, he might have been one of their fans. They'd never seen him before. What's more, they hadn't ever heard of a Kathleen Smith. I found half a dozen of their chaps and girls who had come over to see their team lose. No, he hadn't come over in their bus, and they didn't know him or anything about him. That left me with the village to go through. Seemed easy to me. Mother Smithers would be sure to know." He looked at the inspector and explained. "She's the old woman that's supposed to live in the ramshackle cottage where the roads meet and where the buses stop, in and out."

"Supposed to live? Doesn't she live in the cottage, then?"

"No. She darned well lives on the front garden gate watching them who comes and goes, to see what they've bought or are going to sell. She'd be a dead cert. If an extra fly flew into the village she'd spot the insec' and start trying to find out where it had come from. What happens? 'No, I ain't seen no strange gentleman hereabouts.'" The sergeant mimicked the querulous tones of the old woman.

"I says to her, 'You come to the mortuary and look at him and see if you've seen him before.' She darned near ran there. It was the first time she'd had the opportunity of seeing inside the suicide house, as she called it. Now, if she'd even have thought that she'd seen the corpse when it was alive she'd have said so, just so as to be in the news like. What does the old so-and-so say? 'I ain't never clapt me eyes on him in me life, Sergeant.'" Again the sergeant mimicked. "I'll lay ten to one he never came into the village in a bus, Inspector, or she'd have spotted him. That settled that.

"So then I goes all round the green. I worked out that he would have had to walk along *some* road to reach the chair he was in. And he'd have to pass houses; and houses have got doors and windows; and he was a stranger. But no, nobody could recognize the body. So I said perhaps he had walked to the green after the match had started when there wouldn't be anybody on the road or at the doors, anyway, because they'd all be on the green itself. With that, I had a few words with George Crombie. It's his job to look after the chairs and see they aren't used by any unauthorized person—that means by anybody who isn't a subscriber to the club funds. It's pretty evident that the fellow wasn't a subscriber, and that Crombie ought to have been after him when he took the chair. But he says he never saw him on the green until after he was dead."

"Do you think he's telling the truth?" the inspector asked.

"Why should he lie, sir?"

"I can imagine one reason, Sergeant. He's not supposed to allow anyone not a supporter to have a chair. Suppose the fellow comes up to him, asks for a chair, and shoves half a crown into his hand for the club collection-box. He pockets it himself . . ."

"It's the kind of thing old George Crombie *would* do, Inspector," said Wharton, slanderously.

"Then the fellow goes and gets himself killed in the chair, and Crombie says: 'I let him sit in it.' What's going to happen to Crombie?"

"The club would take his job away."

"Quite. So is Crombie's statement to be relied upon?"

Sergeant Wharton mentally masticated and digested the point. "I don't think he knew anything about it," he decided, at last.

"Well, you know Crombie better than I do, so we'll have to accept your judgment. Where did you go from there?"

"By this time the village cop was back. He found the people who were occupying the chairs nearest to the corpse. They were a Mr. Irving with his daughter on one side, and a couple of fellows and girls on the other side. Neither of them remembers the man taking a seat, or bringing the chair up. Crombie insists that when he put out the chairs he put 'em all together. That was, of course, before the match started."

"And that's all?"

"That's the negative side, Inspector. Now, there's a couple of things that may help. The first I got from the party at Mr. Bosanquet's. That's the man in the big bungalow on the long side of the green, you remember. He was watching the match from his front lawn. Mrs. Bosanquet and three friends were with him. He said that he heard a shot fired while the match was on. At least, he thinks it was a shot, though he doesn't know for sure, of course. He says it came from some distance down the road."

"Down the road? But people don't walk down the road firing a rifle."

"Wait a bit, sir," the sergeant remonstrated. "I got the names of the three friends, and questioned them separately. One was a Mr. Catling. I asked him whether he heard a shot, and he said, 'A shot? Good lord, no!' Then he stopped and asked who said there had been a shot. I replied that Mr. Bosanquet said he heard one. He laughed. 'Oh, old Bossy said so, did he?' he said. 'And when did he hear it?' I replied that it was about a quarter to five o'clock. 'Ah,' he said. 'I heard that. But it wasn't a shot, I reckon. It was a car backfiring. As a matter of fact, Bossy only heard half of it. There were two backfires.'

"The next person I saw was Miss Malcolm. Single young lady she is, and a friend of Mrs. Bosanquet, and has hopes, so I hear, of Mr. Catling, who's a very-well-off young gentleman in the City. And a nice bit of stuff she is, too," he added parenthetically. "She says she heard the backfires. They weren't very loud and seemed to be some distance away. She said the first was exactly at quarter to five, and the second a minute or two later. She's quite sure of that, because the first one made her look at her watch, because she'd promised to help Mrs. Bosanquet with the tea at a quarter to five. So she got up out of the chair, and the second one came just as she stepped into the kitchen. I checked her watch with mine and there wasn't more than a quarter of a minute difference.

"The third guest was a Mr. Watkins, artist gentleman. He said that he heard the explosions, but didn't pay any attention to them because he was watching the cricket. He couldn't even say what time it was that they happened, but knew it was before five o'clock."

The sergeant closed his notebook and put it into a pocket. There was a pause.

"Well, how does all that help?" the inspector asked.

The sergeant countered the question with one of his own. "Have you had any report from the doctor yet?" he asked.

"No. Why?"

"What I'm thinking of depends on the bullet-hole as to whether it's feasible or not."

Inspector Carruthers, after a look at his sergeant's face, reached for the telephone and dialled a number. "Doctor Lumley?" he asked. "Inspector Carruthers here. Have you done a post-mortem on that chap? . . . Oh . . . just looked him over. . . . No. Tomorrow morning will do quite well. But there's one thing that might be a help to me. We'd like to know a point or two about the bullet-wound."

He listened for a moment or two to the doctor's voice, then, covering the mouthpiece with a hand, turned to the sergeant. "He says it was a rifle bullet, probably a .22, but can't be sure yet."

"Ask him the direction of the wound—of the entry."

Carruthers uncovered the mouthpiece. "Can you tell us anything about the direction of the wound, Doctor?" he asked. "What? . . . I see. He says it entered sloping slightly downwards."

Wharton nodded an excited head. "All right," he whispered.

"Thanks, Doctor. That may be a help," said the inspector, and rang off. He replaced the receiver and confronted his sergeant. "Now what is it?" he demanded.

"There were quite a number of cars passing along the road by the green on that afternoon, Inspector," the sergeant began.

"And there were cars parked at the side of the road, on the verge of the green, too," he suggested.

The inspector started. "You mean?"

"Supposing the backfires *were* shots, as Mr. Bosanquet thinks. Supposing they came from some car moving past. The bullet *would* go into the body sloping downwards, because they would be fired from a higher level."

"Good Gad, Sergeant! It's possible. We shall have to look into that. Or, of course, if they were fired from a stationary car at the side of the green, the same would apply. That's a bit of good brainwork on your part. Now, what's the other thing you have up your sleeve?"

"'I'm not sure of the strength of this one, Inspector. It's about old Gaffer Baldwin."

"Gaffer Baldwin? Who the devil is he?"

"Village's oldest inhabitant. Ruddy nuisance he is. Little bent old man. Sits outside the local all day and every day, waiting for visitors. They come to the pub, being very ancient, and looking it. Then Baldwin tells 'em fanciful stories of the village and the pub, and his own mis-spent life, in return for beer and baccy money. Says he's a hundred, the old liar, and won't live much longer seeing as how he has the bronchitis something terrible, and must have a glass of whisky every night by doctor's orders, and him with only his ten bob old age pension to buy it with, as well as having to buy food. I know for a fact that the old scoundrel has five hundred pounds in the bank. I should say he puts a pound towards it every week.

"Anyways, what I was coming to is this. Gaffer, ever since he heard the news has been muttering to himself, but loud enough for anybody to hear, that he knew something was going to happen today. I've been trying to get out of him what he means by it, but it's been such a good selling line that he's practically speechless now, and we had to carry him home to his cottage."

"What exactly has he said?" the inspector asked.

"The words he's used over and over again, sir, are: 'I knew as how something was going to happen this 'ere day. I sez to meself this very morning, "Gaffer, summat's going to happen, and someone's going to die.""""

The inspector emitted a startled gasp. "The devil he did!" he said. He gazed at his sergeant inquiringly. "Do *you* think there's anything in it?" he asked.

"That's what's puzzling me, sir. If there's anything funny going on in the village, old Gaffer Baldwin knows as much, and usually more, than anybody. Fair nose for scandal the old man has, and a mine of information he is. I don't suppose he knew that this chap was going to be shot dead, but I wouldn't put it past him to have known that there was something funny going on."

"I don't like the sound of it, Wharton. We'll have to get some more out of him when he's sobered up. I've fixed the inquest for tomorrow afternoon. You'd better warn all the people you've seen to attend it."

"Including Baldwin?"

"Most certainly Baldwin."

The sergeant had left the room and closed the door behind him when a shout recalled him. He stood, framed in the doorway. "Something else, sir?" he inquired.

"Yes, Sergeant. I've been thinking that if Baldwin *does* know something, and has been spreading an intimation all over the place that he knows it, then he might be in danger. After all, there's a bloke dead. And here's an old toper going round saying that he knew it was going to happen. I think there ought to be a guard over the old fool's cottage."

"Very good, sir. I'll see to that."

CHAPTER THREE
MURDER

LEFT TO HIMSELF, Inspector Carruthers reviewed the facts and fancies which he and Sergeant Wharton had gleaned from round the historic cricket green of Thames Pagnall. Turning them over in his mind he admitted that there was little satisfaction to be found in them. They were few, and those few seemed to have no particular value from a detecting point of view. Turn them which way he would, they still failed to fall into the places in the jigsaw, which places were the connection between the dead man, the match, and his presence in Thames Pagnall.

The man was a complete stranger. He was a holiday-maker. For months, judging by his diary, he had been touring the countryside of Great Britain on a round of sightseeing. He had, apparently, come to Thames Pagnall with the same end in view. That, the inspector thought, was obvious from the diary. The reference to a cardinal, followed, as it was, by the initials 'H.C.', could mean to a sightseer nothing but Hampton Court, and the palace which Wolsey built, and in which he had lived and held princely court. Kingston was, of course, King's stone, where there was still exhibited, enshrined in railings, the coronation stone of some of the Saxon kings of England. The initials 'T.P.' could be assumed, in the inspector's opinion, to mean Thames Pagnall. Thus, he had visited Thames Pagnall in the ordinary course of his sightseeing. Why, then, should a holidaymaker, sitting to enjoy a game of village cricket, suddenly meet with death in the shape of a flying bullet?

Was it accident, or was it murder? Suppose for the sake of argument it was a sheer accident. Why should anyone be firing rifle-shots over the cricket green? And why did nobody see the shots fired? Suppose the alleged backfirings were shots. It didn't make sense. Why should anyone in a car passing the green suddenly start firing shots at nobody in particular?

If it was murder, why should the murderer pick the high spot of a cricket match, and the presence of a thousand people, to put a bullet into his intended victim? Surely he would have waited until the victim was alone, or at least until there were fewer people about to see, even by sheer chance, the fell deed.

And, if it was an accidental shooting, how did the words of the village reprobate, Gaffer Baldwin, fit in; and what did he mean by his reference to "summat's going to happen", and "someone's going to die"? And why must the old fool go and get blind, speechless drunk, so that he couldn't be questioned about it?

No, the more he thought about it, the more mysterious the tragedy seemed to be. The inspector decided to have a talk with his chief constable, and see what that officer of the Law could make of the known facts. He slipped on a light raincoat and, walking to his car waiting in the police-station yard, squirmed into the driving seat and set off on his errand.

Colonel Mainforce received his visitor in the library. The chief constable, like most of his calling, had had nothing whatever to do with the police force previous to his appointment. It is passing strange that in the police circles of this country the last qualifications deemed to be essential for appointment to the position of chief constable is that the applicant should know anything about constables or crime detection. On the other hand, it is of the utmost importance that any applicant should be, or have been, a senior officer of the Army or the Navy: which accounts for a great deal of the not inconsiderable resentment in certain sections of the nation's constabulary; the barrack-square methods of the Army are viewed with misgiving. It is not particularly encouraging to a man who, starting as a constable, has risen to the position of superintendent of police, to know that he has about one chance in a thousand of rising to the rank of chief constable, or of competing with Major Thing-a-me-Jig, who, having served in India for the last twenty years, has rarely even seen a British constable. The system is altogether wrong.

Inspector Carruthers, however, was fortunate in his chief constable. Although Colonel Mainforce had known nothing of police work before he had been appointed to the position, he had, in fact, served a considerable number of years in Military Intelligence. On taking over as chief constable he had at once taken an intensive course of study in jurisprudence, and had accompanied his executive officers on their investigations, in order that he might see, at close quarters, how crime detection was carried out. Moreover, he became easily accessible to all his men, whatever their rank. In his Army days he had aimed at being a friend as well as leader of his men. His regiment thought the world of 'the Old Man'; and he had imbued his police position with the same spirit of fellowship.

It was in such friendship that he now received the inspector, when his butler ushered the latter into the library.

"Ah, come in, Carruthers," he invited. "Take a pew. Now, not a word before you've had an iced lager and a cigar. I'll have one myself. Been like a furnace all the afternoon." He poured out the two drinks and lifted his glass. "Here's your health," he wished.

"And yours, sir."

The two men set their glasses on the arm-rests of the chairs.

"What's all this I hear about corpses being strewed all over the cricket green at Thames Pagnall, Carruthers?"

The inspector recognized the opening gambit, and smiled appreciatively. "That is what I have come to see you about, sir. But there was only one corpse."

"Good God! How many do you want? But I'm not surprised. I've always heard there might be murder done at this Pagnall-Maplecot Olympiad. Not sure that we couldn't stop the event as likely to lead to a breach of the peace."

"The dead man was a complete stranger, sir."

"The devil he was! What's he mean by coming and dying on *our* hands? Tell me the story in your own way."

Inspector Carruthers detailed the events, from the alarm raised by Crombie at the high tea, to the last of the inquiries by the sergeant among the people who had been on the green. The chief constable heard him through without interruption. At the end, he lay back in his chair, and for a few moments blew smoke-rings from his cigar, the while he sorted out possible lines of investigation which occurred to his mind.

"Seems a queer kind of riddle," he said at last. "Nobody saw him come—and nobody, apparently, saw him *go*, either. Who the heck wants to shoot a stranger? What view do you take on that, Inspector?"

"Only that it *may* have been another stranger, sir."

"Eh? . . . True. Yes, of course. But on the green. He took an outsize in risks, didn't he? Of what are you thinking? Gang war?"

Carruthers turned the point over in his mind. "Might be, sir," he said. "Shots, if they were shots, seemed to come from the road, presumably from a passing vehicle. But if the explosions were backfires, then the theory drops right out."

"It would be pretty good shooting, you know, Carruthers—from a moving car." The chief constable had been a bit of a marksman himself in his Army days, having shot tigers from an elephant's back, and for the King's Prize at Bisley.

The inspector countered with a shrewd thrust. "Could you not have found the mark sir?" he asked.

"Perhaps I could have done, then," he agreed with a smile. "But not now. Did you find any trace of a second bullet?"

The inspector shook his head. "Wharton says not, though he searched. You'll bear in mind that we don't know the range, sir—and looking for a bullet in the grass of that green in those circumstances is like looking for a needle in a bottle of hay."

"If the explosions *were* backfires—perhaps some of the people sitting near the road may say they were—then it's more of a mystery than ever," commented the chief constable.

"And a remarkable coincidence, too, sir, that there should have been such backfires at the precise moment when the doctor thinks the man was shot. Kind of coincidence that your friend Doctor Manson, of Scotland Yard, would look upon as sort of unnatural, he being of a very suspicious turn of mind, as I've heard you say."

The chief constable looked sharply across at the inspector. "What do you mean by that, Carruthers?" he asked. "Do you think that I want the Yard called in? You know I shouldn't do that if you believe that we can handle the case ourselves. I'll give my men every opportunity to find their feet."

"I know that, sir"—gratefully—"and we like you for it. The point I was making is that we shall have to call on Scotland Yard for help in any case, to identify the man. We've got his prints and we shall have to have the records searched. If he was a local man, or somebody who had been here before, I'd be prepared to take a chance. But we have not the ghost of a line to work on, and if we waste time we'll be blamed for not calling in the Yard before the trail is stone cold. I'd sooner, for the credit of the

Force, see the police get the man, even if we lose the credit, than try on my own and fail.'

"That is well spoken, Carruthers, and I give you full credit for it. I like that team spirit. What do you want me to do?"

"Well, sir, I thought if I could place the facts before Dr. Manson he could, perhaps, give me a hint or two. And if I had your permission to use my own discretion when I hear what he has to say, then I could decide whether I thought we should ask the Yard to take over or not."

"Do it gladly, Carruthers. I'll telephone the Yard and tell them you are coming. Going right away?"

"Yes, sir. I can do the journey in half an hour or so."

"Right you are. Off you go. And take a couple of cigars with you. Give one to Dr. Manson with my compliments. He'd pinch one if he was here, in any case."

Inspector Carruthers made the short journey to the Yard in a minute or so over the time he had set himself. He parked his car in the courtyard, and walked, not to the imposing entrance of New Scotland Yard, but to the narrow backdoor which led direct to the Criminal Investigation Department. He asked for Dr. Manson.

"You Inspector Carruthers, sir?" the commissionaire asked. "The Doctor is waiting for you in the laboratory." He led the way to the lift, and the couple left it at the top floor of the Yard building. Pushing open a door at the end of the passage the commissionaire ushered in the visitor. "Inspector Carruthers, sir," he announced.

The Yard's scientific investigator was standing with his back towards the fireplace in earnest conversation with a tall, soldierly-looking companion with a pleasant face and hair greying at the temples. His fingers were playing with a monocle dangling at the end of a black silk cord. Carruthers stood, hesitatingly, inside the door now being closed behind him. Dr. Manson broke off in his talk and came forward, hand outstretched, in welcome. "Come in, Inspector," he invited. "Colonel Mainforce telephoned me that you wanted some advice. You know Sir Edward Allen." He nodded towards his companion. "The assistant commissioner. He thought he would wait and hear your story. It is the Thames Pagnall business, of course?"

"That's right, Doctor," stammered Carruthers, a little over-awed at the presence of the assistant commissioner. "It's a bit of a queer business all round."

The assistant commissioner chuckled. "Well, well. Inspector you've come to the right man. Dr. Manson has heard a few queer businesses in this room in his time—and managed to show that they aren't so queer after all," he said. "I only hope you've brought him something at which he can peer through a microscope. He'll be dashed disappointed if you haven't."

"I've only a finger-print to show with the story so far, sir," explained Carruthers, and produced a record card from a pocket.

"Well, well, that's better than nothing."

"Let's sit down, Inspector," broke in Manson. "We can talk more comfortably." He pulled forward a chair for his guest between those of the A.C. and himself. "Now," he said, "we'll have a cigarette to help our thoughts."

"Oh, sorry, Doctor. I forgot." The inspector produced a cigar from a cardboard case. "The chief constable sent this, with his compliments."

Manson chuckled delightedly. "He remembered that I only visit him when I want one of these, did he? That man has the finest cigars in England. Can't think where the dickens he gets 'em. Got another? Well, light it up. The A.C. can smoke one of his own."

The three men lit up, and Manson took the finger-print card from the inspector. He studied it through a magnifying glass which appeared as though by magic in his hands. For a full minute he eyed the whorls and loops. "Nothing outstanding in it that I can see," he commented at last; and rang a bell. "Take this to Prints and ask if we have a record," he said to the constable who answered the summons. He paused until the man had left the room. "Now, Inspector, let us hear your tale of woe," he invited.

"Yes, Doctor. How much do you know already?"

Dr. Manson frowned a little. "Never mind what I know, Inspector," he protested. "Assume that I know nothing at all. Tell

me exactly how the thing happened from the start. Tell it naturally, as it comes to you. Do not try and put it in any kind of
sequence. And try to tell me everything, even the smallest detail,
even to those things which do not seem to be of any importance
to you, or to the story. Facts are what I deal in, and even the least
of happenings may, in some way, fit into a fact which may only
be discovered later on in the case. Assume, then, that all I know
is that a man was found dead on the village green at Thames
Pagnall. How did he die?"

"He was shot, Doctor."

"Anybody see it happen?"

"Not a soul."

"Anybody there at the time?" Manson was sitting back in
his chair as he asked the question, the fingers of his right hand
tapping nervously on an arm of his chair. His eyes were closed.
Though it rather worried Inspector Carruthers to be talking to
a man who looked as though he was so little interested that he
was sinking into a doze, the attitude was a normal one with the
scientist when he was listening to, or studying, a problem. Carruthers waited as though for the eyes to open and focus themselves on the tale and the teller. "Anybody there at the time?"
asked Manson again.

"About a thousand people," Carruthers replied. It came
simply, unconsciously simply, as though there was nothing unusual in a thousand people being present during a sudden death
by violence.

The scientist's eyes shot open in surprise. Had Carruthers
known, he could have congratulated himself on surprising Dr.
Manson, for the scientist was a brilliant poker player in theory,
if not in fact, in that his face was hardly ever a register of his
interior feelings. The assistant commissioner, watching, chuckled inwardly, and made a point of remembering the incident to
confront the doctor when next occasion arose to 'bait' him on
his unresponsiveness to emotion.

The suddenly opened eyes flickered over the inspector's
face, as though searching to see whether the remark was made
sarcastically or in pure innocence. They seemed satisfied, for

almost immediately they closed again. "Now, that sounds interesting, Inspector," Manson commented. "Start from the beginning—and the beginning would seem now to be the reason for the gathering of that large concourse of people in the little village of Thames Pagnall."

For a quarter of an hour Inspector Carruthers talked. Gathering confidence as he went, he outlined the case with the freedom with which he was wont to present a case for inquiry to his sergeant. He told of the century-old rivalry of the two cricket clubs of Thames Pagnall and Maplecot, and their quarrels. He described the meanderings of old George Crombie with his barrow and chairs, the tragedy of the unfinished high tea in the 'Green Man'. He detailed the tale of the wanderings of the dead man until the day that he embarked on his last and longest journey; and finally told of the strange words of Gaffer Baldwin, who knew that something would happen that day and that somebody would die. Only once did he lapse into silence; that was when the telephone shrilled out a demand. Dr. Manson, reaching forward to the receiver on the table by his side, lifted it and replied. "Thanks," he said, and, without any explanation, resumed his pose, and his listening, after motioning the inspector to proceed.

The recital at last ended in Carruthers clearing his throat in warning that his tale was completely told. He sat back in his chair and, knocking off the ash from his now extinguished cigar, relit it—to the horror of the assistant commissioner—from his petrol lighter!

For a minute—two minutes—Dr. Manson sat as he had listened, eyes closed, head back, and his fingers tapping on the arm. Then, suddenly, as though wakened abruptly from unconsciousness, he turned his gaze on the story-teller.

"And what, Inspector, do you want us to do about it?" he asked.

"W—w—well. Doctor, Colonel Mainforce and I thought that perhaps you might be able to give us one or two points on which to work. We—"

"That, Inspector, is a simple matter. What kinds of points have you in mind?"

"His death, chiefly, Doctor. . . . Among a thousand people. . . . It seems to us a complete mystery without any visible reason."

"There is no mystery at all about his death, Inspector," was the reply.

"No mystery?" queried Carruthers—and looked as though he thought the scientist was, to put it baldly, out of his mind.

"Certainly no mystery," was the retort. Dr. Manson's eyes were alive now. They gleamed cold as steel from their deeply-sunk sockets. The assistant commissioner, watching, recognized the signs. He had seen them so often before. The doctor had found in the story an end which would unwind from the tangled skein of tragedy. Sir Edward knew that he ought to know what that end was; but he did not. He knew that Dr. Manson had heard no more than that to which he had himself listened. He had, over the past two years, followed from start to finish the doctor's investigations, and had had opportunity after opportunity of seeing the web of scientific thinking and logical deduction of the doctor's methods. In the present case, he had tried his hardest to follow the story of the inspector, and work out the logic of it in the doctor's way. He had endeavoured to see those things which the doctor had, it was plain, obviously seen. And the result was—nothing. He could visualize no 'lead' to justify the scientist's confident assertion that the death was no mystery. So he waited for the as always *dénouement*.

Dr. Manson ticked the points off for the inspector on the fingers of one hand:

"The man was deliberately murdered," he said.

"The murderer, or an accomplice, but most likely the murderer himself, was on the green.

"He took something from the dead man's pockets."

Silence hung like a black curtain over the laboratory.

Inspector Carruthers sat staring at the scientist, fascinated. He looked as Lot's wife must have appeared, when changed into a pillar of salt. His expression was comparable only to that of a boy at his first conjuring exhibition, who, having examined his father's hat, and being quite confident that, of all things that might be inside it, a rabbit certainly wasn't, sees the conjuror promptly hike one out by the ears!

And, maybe, the reader is also puzzled. The authors, following their usual custom in the Dr. Manson stories, having introduced you into the conference in Scotland Yard, invite you to study the description of the tragedy on the green at Thames Pagnall, and pit your wits against those of Dr. Manson.

Why is the doctor so certain that the man was murdered? Why is he sure that the murderer, or an accomplice, was on the green, and removed something from the body?

And, finally, what was the something he removed?

CHAPTER FOUR
OMEN

THE ASSISTANT COMMISSIONER looked from the puzzled face of Inspector Carruthers to the calm, in fact contemplative, gaze which Dr. Manson was bestowing upon the cigar wafted to him from Colonel Mainforce. And as he looked he smiled quietly within himself. Detective officers of all ranks coming, for the first time, against the prognostications of the doctor were wont to look like an unsuspecting rabbit suddenly confronted by a snake in search of a tit-bit in the menu. There was the same fascination in the eyes of Carruthers; the fascination that kept the officer's orbits on the doctor's face, while the brain attempted, without success, to follow the trend of thought that had worked out the pattern of murder.

Sir Edward had seen it so often, and always accompanied by the same expression. He knew that Manson, though apparently unconscious of the inspector's attention, and feigning to know of no reason why there should be thought any reason for surprise at his dictate, was, indeed, very well cognizant of just what Carruthers was thinking and doing, and was chuckling inside himself at both his companions; for the A.C. knew perfectly well that the scientist was aware that he, too, was in ignorance of the line of thought which had produced the four points. But Sir Edward said nothing of this. It would not do, he counselled himself, for the inspector to be even suspicious of the fact that the assistant commissioner was also in the dark. It would be bad for discipline. His line of country was to ignore the doctor's decision. In that way, Carruthers might well assume that what was a closed book to him was as open a page to Sir Edward as to the doctor himself. He therefore, like Brer Rabbit, laid low and said nuthin'. At least, he said nothing on the summing-up of his scientific colleague. What he *did* say was addressed to Carruthers.

"Well, there you are, Inspector. The doctor has given you the points for which you asked," he said. "Are they of any assistance?"

Carruthers demonstrated no enthusiasm at the A.C.'s question. Nor did his outward and visible appearance belie his inward and spiritual view of the situation. As he saw it, the doctor's aid had confused more than assisted him. The case of violent death which he had presented to the Yard on a platter had been returned to him as one of wilful murder. That would not, perhaps, have been so bad if he had been able to see in which direction the murder lay. or any reason for it. It would have been a little encouraging, and possibly of some assistance, if he could see why Dr. Manson was so certain in his own mind that it *was* murder. If he (the inspector) was unable to track that final point down— and he certainly could not, so he told himself—how the deuce would he be able to hunt, unaided, the murderer? Much as he disliked giving up without an effort, and handing over his case to others, he felt that in the circumstances it was the only move he could make if the village was to be cleared of a homicidal maniac, for a maniac it must be who killed, deliberately, a harmless visitor to its annual cricket match. The chief constable had given him full liberty of action to undertake what arrangements he liked. The inspector made up his mind.

"I am afraid that they do not help me at all, Mr. Assistant Commissioner," he replied. "I have no doubt that Dr. Manson is correct, but I cannot see—I confess it—the grounds he has for saying what he has said. And I do not see how I can implement the information, in those circumstances."

Sir Edward nodded approvingly at the candour of the inspector's statement. "Then, is there any other help we can give you—any elucidation, or amplification?"

The inspector jumped in at the opportunity. "I would like to call in Dr. Manson, sir," he said.

Sir Edward frowned. "Surely there should be some consultation with your superiors about that, Inspector, should there not?" he asked.

"The chief constable and myself went over that before I left to see you, sir," was the reply. "He gave me full authority to speak for him on the matter if, after hearing Dr. Manson, I thought it desirable that the Yard should be asked to take over the investigation, in the interests of Justice. I *do* feel that way, sir."

"That is, of course, a different matter." He looked across at the scientist. "What do you think of that, Doctor?" he asked. "Can you spare the time from the other matter?" He emphasized the latter point to the inspector. "Dr. Manson is pretty well occupied at the moment with a matter of some importance."

Dr. Manson nodded agreement. "Nevertheless, A.C., there are one or two peculiar points in Carruthers' story which interest me," he said. He thought for a moment, and then turned to the inspector.

"When are you holding the inquest?" he asked.

"Tomorrow afternoon, Doctor," was the reply.

The scientist turned to Sir Edward. "I think it might meet the case at the moment if I attended the inquest in my legal capacity as a barrister. I could be watching the case on behalf of the chief constable. That would give me an opportunity of questioning some of the witnesses if I think it necessary, and also a chance to look round the scene. It may be that I may see a course of action which Carruthers, here, could follow with assistance from me, or we might, in certain circumstances, spare Sergeant Merry. That would relieve me of too close an attention to the problem, leaving me pretty free for the other. What do you say to that?"

"Just as you like, Doctor. Corpses are your failing. It takes a bit to keep you away from one."

"Very well, Carruthers. I will attend the inquest. In the meantime I would be glad if you will endeavour to find out how the man came to the village. He must have arrived there some way, despite the evidence to the contrary. There are, if I remember correctly, several bus routes, and there is a railway station. I suppose you have marked on the green the spot on which the chair was standing?"

"Yes, Doctor. The position of the legs have been pegged and a tarpaulin is covering it."

"Right. Then I'll see you tomorrow."

"A remarkable story, Harry," the assistant commissioner commented after the door had closed on the inspector.

"Very remarkable, Edward," was the reply. In the privacy of their own company these two reverted to the position of close personal friends and fellow clubmen. In the presence of their colleagues, discipline made it imperative that they should be the assistant commissioner and Chief-Detective-Inspector Dr. Manson; but in the privacy of themselves they were Edward and Harry.

The scientist looked up at his friend. "And the most remarkable thing about the story, Edward, is the thing which has aroused my particular interest."

"That being, Harry?"

"That the man is shot and murdered despite the fact that he had not been seen, generally, around the village. Do you realize what that seems to imply? It suggests that he came to the village after the match had started, sat down to watch the cricket, and was shot. By whom? *By somebody who saw him on the green, and only on the green.* That is the only suggestion or explanation I can see. I may be wrong. I have not what I regard as the full facts, probed by myself, but only a statement by two or three officers who may not have looked for what I should have looked. But we can be sure of this: the person who fired did not see him round the village and *plan* to murder. He saw him at the match, and killed on the spur of the moment.

"Then, again, the man's chair stood away from the others. Why? Was it moved there by the murderer, to leave him free from observation? Or was it moved there by the victim to escape from the proximity of the murderer? It is all extremely interesting, and a problem after my own heart. That is, of course, on our present knowledge.

"There are other features of importance. Were the shots fired from the high road, and were the backfires, which various people heard, the shots? It would be a good marksman who could be certain of shooting dead a person from a moving vehicle. It would have to be a moving vehicle, you know, to allow the shots to be mistaken for backfiring. And it would be an extraordinarily good shot who could kill from a moving vehicle a person *he couldn't see.*"

"A person he couldn't see? I don't get it, Harry."

"He was lying in a canvas chair, and he was shot *through the back*, Edward. You've sat in a canvas deck-chair a few times at Roehampton and Henley. Do you think you could be seen from the back? Then how did the person know he was there, unless he had been on the green and seen him? Seen him from the front. Or unless, as I have already said, he moved the chair and knew that 'X' seated himself in it. And how sure he was of himself as a shot. He had to be certain of killing, you know. He *had* to kill, had to, you understand. If he had only wounded him, 'X' could have spilt the beans.

"Except for one thing I would have said that the shot might have been accidental murder. Murder because a lethal weapon had been discharged unlawfully within reach of the highway, with fatal results, and accident because the shot had, by a thousand to one chance, killed that particular person. But accident is ruled out by the something taken from the body of the dead man. There, again, it might have been taken from him either before or after death. I don't know which. But it was most likely afterwards."

"Quite. And that reminds me, Harry. What *was* it that was taken from him?"

The scientist looked reproachfully at his friend. "You mean to say you don't know, Edward?" he asked. "Now, I thought you would have seen it right away. You know my methods, Watson," he added humorously.

"But I haven't your suspicious mind, Harry," was the retort. "I can no more see what it was than Carruthers could."

Dr. Manson leaned forward and spoke for a few seconds. "Doesn't that strike you as a perfectly reasonable deduction?" he asked.

"Of course . . . yes. Simple, of course. Beats me how it is that I never saw it."

"Just lack of logical thinking, Edward. You were never taught to think logically, my lad. That's your trouble. It is also the trouble of nine hundred and ninety-nine people out of a thousand. Well, I'm off for a spot of dinner. I am a couple of hours past my time, thanks to Carruthers."

* * * * *

The inquest on the mysterious stranger was held in the Church Hall, at Thames Pagnall; and the village, or all that part of the village as had no daily round or common task to perform in the adjacent city of London attended in strength. Eleven good men and true sat on the stage where, a week ago that very day, the local amateur dramatic society had killed off a character in their annual play.

The coroner was also on the stage, on their right; the kitchen table of Mrs. Rossemer, the hall caretaker, extracted by persuasion, forming his official rostrum. A green baize-covered card-table and a chair evolved themselves into a witness-box. At a table below the stage, and facing it, sat Inspector Carruthers, with a vacant place next to him reserved for Dr. Manson. A few yards away, gentlemen of the Press sat at a long trestle desk, their note-books open and pencils in their hands. The stage was set—in very truth.

The coroner bustled to his seat, laid open his note-book, official paper, and medico-legal works. When he was not one of His Majesty s coroners he was Mr. James Meech, solicitor, of Kingston-on-Thames. While the jury were viewing the body he had a word or two with Inspector Carruthers. The result was heard when the jury returned and filed into their seats.

"Before we begin the actual proceedings, gentlemen," said the coroner, "the police have requested me to ask you a question. You have seen the body of the deceased. Have either, or any, of you seen the man before, inside the village or outside it?"

The jury whispered among themselves for a few moments, and the foreman then rose. "Mr. Coroner," he announced, "none of us has ever seen the gentleman—I mean the deceased." He corrected himself, apparently under the impression that no deceased could possibly be a gentleman.

"Very well, gentlemen. We will proceed. I shall call Detective-Inspector Carruthers to the witness-box."

The inspector deposed, on oath, that he was called to the cricket green at Thames Pagnall, at about six-thirty o'clock the previous evening. "I saw the deceased sitting in a canvas deck-chair. He was lying back in the chair, with his hat over his eyes. He looked asleep."

"Did you know that he was dead?" the coroner asked.

"I had been told that he was dead."

"Was there anyone else there when you arrived?"

"Nearly all the village," the inspector replied, grimly.

"I take it that the man was, in fact, dead before you arrived there?"

"Yes, sir. I could find no trace of life."

"Did you know how he died?"

"Not then, sir. The doctor arrived a few seconds after. On examining him he found that the man had been shot."

"Have you any intimation of the kind of weapon from which the shot was fired?"

"Yes, sir. The bullet has been handed to me by the doctor It was projected from a .22 rifle."

"Do you know of any such weapon owned by any person in Thames Pagnall?"

A murmur ran round the hall; the village leaned forward to hear the inspector's reply. He paused for a moment, eyeing the crowded hall with a glint in his own eyes. Had he been an actor, instead of a police inspector, he might, with some justification, have been accused of playing to the gallery. The good actor would have said that his hesitation had that touch of 'timing' which betrays the artist.

"I have made careful inquiries, sir, and I can find no one in the district who owns, or has ever owned, a rifle of this description."

"I understand that a cricket match had been played on the green that afternoon between the home club and that of Maplecot. Have you inquired whether a resident in Maplecot possesses a rifle of this description?"

"I have, sir. A Mr. Ferris has such a weapon."

"Ah-h-h!" The exclamation came in a loud rumble from the hall. What it meant, really, was: "Ah! we told you so. Nothing is beyond a team which will play a county bowler who had only been in the village for twenty-four hours."

The coroner frowned at the interruption. He waited until his frowns had restored order. Then: "Have you examined this rifle, Inspector?" he asked.

"I have, sir. Mr. Ferris informed me that he had purchased it some ten years ago, and that it had not been in use for at least five years. I convinced myself that it had not been fired recently. It could not have been fired. The barrel was very rusty, and any attempt to fire it would probably have burst it."

"And you have found no traces of a weapon other than this one, which has not been fired recently?"

A disturbance at the back of the hall caused the inspector's 'yes' to be inaudible. There was a scraping of chairs on the wooden floor, and through the gap made, a tall, scholarly-looking figure negotiated a way. He walked up to the table below the stage.

The coroner registered stern annoyance. "Really, this is the second time these proceedings have been interrupted," he announced, testily. "What is the meaning of this intrusion? And who are you, sir?"

Inspector Carruthers leaned forward and whispered a few words in the coroner's ears. That official nodded, and turned to the intruder. "I understand, sir, that you are Dr. Manson of Scotland Yard, and that you are legally representing the police, and are also concerned in these investigations?"

"That is so, Mr. Coroner. I must apologize for my late arrival, and for the interruption. It was caused by the car in which I was travelling breaking down on the way. With you, I deplore late arrivals and interruptions at an inquiry."

The coroner, mollified, acknowledged the unavoidability of the doctor's delay. "The inspector is the first witness, Dr. Manson. He has told us that he was called to the green, found the man upon whom we are holding this inquest dead from a shot from a rifle of .22 calibre. He has just stated that a rifle of this calibre is owned by a member of the team which was playing against Thames Pagnall, but that it had not been fired for a considerable time, and could not, in fact, be fired without bursting the barrel."

"Thank you for your courtesy, Mr. Coroner," the scientist acknowledged.

The coroner now turned again to the inspector. "Did I understand you to say, Inspector, that you can find no rifle other than the one you mentioned, as being owned by anyone in this district, or in the district of Maplecot?"

"That is so, sir."

"I see. Now, Inspector, regarding this shot. Do you know when it was fired and from where?"

"I do not know of my own knowledge, sir. But I have witnesses who will speak of a certain explosion or explosions which may, or may not, have been the shot or shots."

"Then we will seek the information from them, Inspector." The coroner consulted his notes, reading them over to himself and considering whether there was anything further he might obtain from the witness. "And I understand that, so far, you have been unable to establish the identity of the dead man?"

"Quite unable, sir."

"Very well." The coroner looked across at Dr. Manson. The scientist shook his head at the invitation.

"Call George Crombie," the coroner demanded; and old George stepped on to the stage and into the limelight. The coroner addressed him.

"You are George Crombie. You are sixty-eight years of age, and are a general handyman. It is your duty on behalf of the cricket club to take charge of the chairs and other seating accommodation—to set them out, and to collect them at the end of the match. Is that correct?"

"Yesser."

"And that it was while you were engaged in the performance of those duties that you saw the deceased?"

"I thought as 'ow he was a-sleepin', mister," announced George.

"Why should you think he was sleeping?"

"He was a-lyin' back in the chair, mister, with 'is 'at over 'is eyes, like anybody 'ud be lyin' asleep in a deck-chair. Lots of people goes to sleep in 'em at a match. Dunno wot they comes to the cricket for at all, when they could go ter sleep more comfy in their beds."

A ripple of laughter ran round the hall. There was more than a hint of philosophy in Crombie's view of spectators.

"Anyhow," the coroner said, "you thought he was sleeping, and you wanted the chair, so you tried to wake him?"

"'S'right. I calls him, then I nudges him, and then I shakes him."

"And when he didn't wake up, then what did you do?"

"Hared it to the 'Green Man' to tell the squire, mister."

The coroner frowned again at the burst of laughter which greeted the description of Crombie's hobbling as "haring it to the 'Green Man'."

"Leaving the body in the chair?"

"No, Mr. Bosanquet was there. It was him as told me to fetch squire. He'd come about his fowls. Dratted nuisance them there fowls is."

The coroner looked puzzled. "Fowls?" he echoed. "What have fowls to do with it? And where were they?"

Inspector Carruthers whispered to him.

"Oh, quite . . . quite. Had you seen the man at all before this, Crombie?" he continued.

"Never seen a sign o' him."

"Do you want this witness, Doctor?" The coroner looked across at Manson, who nodded and rose.

"Mr. Crombie, do I understand that, on the occasion of a match, you bring the chairs and forms to the field and set them out?"

Old George nodded.

"How do you set them out? I mean in what order? Are they just put down for people to fetch and take where they like?"

"No blooming fear, mister," answered George, with emphasis. "I puts all the deckers—that's them with the long backs—alongside each of the tents. Them's for the gentry and the members of the club to use. Then I puts the upright chairs, them what shuts up, a bit further off. And the forms, wot ain't got no backs, goes along the boundary on t'other side o' ground. So as there's people all round the field, like."

"I see. Bit of an art in it, eh? And did you put them that way yesterday?"

"Aye."

"Now, when you found this man apparently asleep, his chair, one of those which should have been with the others of its kind near the tents, was some distance away, was it not? Did you see that chair taken away from the others?"

"Not bloomin' likely. Else I'd a' fetched it back, quick."

"Is it part of your duties to watch the chairs?"

"No. But I mostly does. I only fetches 'em to the ground, and takes 'em away agen, official."

"And you saw nobody move the chair, and you don't know how it came to be where it was?"

"No."

"But, anyway, you are quite sure that the chair was taken away by somebody, and placed where the man was sitting in it?"

"Sure, mister, yes."

The next witness was Mr. Alfred Bosanquet. The coroner eyed him questioningly. "How do you pronounce your name, sir?" he asked. "I know that you gentlemen of that clan have various theories of pronunciation."

Mr. Bosanquet smiled. "I like it pronounced Bow-*san*-kay," he replied. "And with the emphasis on the 'san'."

"Then we will use it that way," the coroner conceded. "I understand, Mr. Bosanquet, that you reside in a bungalow which faces the cricket green?"

"Green Shutters, sir. That is so."

"What are you by profession?"

"An importer of general merchandise. My offices are in Temple Avenue, London."

"And on the day in question at this inquiry, you were watching the progress of a cricket match on the green?"

"I was entertaining a few friends, sir, and we were sitting in chairs on my front lawn. The lawn commands a view of the cricket pitch, which was the chief reason that I took the property. I am a village cricket enthusiast."

"The witness Crombie has told us that you sent him for the squire, and remained yourself by the dead man. How did you come to be on the green? You were entertaining friends, I understand."

"I wanted to get hold of Crombie, sir, and looking out of my windows I saw him with his barrow and chairs on the green. I walked across to him."

"Would that be over the matter of fowls, sir?"

"It was. I wanted Crombie to catch them, and repair the damaged wire through which they had escaped. I saw that he was a bit disturbed, and asked him what was the matter. He replied that he couldn't wake up the man in the chair. I bent over the man and shook him. He didn't move. So I slipped my hand inside his waistcoat and felt his heart. He was dead. I thought it better that Crombie should go for assistance while I remained to see that the body was not disturbed in any way."

"Had you recognized the man?"

"I had not, then, even seen his face, sir. His hat was over his eyes, completely hiding the features. When I had shaken him, without effect, I felt the body to be a dead weight, if you understand me. It presented heavy resistance. It was that which made me feel for his heart. When I found he was dead, I made no further investigation. I was quite sure that the police would object to the body being disturbed. Had the man been still alive, I should, of course, have endeavoured to render him some assistance, which would, doubtless, have meant disturbing his position in the chair."

"A very commendable action on your part, if I may say so, Mr. Bosanquet. And an example to other people who may come across people who have died suddenly."

Dr. Manson had looked sharply up at Mr. Bosanquet's statement. He now studied the man with an interested gaze. Little wrinkles appeared round the corners of his eyes, and furrows corrugated his broad and high forehead. What he saw seemed to satisfy him but he made a note in a note-book open in front of him before accepting the coroner's look of invitation. He rose.

"I think, Mr. Bosanquet, that you told Police-sergeant Wharton that you heard a shot fired. What time would that be?"

"Oh, as to that, sir, I am told that what I heard was a backfire from a motor vehicle."

"Never mind, for the moment, what you were told." retorted Manson, quietly. "Never mind whether it was a shot or a backfire. Let us say that you heard some kind of explosion. What time would it be?"

"As near as I can say, about a quarter to five."

"Did it come from far away?"

"I could not say about that. I mean, I heard a sound. I wasn't listening for anything, and did not take much notice of it. I just heard it, and remembered the fact when the doctor stated that the man had been shot."

"Do you know the sound of a shot, sir?" asked Manson.

"I know nothing whatever about firearms. I have never shot anything in my life."

"Anyway, you heard some sound at about four-forty-five, and nothing afterwards?"

"That is so."

During the evidence of Mr. Bosanquet, Dr. Lumley had entered the room. He now came forward and addressed the coroner. "I should be glad, sir, if you could take my evidence at once, since I have to return to a patient at the earliest possible moment." A nod from the coroner, and he took his place at the witness-stand. He deposed that he was called to the green, and found that the man was dead. On making an examination he discovered that the man had a bullet-wound in the back. He had since conducted a post-mortem examination.

"And you found?" asked the coroner.

"I found that the body was that of a well-nourished and well-developed person, of between fifty and sixty years of age. The only mark of violence visible on the body was a small puncture in the back, between the shoulder-blades. It was obviously the entrance of a bullet. On opening the body, I found a considerable quantity of blood in the chest cavity and in the tissues below the breastbone. Behind the chestbone I found a bullet which I handed over later to Inspector Carruthers. The bullet had passed through the main artery of the body which leads from the left chamber of the heart, the aorta. The wound in the walls of the heart-bag measured three-eighths of an inch in length, and about half an inch in width. The breastbone was bruised apparently in stopping the course of the missile, which would otherwise have emerged from the body. I found no evidence of disease, all the organs of the body being healthy, with the exception of the liver, which was somewhat fatty. I came to the conclusion that death was due to the wounding of the aorta of the heart, caused by the penetration of a bullet."

"Can you say, Doctor, from what distance the bullet was fired?" asked Dr. Manson.

"I am afraid not, sir," was the reply. "I am not an authority on ballistics, nor an expert witness."

"Perhaps we can find that you are both, in spite of yourself," retorted Manson, with a pleasant smile. "For instance, in what direction did the bullet enter the body?"

"Slightly downward."

"Could you say how many degrees out of the horizontal?"

Dr. Lumley considered carefully before replying. "Yes," he said, at last. "I should say it would be between thirty and forty degrees."

"I assume from that, Doctor, that the entrance hole was not round in character, but slightly conical?"

"That is correct."

"Now, were the margins of the entrance well defined, allowing, of course, for the retraction of the tissues, or were they, shall we say, ragged?"

Dr. Lumley started in surprise, and a gleam came into his eyes. He looked up at the scientist. "I see your point, sir," he said. "As a matter of fact, the entrance was *not* sharply defined."

"There you are, Doctor, you see. The perfect expert witness," retorted Dr. Manson. "Can you say whether any part of the dress was driven into the wound?"

"There was no extraneous matter in the body, other than the bullet."

"Can you say whether death was instantaneous? Contrary to general belief, a wound in the heart is by no means an immediately fatal wound, as you and I know very well."

"That is so. But in this case I think death was instantaneous. I base that, principally, on the position of the body when I saw it. It was lying restfully and peacefully in the chair. Had there have been life after the bullet pierced the heart, I should have expected to have found evidence of movement of some kind, possibly of contortion from pain. I found nothing of the sort."

"Quite so. How long had the man been dead when you first examined him?"

"I told Inspector Carruthers before the post-mortem that he had been dead not less than two hours and not more than three hours. I see no reason to change that opinion."

"Thank you, Doctor."

Mr. Horatius Catling took the doctor's place in the witness-stand. His examination by the coroner was brief.

"You told the police-sergeant that you had heard two explosions during the course of the cricket match. Can you give the time?"

"About a quarter to five."

"Were they, do you think, shots?" asked Dr. Manson.

"I said they were backfires when the sergeant inquired of me. It was Mr. Bosanquet who said he heard shots," was the reply.

"Do *you* know the sound of a shot, Mr. Catling?"

"Of revolver shots, yes; but not rifle-shots. And I know the sound of backfires. I should do. I've got a stinker of a car."

"So have I," sympathized Dr. Manson. "Anyway, they were not revolver shots that you heard?"

"They were certainly not."

"You are, by the way, quite certain that you heard two explosions? Where were you when they occurred?"

"There were two right enough. I was sitting on the lawn of Mr. Bosanquet's house, watching the game."

"With, of course, Mr. Bosanquet, Mrs. Bosanquet, Miss Malcolm and Mr. Watkins?" The scientist waited for the answer. Had Superintendent Jones, or Inspector Kenway, of Scotland Yard been with him, they would have said that he waited *warily* for the answer. But the only evidence of this was the reappearance of the wrinkles and the furrows. And these conveyed nothing to the coroner, the witness or the court.

"As you say, sir, I was sitting with all the others."

Only one witness now remained. "James Baldwin," called the coroner. Excited whisperings broke out as Gaffer Baldwin tottered his way down the hall to the stage and into the witness-chair. Everybody knew that Gaffer had something to tell. The cryptic utterances, which had earned for him more pints in one night than he was usually treated to in a month, had been noised abroad by all who had heard them. The rumours were many and varied, from relating how Baldwin had actually seen the man shot, and had been terrified into silence by threats of being sent the same way, down to the mere seeing of a strange man with a gun in a cricket-bag. And, it was pointed out, Constable Lambert had been on guard over Gaffer at his cottage all night. All attempts the previous night, and throughout the day, at getting anything out of Baldwin had failed. Gaffer was not so great a fool as he looked; and while he kept his secret knew that he could enjoy glasses of beer lavished on him with the intention of making him tell it! Now, however, he was in the witness-box, and had to tell, beer or no beer. The village waited.

The coroner eyed him without enthusiasm. Gaffer was pretty deaf, except to the words he could read on a benefactor's lips— "What'll you have, Gaffer?"

"How old are you, Baldwin?" he asked at length.

"Wot's he say?" asked Gaffer of Sergeant Wharton.

"He says how old are you—and you tell him the truth, see."

"I'm a hunnerd," said Gaffer.

"He's not, sir," put in the sergeant.

"Wot?"

"I said you aren't a hundred, you old nuisance!" bellowed the sergeant. "You're only eighty-two."

"I tell 'ee I'm a hunnerd. And don't 'ee start takin' away me word, young Wharton. Many's the time I've dusted yer breeches for stealing old squire's apples, and I'll dust 'em again if yer takes me good name away, hunnerd though I be."

A roar of laughter greeted the reminiscence of the old man, and Sergeant Wharton turned a beetroot-red face to the coroner. "He's eighty-two, sir. I've seen his birth certificate."

"I'll make it eighty-two," the coroner decided. He raised his voice. "What do you do for a living?"

"Livin'? Me old age pension, master. What don't properly keep body and soul together. Many's the night—"

"Never mind that, Baldwin. It's been reported that you've been saying that you knew somebody was going to die on that green yesterday. Is that true?"

"Wot's he say?"

"You said you knew somebody was going to die in the village!" roared the sergeant in his ear.

"Oh . . . aye . . . that's right."

A rustle of excitement swayed the crowd forward. Ears were cocked for the old man's story.

"I was a-waitin' for it, o' course."

The rustle became a movement, and the whispering a gasp. The coroner gazed at him as though mesmerized.

"You . . . were . . . waiting . . . for . . . a . . . man . . . to . . . be . . . killed . . . and never . . . gave . . . a warning that it might . . . happen?" he asked.

"Warn't no good giving no warning, master. Nobody could'a stopped it."

"N—n—nobody c—could have stopped it?" The coroner was in danger of developing apoplexy.

"Not arter wot I seed, no."

"Oh! You saw something, did you? What did you see?"

"Aye, I did. As soon as I see'd it I sez to meself, 'Gaffer—'"

"Yes, yes, we know all that, Gaffer!" roared Sergeant Wharton. "The gentleman wants to know what you saw and when you saw it."

"When I seed it? When should I ha' seed it 'cept when I was a-havin' o' me walk at five o'clock, me being kep' awake by the cold, havin' no blanket, on account o' me old age pension?"

"You mean when you were going to look at your rabbit snares afore anybody was up," put in Wharton. "I'll catch you at it one of these mornings."

"I was a-takin' o' me walk round the green," went on Gaffer, ignoring the poaching allegation, "when all o' a sudden I sees him. I sez, 'Gaffer—'"

"Will you tell us *what you saw*, you old nuisance!" bellowed the sergeant.

"He went acrost the green whiles I watches 'un, and I sez—"

"WHO WENT . . . ACROSS . . . THE . . . GREEN?"

"Flew acrost, 'e did."

"FLEW across?" from the coroner, bewildered.

Sergeant Wharton, his patience exhausted, seized the muttering old dodderer by the jacket collar and shook him. "Will you tell the coroner and the jury who or what you saw!" he shouted. "What, or who, did you see fly across the green?"

"A magpie—that's wot I see'd."

"W—w—what!"

The coroner's dumbfounded ejaculation was drowned in the great burst of laughter which shook the court. It was thirty seconds before the villagers, seeing Gaffer's lips still moving, lapsed into silence to hear what he was explaining.

". . . and I sez, 'One is fer sorrow, two is fer mirth, three fer a wedding, and four fer a birth.' So I know'd summat was a-bound t'happen."

The coroner, who throughout this recital had been speechless, now found his voice. "Do you mean to tell me that you have been wasting my time and the time of this court on a cock-and-bull, old wives' tale of superstition?" he howled. "I've a good mind to commit you to prison for contempt of court."

"Wot's he a-sayin'?" demanded Gaffer.

A choleric sergeant shook him again. "He says he's going to send you to the lock-up for wasting his time with old wives' tales."

"Old wives' tales be danged," said Gaffer. "I sez as 'ow it wur an omen, an' it wur, wurn't it? I sez as 'ow somebody 'ud die. An' they did. Any fool knows as seein' one magpie by hisself means a dyin' man or 'ooman."

"He's got us there, Mr. Coroner," commented Dr. Manson, tears of laughter in his eyes. "The Augur spoke truly this time, at any rate."

While Sergeant Wharton bundled Gaffer unceremoniously out of the door, the coroner summed up. "You have heard, gentlemen, how the body of the deceased was found," he said. "You have heard that he died from a bullet-wound. You have heard, also, that no evidence has so far been found as to how he came to be shot; and that the police have not, as yet, been able to identify the victim.

"There are four verdicts which you can return. You can say that the man committed suicide. I must tell you that there is no evidence of that. On the contrary, the evidence is against it. You can say that he was the victim of an accident. You can say that he was murdered. In neither of these is there, in my view, evidence sufficient to justify such verdicts. Or you can say that the man was found dead, which is, in fact, an open verdict; and leaves the police free to pursue further inquiries."

"Yes, sir," said the foreman.

"You mean that you return an open verdict?"

"That's it, sir."

"Very well. Then that closes the inquiry."

CHAPTER FIVE
FIRST FITTING

"THE CHIEF CONSTABLE'S compliments, sir, and I was to say that he hoped you would step round for a cup of tea and a chat after the inquest."

Inspector Carruthers conveyed the invitation as the village population was filing out of the Church Hall to return to its neglected homes.

"I shall be glad to, Inspector. A cup of tea would be very welcome at the moment. I can drive you over in my car, if you like. But first, I would prefer to have a look at the body of the man."

"The mortuary is just behind this hall, Doctor," the inspector responded; and led the way. Manson, standing presently in front of the corpse, looked it carefully over. He examined the body for any sign of violence, other than the shot-wound, peering through a glass at any mark, however small, which disfigured the skin. Finally, with the aid of the inspector, he turned the body over, and paid close attention to the bullet-wound. His glass came into play again as he examined the edges of the entrance of the bullet. What he saw seemed to satisfy him, for twice he nodded his head in agreement at some conclusion which he had seemingly found evidence to confirm. This cursory examination ended, he settled down to a more detailed one. From a pocket-case he took a glass rod, some six inches long. This he gently edged into the wound. It was a careful operation, for the natural retraction of the opening made it difficult to slide the rod into its depths, slim though the rod was. The inspector watched the operation with lively curiosity; he bent forward and leaned over the body, the better to observe it.

"One has to go pretty gently, Inspector," Dr. Manson explained, noting the interest shown. "Forcing might penetrate the sides of the wound under the skin, and that would give a wrongful conclusion to the experiment I am making. I must have the implement lying straight through the centre of the bullet-hole if my calculations are to be correct." As he spoke, he slid the rod slowly up and down, and, finding the action easy and free, expressed his satisfaction in a "Ha! I think that will do. Seems quite tight, too. Now, a protuberance of about three inches should be suitable." He adjusted the rod, stepping back once or twice, to note the effect, and making some slight adjustment. His next move was to take from his pocket-case a protractor. This he contacted on the skin of the man, gradually and slowly edging it towards the protruding rod, until the latter cut across the face of the instrument. Noting the angle of contact on the face of the protractor, he repeated the action from the opposite side of the rod. Three times the experiment was continued before the scientist was satisfied, and replaced the rod and protractor in his case. He wrote the result in his note-book—'Angle 30.25 degrees.'

The calculations, however, were not yet concluded. Dr. Manson dipped again into the case and his hands emerged this time holding a small 'T'-square. It differed somewhat from that familiar on a drawing-board, in that it was fitted with a base some three-quarters of an inch thick. The tail of the 'T' ran to some twelve inches length. Set vertically in the length was a two-inch spirit level, and in the base a similar level had been inserted horizontally. Laying the square on the skin of the dead man's back, he drew, with an indelible pencil, a straight line from the point of the entry of the bullet upwards towards the shoulders. The line extended for some two inches from the wound. This done, he stood the 'T'-square on its base, forming a right angle to the drawn indelible line, and exactly one and a half inches in front of the bullet-hole. It was now evident that the bullet had not only entered the body with a downward angle, but also from an oblique direction, for the glass rod cut across the 'T'-square leaving a gap of definite measurement between.

It was at this point that Inspector Carruthers saw the purport of the experiment. "Gosh, Doctor, that's pretty cute," he ejaculated. "Gives you an almost perfect idea from where the shot was fired."

Manson smiled. "I already knew the direction from which the shot was fired, Inspector," he said. "The rod extending from the wound gave that quite clearly. It is a point to be remembered in all wounds that a mere visual examination cannot supply precise mathematical data as to how it was inflicted. Seeing the direction from which the shot came was a simple matter of eyesight; but that is not sufficient. I want to be able to demonstrate to a jury, if necessary, the position when the body is no longer available for them to see it for themselves. Also, I want to know the exact position whence the rifle was aimed, if it is possible at all to get the position."

"And this will give it?"

"That remains to be seen. But I should be failing in scientific investigation if I had not taken these measurements." As he spoke he was measuring with a micrometer rule the gap between the 'T'-square and the centre of the projecting rod. "Seven-sixteenths," he announced, and added the calculation to the earlier one in his notebook. "You see, Inspector," he explained, "it is now a simple mathematical calculation to arrive at the distance on the left of the man that the murderer was standing when he fired, let us say, at two hundred yards' range, or a thousand yards' range. Work it out, starting at seven-sixteenths of an inch deviation at the point of impact."

Carruthers waxed enthusiastic. "I see it now, Doctor. You can say with absolute certainty where the man who fired lay in wait, as it were. We thus know the line of fire, and have only to find who was at that spot you mark at the time."

"Oh dear, no! It is not so easy as that, Inspector. We do not know the range, though I may be able, later, to give some idea of that. Then, again, the angle I have taken from the body depends for its accuracy upon how the dead man was lying in the chair. Half an inch either side of dead flat will vary the position very greatly, and throw all the calculations out. The most it does, so far, is to limit the position of the rifle to a certain width. I may be able to limit that width still further when I reconstruct the man's position in the chair—and when I have examined the photographs which you had taken—I give you full points for those valuable aids."

During this dissertation, Dr. Manson was examining the clothes of the dead man. He turned them, and once or twice peered through his magnifying glass at the cloth. Next, he crossed to a deck-chair, standing against a wall. "This the chair?" he asked; and received a confirming nod from the inspector. Without touching it, he looked closely at the canvas at the point where it was perforated by the entrance of the bullet. "Well, I think that is all I can do now," he said at last. "Perhaps, however, you will get the constable to parcel up these clothes and have them ready for me on my return. That done, we will keep our appointment for a cup of tea."

The tea was waiting. The buttered scones were waiting. And Colonel Mainforce was also waiting. He welcomed Dr. Manson as an old friend. "So you're paying me a visit at last, Doctor?" he jested. "It has taken a corpse to drag you down, eh? When Carruthers, here, suggested that he should ask you if you would take over, I knew for sure that I should be entertaining you. You will never be able to resist the attraction of an unknown body—if it *is* still unknown?" he added, questioningly.

"Still unknown, Colonel. Yes, still unknown. I'm not a magician, you know."

"I've my doubts about that, Doctor." He turned to the inspector. "What happened at the inquest; and what did Baldwin say?"

Carruthers snorted. "Baldwin! I'd like to wring the old fool's neck," was the reply.

"Not here, Carruthers. Not here. Damn it, suppose somebody *does* wring his neck, where do you suppose the Doctor's going to look?" The colonel chuckled at his little joke. "What's wrong with Baldwin's story? I thought he knew something or somebody was on the point of dying."

"So he did—according to him." Carruthers told the story, and told it dramatically, up to the *dénouement*. The chief constable laughed until the tears ran down his cheeks. "A magpie!" he gasped. "Oh, my sainted aunt! And you guarded his cottage all the night! Ha, ha! Waiting for a blessed magpie! Damn it, Doctor, I haven't heard that old tale since my boyhood days, when old Farmer Beddowes who was our neighbour, came back home walloping his horse into a gallop, because on the way to the bank to put in £250 he saw a magpie fly across the road in front of him. He came back with the money still in his pocket. Ha, ha!"

He stopped suddenly, and sat up. "And now I come to think of it, the dashed bank suspended payment next day, and old Beddowes saved his money. Darn it, that's funny. And now it's come true again. I've a couple of magpies come fetching my peas—"

"That's all right, Colonel," Manson chuckled. "Two is for mirth, according to Gaffer Baldwin. But don't go shooting one of 'em."

"That's comforting, at any rate. So you got a 'found dead' verdict, did you, Carruthers; and now it's up to the doctor, eh?"

"I hope so, sir." He looked at the scientist.

"I think we will have a shot at it, Carruthers—you and I, together," was the reply.

The eyes of Inspector Carruthers lit up. The chief constable, catching the glint, nodded mentally to himself. Dr. Manson, too, saw the brightening in the inspector's face; and knew that his judgment of the man was correct. It was the working method of the scientist to gain the goodwill of the provincial men who had to come into his investigations. The task is not always an easy one; local C.I.D. men are apt to resent the calling in of Scotland Yard. Too frequently it means that all the credit goes to the big names of the Yard men, while their own hard work is unheralded and unsung. The 'Yard' did the investigating—at least in the eyes of the general public.

Dr. Manson's partnership compact awakened all the enthusiasm of Inspector Carruthers. The scientist, remembering the inspector's attitude at the Yard conference, had judged that it would awaken thus. And he was content. Carruthers, working in partnership with the great Scotland Yard scientist, was more than content.

"Then that is comfortably settled," commented the chief constable. "Now the point is: where are you starting? Do you still say that it is murder, Doctor?"

"More emphatically than at first, Colonel. There is no shadow of doubt about it."

"Um! Carruthers gave me the gist of your summing-up at the Yard, but I confess that I do not follow the reasoning."

"Well, Colonel, let's spend a few minutes going over the points. Now, before I went in to the inquest I spent a few moments walking across the green—"

"Not, I hope, on their sacred pitch, Doctor?" put in the chief constable.

"I was very careful to avoid the pitch, Colonel," said Manson, gravely. "You know the green, Carruthers, and you saw the body in the chair, which I did not. You know that the man was killed by a shot. From which direction do you say the shot, or shots, came?"

"From the road behind him," replied Carruthers, without hesitation.

"Are you sure about that?" The question came in a slow drawl from the scientist.

"Well . . . un . . . unless you have something which I do not know . . ."

"I haven't anything which you do not know, Inspector. I am not trying to trap you into anything. I want you to say just what you think. It will not do any good for you to hang on to my coat-tails like a Tory to his party whip, and say 'yes'. I am not infallible by any means. I merely want your assurance, as the man on the spot, that you are quite sure, from your own knowledge and judgment, that the shot came from the direction of the road. Are you sure?"

"Yes Doctor."

"And that it was, in all probability, fired from a car?"

"Yes. It couldn't have been fired openly from the road, or from anywhere on the green. The inside of a closed car would have provided ideal cover for the operation."

"Of course."

"Any other motor or carriage road run past that green, in-spector?"

"No, Doctor; only that main road. The others are kinds of footpaths approaching the houses. Their garage roads and tradesmen's roads are at the backs of the houses."

"Then, since the man was sitting hidden in a deck-chair, In-spector, and was shot in the back, from a car on the road at the back of him, how do you suggest that the marksman knew who he was, or even that he was there at all?"

The inspector stared. "So *that's* what you meant when you said at the conference at the Yard that the murderer had been on the green," he said.

"Partly, but not quite all that I meant," replied Manson. "But you see the point, don't you? Suppose someone in the village happened to take out their car shortly before four forty-five o'clock; and suppose they had previously been on the green. Their movements would need some very cautious, but thor-ough, inquiry. Particularly if they came back to the green shortly afterwards," he added, pointedly.

Colonel Mainforce interrupted the dialogue. "Suppose it was an accidental shooting, Doctor?" he asked.

Dr. Manson eyed the questioner thoughtfully. "Very well, Colonel, we will assume that you are passing the green in your car. By accident, a rifle which you are holding is fired. Since you cannot see the flight of the bullet, you do not know where it has found a billet. Why on earth are you, later, on the green robbing the dead man? I should have thought that you would have ac-celerated and put as great a distance between you and the scene as you could."

"It is this robbing the dead man that I cannot fathom, Doctor," put in Inspector Carruthers. "You said the same thing at the Yard, I remember. Why do you assume that the dead man had been robbed?"

"Careful, Carruthers," put in the chief constable. "If there is one thing that the doctor doesn't do, it is to assume anything. If you start any assumptions he'll be down on you like a ton of bricks."

Manson smiled. "Well spoken, Colonel," he agreed "No, as the colonel has said, Carruthers, I do not assume. Assumption in crime detection is the resort of the incompetent, or the careless. It means that the officer who has arrived at an assumption proceeds to search for clues to fit that assumption, or clues which seem to fit it. And he thereby ignores, or fails to appreciate, anything that does not lead him in that direction. When his assumption falls down, he has no other leads in his bag. There is another method in investigation, and that is to collect facts—not fancies, but plain, hard facts—whether they seem to be of any importance or not. Put them all in order, and then see where they lead. It is assumption reversed. Now, before I answer the question you asked me, let me put one to you: have you discovered, or are you on the way to discover, Kathleen Smith?"

"No, Doctor."

"What steps have you taken?"

"I have had the area round here combed for a family of that name, but no such person can be found."

"Why around here?"

"Well, Doctor, he had been invited to spend a week-end. The letter was in his pocket. If he had already spent it, he would have destroyed the letter. As he was in this neighbourhood on Saturday, I supposed he was going over to the visit."

"I see." Dr. Manson eyed the inspector. "That is the very type of assumption which I abhor," he enjoined. "Now let us take the *facts*. I have here a man. He has an invitation to a week-end visit. On Saturday afternoon, early, he is killed in Thames Pagnall. What was he doing in Thames Pagnall? Was he on his way to the week-end visit? I have his body. I have his clothes to aid me. I find that he has a ten-shilling note, and eight shillings and twopence in coin. A queerly inadequate sum, I say to myself, with which to go spending a week-end visit. He might find other guests present. He might be asked to join in a game of cards. He might even take his host and hostess to a drink in the local. And, afterwards, he has to return whence he came—all on eighteen and twopence, Inspector.

"Then, however carefully I search his belongings, I find no tooth-brush, no razor, although the man is clean-shaven, and I find no pyjamas. And this is a man who has spent several weeks on a sightseeing holiday. So I say to myself, taking all these *facts* into consideration, I am *entitled* to *assume* that he was not on his way to stay with Kathleen Smith when he was killed. Ergo: Kathleen Smith is not likely to be in the vicinity of Thames Pagnall. Thus, I must search wider."

The doctor paused, as though inviting any comment from the inspector. But Carruthers, who, with the chief constable, had been listening with marked attention, made no sign. The doctor continued.

"You asked me why I was so sure that the man was robbed. The deduction seems to me to be not only simple, but logical. Maybe that is because I have always subordinated all the processes of my mind to pure logic—and, therefore, factual deduction. I say to myself that here is a man, a sight-seeing visitor, travelling at large round the country. He has on him a small sum of money. He has no visiting cards. He has no letters addressed to him by name, such as, for instance, confirmation of rooms booked in hotels for the future. He has no receipted bills, no cheque-book; in fact he has nothing by which, should he be involved in an accident, or any incident, he could prove his identity. He has a single, solitary letter inviting him to spend a weekend. For safety's sake, since a piece of notepaper can easily be pulled out of a pocket and be lost, he has carefully cut off the address. *Show me your warrant card, Inspector.*"

"W—w—what d—did you s—say, Doctor?" asked the staggered Carruthers.

"I said show me your warrant card. Here am I, talking of crime investigation and identity, and I have not, myself, taken the slightest precaution. I have only your word that you *are* a detective-inspector. If you are, you should be carrying a warrant card, giving your name, rank, and authority. *Let me see it.*"

Inspector Carruthers sat as though transfixed. Surprise, consternation, and incredulity chased each other over his face as he stared at the scientist. "My . . . warrant . . . card," he stammered, slowly. Manson nodded, and held out his right hand.

Carruthers slipped a hand into his inside jacket pocket and brought out a leather wallet. He extracted from it the small folding leather-backed card of authority and held it out to the scientist.

But Dr. Manson made no move to take it. He sat silently, for the space of fifteen seconds, eying the inspector's *left* hand, which still held the open wallet. *"I take it, Inspector, that you keep all your personal memoranda in there—a few Treasury notes, too, I see."* His gaze moved from the wallet to the inspector's face—and remained there.

Carruthers dropped the wallet as though it had suddenly stung him. *"That's what's gone from the body, Doctor. He had a wallet!"* he ejaculated, in a shout.

"Of *course* he had a wallet! Every man in his position has a wallet, or a pocket-book of some kind. And of *course* he cut off the address from the letter to place it in safer keeping in his wallet, as you would do yourself. As I do myself. Now, do you see why I was so sure at the Yard that the man had been deliberately murdered, and that the murderer, or an accomplice, had been on the green, and taken something from the body? *Who but a murderer would want to take the man's identity, and all the things that could give his identity, away from a shot person?"*

The reader is referred to the problem set in chapter 3.

"There is no making facts fit the assumption there Carruthers," the scientist continued. "You see what I mean when I say that I work in reverse—make the known facts give me the assumption.

"Still," he added, "all this does not help us in finding how the man was shot, and who shot him. There is one point that occurs to me on that. You told me that the small waistcoat pocket diary found on the man had an entry, 'T.P. Saturday'—by the way, I would like to have that diary for examination, later. Since all the other places he visited are marked by initials, T.P. probably represents Thames Pagnall. That being so, his visit was not the chance one that his unheralded appearance would seem to suggest. What is there in Thames Pagnall for a sightseer to enthuse over, or make a special journey to see? And how did he come to know that the place existed, so much so that he made a special entry in that diary? These are questions which seem to demand answers. In the meantime, however, I think you should concentrate on the question of identity."

"Those finger-prints, Doctor?" suggested Carruthers.

"Sorry, Inspector. I should have told you before. They are not in Records. Now, the person who can best tell us the identity is obviously Kathleen Smith, who issued an invitation to Mr. L— for a week-end. I suggest that you circulate to the Press copies of the photographs of the man you had taken, together with a request to Kathleen Smith, who issued that invitation, to communicate with you at once. I have no doubt that the national Press will oblige you by printing both the photograph and the request. They are decent fellows."

"I'll do that right away, Doctor."

"Right. There is nothing more that I can do at the moment. But tomorrow I would like to carry out one or two experiments on the green. What would be the quietest time? We don't want another thousand people round."

"Say ten o'clock, Doctor. The place is pretty quiet about then."

"Good. Ten o'clock it shall be. If you can persuade the doctor to come along, and the constable, and, of course, yourself. Now I'll drive you back to Thames Pagnall, and pick up the clothes and the diary. I will go over them in the laboratory."

"Wait a minute, Doctor." It was the chief constable who spoke. He had listened to the dialogue between the scientist and the inspector without comment, and had formulated an idea. He proceeded now to elaborate it. "I suppose we are not creating difficulties where they do not exist?" he asked. "We are taking it that the shot was fired from a car on the road, and that the murderer came, later, on the green and took all traces of identity. Might he not have been on the green all the time?"

"You mean that he might have shot from the green?" asked Manson.

The chief constable nodded. "If I were desirous of killing a man in such circumstances, I could think of no safer plan—his chair being where it was—than to stroll casually past him from the rear and fire as I passed."

"The noise of the shot, sir," protested Carruthers.

"Wouldn't be heard with a silencer, my boy."

Dr. Manson shook his head. "Ingenious, but I'm afraid right out, Colonel," he said. "The bullet was, I am told, a .22. That fact would not necessarily condemn the theory; I can think of circumstances which might cover it. But the other arguments are conclusive. I have seen the deck-chair, and I have examined, cursorily, the clothes. There is not the slightest sign of any zone of burning or blackening, nor of scorching. Any man committing murder in such a fashion would be compelled to be so near his victim as almost to be touching him, otherwise people in the vicinity would, without doubt, see the flame of the discharge. Blackening would be tattooed on the texture of the canvas back of the chair from a revolver fired less than three feet away—"

"With smokeless powder, Doctor?" the chief constable queried.

"No, there would not be blackening, if modern smokeless powder was the charge in the cartridge, but there would still be scorching. There is, however, further, and I say conclusive, evidence. I questioned the doctor closely at the inquest. He replied that the edges of the entrance wound of the bullet were not sharply defined. He said that nothing extraneous was in the wound, other than the bullet. Now, the effect of a shot at close quarters, such as you suggest, Colonel, would be so terrific an impact as to drive a fragment of the dress into the wound with the bullet. Also, the entrance hole would be defined and definite, and the skin round it would show very marked signs of bruising, consequent on the violent thud of the bullet. The circumference of this wound is ragged. The penetration of the canvas back of the chair is also ragged. That, in my belief, would *be caused only by a spinning bullet as it cut through the obstruction from such*

a distance that it had passed the centrifugal acme of its range.
Only one kind of bullet that I know of spins—that shot from a
rifled barrel. And an automatic is not rifled."

The chief constable capitulated. "Doctor, you make abstrusi-
ties appear very elementary," he said.

"On the contrary, Colonel, the truth is that you argue the elementary into the abstrusity. See you tomorrow."

CHAPTER SIX
THE BOX OF TRICKS

NOW, BEFORE HE became chief inspector, Harry Manson,
Doctor of Science, was a dilettante in science, and had for some
years taken a more than passing interest in medical jurisprudence. His introduction into police circles was the result of a
dinner-party at the house of a friend. Among the guests was
Sir Edward Allen, Assistant Commissioner at Scotland Yard.
During the course of the dinner-table conversation, crime was
bandied round. Harry Manson, unaware of Sir Edward's calling,
criticized the lack of any scientific method in police detection.
As an example of what he meant, he detailed a case then promi-
nently before the public, and in which no arrest had been made
after some weeks of effort. He proceeded to give a reasoned
possible solution of the mystery, based on scientific and logical
argument, adding that, had he access to two particular items,
which he enumerated, he believed that the solution of the riddle
was only a matter of minutes.

To his astonishment and dismay, Sir Edward, who had listened to the arguments with lively attention, offered to place the
essentials at his service. It was then that Manson learned, for
the first time, his fellow guest's official status. Apologies were
waved aside. Dr. Manson next day carried out the experiments
he had outlined in argument; and within a few hours the police
case was complete.

An offer to join Scotland Yard as the C.T.D.'s scientific investigator was gleefully accepted by the doctor. His first action was

to co-opt his fellow-graduate of University days, James Merry, B.Sc., as deputy scientist. Together, they converted the top-floor rooms of Scotland Yard into a modern laboratory; there they experimented, planned and deciphered, and hooked offenders against the law.

But there was one fly in the laboratory ointment; when, as frequently happened, investigation had to be carried out at some distance from Scotland Yard, the laboratory was robbed of much of its usefulness as an aid to detection. Not only was time lost in getting to it and back again for the testing of any article, but where the article was undetachable from its surroundings it could not be tested in the laboratory at all. The two men set out, therefore, to overcome this obstacle to investigation. The co-operation of scientific instrument makers resulted in the fitting up in the interior of a leather suit-case of a miniature laboratory, perfect in every detail and requirement. The miniature microscope had the power of a full-sized model; a miniature Bunsen burner and stand served in place of its bigger brother; and beakers, test-tubes and microscope slides were all made on the lesser, but no less useful, size. A chemical rack, with glass-lined flasks for reagents, was included.

The earliest appearances of this portable laboratory at the scene of a crime led to much mirth among the older members of the Force. Chuckles were only half suppressed when, at the seat of the inquiry, Dr. Manson opened the case and fiddled around with microscope, reagents and micrometer rules. But by and by the chuckles ceased; officers came to be more and more solicitous for help from the little laboratory on the spot; and before long the case had bestowed on it by them the nickname of the 'Box of Tricks'; because, as Superintendent Jones, the Fat Man of the Yard, put it, "It's always doin' the trick."

It was this 'Box of Tricks' that Dr. Manson and Sergeant Merry carried on to the green at Thames Pagnall at ten o'clock next morning. Dr. Lumley and Inspector Carruthers accompanied them, followed by Constable Lambert carrying the deck-chair which had held the live, and then the mortal, remains of the unknown on that day that death ended his innings while the last innings of the annual match was also running towards its close, in front of his eyes.

The party halted at the tarpaulin-covered spot on the green. The inspector rolled up the covering, exposing beneath four small wooden pegs. "They have been put dead centre of the cross-pieces of the chair where they were resting on the ground," he explained.

"Excellent," replied Manson. He went down on his knees and peered carefully and cautiously over the area that had been covered by the chair. He inspected it through a large-area lens. If he found anything of interest he made no comment. After a glance round the green, to get his bearings, through, as it were, the eyes of the dead man, he motioned to the inspector.

Carruthers took the chair from the constable.

"Fingerprints?" queried the doctor.

"Have been photographed," was the reply; and an approving nod from the scientist acknowledged the precaution.

The deck-chair was opened up, and, with the help of Constable Lambert, was placed in position between the pegs. Dr. Manson, standing first at right angles to it, eyed its position against the line of trees starting the green. A second panoramic view was taken from the other side. Finally, he stepped behind the chair and looked over the pitch upon which the game had been played on the Saturday of the tragedy, and then, from the front, examined, over the chair, the vista behind. Running parallel with the chair, some two hundred yards behind it, was the high road, a by-pass highway to the coast, a long, white and busy road, never for a moment in the twenty-four hours of the day entirely devoid of some vehicle or other.

It cut across the end of the green at an angle. This fact seemed to worry the scientist, for he walked over to the corner nearest the chair, and from it stared at the opposite corner. Returning, he opened the 'Box of Tricks' and from it lifted a square frame of metal of some six inches. Held in the quadrangle of the frame was a piece of glass, across which ran a number of fine lines, bearing numbers at the top and bottom. An upright and a horizontal line, more clearly defined, cut the glass at right angles. It looked like an outsize direct viewfinder for those cameras, the sighting and focusing for which is done from eye-level. And that was, more or less, an accurate description of it. It was of the doctor's own designing and making in the laboratory; and he now proceeded to demonstrate its use. Returning to the corner of the green, he held up the frame as though sighting a camera. Getting a perfect horizontal by means of the inset spirit level in the base of the frame, he noted from the intersecting lines the divergence of the line of the road from the right angle. Marking the figure on a card, he returned to the chair, and, by similar means, obtained the divergence of the width of the chair from the same angle. This, also, he recorded. A further peering, this time from in front of the chair, gave another calculation. From the 'Box of Tricks' Merry extracted a slide rule; the two scientists whispered together for a few moments, and then Dr. Manson nodded an emphatic satisfaction.

Inspector Carruthers, who had watched this byplay in growing bewilderment, now sought enlightenment. "Those calculations were of the utmost importance, Inspector," explained Manson. "You saw me, yesterday, take the angle at which the bullet had penetrated the body?" The inspector nodded. "Well, it must be evident to you that such angles as I took must depend for their usefulness on the position of the body—and of the chair. Let us take an example. Suppose we find that a dart, fired from an airgun, went into a target at an angle of twenty-five degrees to the left. We have a faithful marking of the position in which the target was fixed. Very well, nothing is more easy than to follow the angle of twenty-five degrees back from the target to the firing position. But suppose that we are not aware that the target at the time *was held by some projection so that it was itself out of the straight by five degrees on the left-hand side*; do you see what a mess that is going to make of our probable shooting position? The same thing applies here. Before any calculation can be made as to the possible whereabouts of the position from which the shot was fired, we must be quite certain that the respective angles of the road and the chair are brought into proper relation. As it happens here we are particularly fortunate; the sloping-away angle of the chair width is almost—within the twenty-fourth part of an inch—the same as the going-away of the course of the road. That means that the chair was parallel to the road (but not to the cricket pitch) except for a minute variation. That is a piece of luck, because it seems at the moment that it is the road with which we are concerned rather than the green; the shot came from behind the man, who was watching the play."

Inspector Carruthers nodded comprehendingly. "I see that, Doctor, although I must say it would not have occurred to me to go as closely into it as all that. But how is it going to help us? Possibly, had the investigation been carried out while the body was still here, it might have given us an idea—"

"I am hoping that we may be able to overcome that difficulty, Inspector," was the reply. "You will remember that I made certain experiments in the mortuary yesterday. The further possibilities of those experiments is what I propose now to test."

He turned to the 'Box of Tricks', and extracted a contraption constructed of aluminium. Opened out, it revolved itself into a tripod with a small, flat and square head. In appearance it was much like a cine-camera tripod with revolving table. While the scientist busied himself extending this, Sergeant Merry, taking four long metal staples from the 'Box of Tricks', proceeded to pin the chair firmly to the ground in the position marked out by the inspector.

"Now, Inspector, if Constable Lambert will sit in the chair, we will endeavour to arrange him as near as possible to the position of your corpse," said Manson.

The constable seated himself with a lack of enthusiasm amounting almost to repugnance; and Manson beckoned to Dr. Lumley. "What I want from you, Doctor," he explained, "is the position, the exact position, of the wound in the back."

The medico consulted his note-book. "I made it some four and three-quarter inches from the top of the spinal column and one and a half inches to the left of it," was the reply. With a piece of chalk, Manson marked the position on the constable's tunic.

"Our object now," he explained, "is to get that chalk mark opposite the bullet perforation in the canvas of the chair."

The constable was modelled into position. Satisfied at the accuracy of the arrangement, the scientist, enjoining complete immobility on the part of Lambert, proceeded with the experiment.

He placed the tripod behind the chair, lowering it until the table was an inch below the level of the bullet-hole. Then, taking from the 'Box of Tricks' a lump of modelling-wax, he kneaded it into softness and, moulding it roughly into a ball shape, fixed it firmly on the tripod table. As this operation was completed, Sergeant Merry stepped forward with an open box in his hand. From their bed of cotton wool, two hollow glass rods, or tubes, were lifted. Taking the first of them, and putting a sharply pointed plug in one end, Dr. Manson inserted it in the wax, gently urging it forward until it penetrated through the inner side. A similar operation was conducted with the second tube. Both tubes were then further extended until each rested against the canvas of the chair. Making certain that the constable had not changed his position, Dr. Manson edged the end of the first tube into the centre of the bullet-hole. Then, working gently, but quickly, with the aid of his protractor he elevated the rod until it lay at an angle of 30.25 degrees. Pressing the wax firmly round the tube, to ensure that there was no possibility of its moving, he began a manipulation of the second tube. Consulting his note-book, he drew an imaginary line at right angles to the bullet-hole and, setting his 'T'-square on the table, arranged the second tube until his micrometer gauge showed the same definite gap that had resulted from his experiment with the wound in the dead man. A final check of the position, both by himself and Merry, resulted in each giving approving nods.

"Then, Constable, if you will very carefully move out of the chair, we can complete the experiment," said Manson.

With the utmost caution, Merry pulled out the metal staples from the turf, and the chair was drawn away. It left the tripod with its wax top and the tubes protruding from the front and back.

Dr. Manson, pulling out the pointed plugs, knelt on the grass, applied an eye to the hollow centre of the first of the tubes, and peered through it for some moments. He looked away and took a rule from a pocket. This he held on a level with his eyes, much as does an artist with his pencil when seeking perspective. He made a note or two in his note-book, and then turned to the second tube, again peering through the hollow centre of it. Once more noting the result, he stepped back and motioned the deputy scientist to take his place. Merry, having taken his peering, compared his calculations with those of his chief. He made way for Inspector Carruthers. That officer, having dutifully peered, scratched his head in perplexity.

"Well, Doctor, where does that lead us?" he asked.

Manson smiled. "You must not be too impatient, Carruthers," he abjured. "At the moment it appears as though the miscreant was suspended about eight feet in the air at a spot some forty feet to the left of that bungalow. Whose bungalow is it, by the way?"

"Mr. Bosanquet's, Doctor," answered the inspector, his face falling in disappointment.

"If it is any consolation to you, Inspector, the experiment was never intended, by me at any rate, to bring any certain result. I should have been most agreeably surprised had it done so. There are too many unknown quantities for it to produce definite evidence."

"What would they be, Doctor?"

"For one thing, we have had to assume that the man was sitting squarely in the chair. If he was turned, such as is a man when he sits with his legs crossed, then our present angle is bound to be incorrect. All that I hoped for was that I might get from the experiment some starting point, some working guide. Because there were possibilities, I *had* to carry out the test. Science, like your police work, Inspector, has its routine, you know."

"And has it given you any working result, Doctor?"

"It has given me more than a working result, Inspector." The scientist's voice was grim. "One feature of it was correct at any rate. You need not, Inspector, worry about anyone in the village taking out a motor-car about four forty-five o'clock. The shot was not fired from a motor-car."

He met the inquiring gaze of Inspector Carruthers—and teased it. "Have a go at working it out," he said; and turned to the repacking of the 'Box of Tricks'.

CHAPTER SEVEN
CLUE THE SECOND

THE NEWSPAPER REPORTER and the man of science are like Kipling said of the Colonel's lady and Judy O'Grady; they are sisters, or rather brothers, under their skins. For each spends his life collecting facts, and writing about them. A reporter would no more think of writing his report of any news to which he has been assigned before he had obtained the facts necessary to present a news picture than a man of science would seek to propound some "new theory before he had acquired the data for which his colleagues are entitled to ask in proof of his treatise.

Dr. Manson was a man of science; and science includes not only those material experiments which can be carried out with the visible aids of a Bunsen burner, beakers and test tubes: science is also of the mind. Like the reporter, Dr. Manson made no attempt to weave a theory until he had collected all the facts that could be gathered relative to the inquiry in hand; and there was bred in his brain that unique facility of being able to keep a perfectly open, unbiased mind until his accumulation of facts was as complete as could reasonably be anticipated. Not till then did he sit quietly down and attempt to marshal the facts into some semblance of order, so that, strung together, they guided his mind to the telling of the complete story, just as the reporter's facts, also set in their order, tell the story of this or that piece of news. That had been the purpose of the experiments on the green at Thames Pagnall. He had told Inspector Carruthers that he did not expect any definite result from them—then. But, in his view, they represented a very necessary adjunct to what the late Mr. Neville Chamberlain would have referred to as 'the exploring of every avenue'. What the experiment had served was to provide him with one more fact, the fact which he had confided to Inspector Carruthers: that the shot had not been fired from a motor-car.

Now, in his laboratory, he began to search for other facts. Laid out on the large glass-topped table in front of him were the dead man's clothes and the other few possessions found on him; and on the scientist's blotting-pad was the diary which had been in his waistcoat pocket.

It was to the latter that Dr. Manson first turned his attention. The book was one of the miniature pattern, popular for telephone numbers and dates, which fitted comfortably and flatly the upper pocket of a waistcoat. The cover was of soft leather, silk-lined, and the pages were of that thin texture erroneously spoken of as India paper. The doctor first submitted it to a general examination. Opening it, he turned to the index page and read the inscription. With a frown of surprise, he turned over the pages to the end of the book, and there sought the imprint of the publisher's name. There was none. "Now that," he said to himself, "is definitely unusual. No identity of the printers . . . certainly unusual." Having made certain that the clue he sought had not been missed, he settled down to digest the various entries. He read slowly, pondering over the notes, though they seemed simple enough.

Then, having reached the end, he laid the open diary face downwards on the table, and lay back in his chair with closed eyes, and with the wrinkles crossing the forehead of him, and the crinkles in the corner of his eyes. It was thus that Sergeant Merry, entering, found him.

"And what is worrying you, Doctor?" the sergeant asked.

"There is a message in this diary, Jim," the scientist responded. "But I cannot find it. Yet, I feel that it should be able to tell us something."

Together, the pair went again over the entries. "Take the initials first," said Manson. "There is R.H. and mention of Sherwood Forest and a castle. Taking that in conjunction, I think we may regard R.H. as Robin Hood, especially as the word 'grave' is mentioned also, and Robin Hood's grave is in the vicinity. 'Car-

dinals knew a thing or two in those days—H.C.' must mean Hampton Court Palace."

"Quite," agreed Merry, "because, after seeing Kingston, he is at H.C. again."

"Then we get the note on the day he died—*'T.P. Saturday.'* That seems to refer to Thames Pagnall. But where is 'S.F.'?"

"'Saw S.F. today. Strange. Must look into it. May be interesting,'" read out Merry from the page. "He doesn't seem to have moved out of the area, so S.F. must be somewhere around."

Dr. Manson walked across to a bookcase and took down a guidebook of the county of Surrey. Patiently, the two men searched through the sightseeing pages of the volume, but without finding any 'exhibit' S.F. which might have exercised any attraction for a visitor to the county. "Nothing here," was the doctor's comment. "Let us finish the other part of the entries, and then come back to this."

Sergeant Merry read out the longer of the entries:

"'B. told me that I'd find the Yorkshire moors as adventurous as I should like. Too right he was. Lost in the fog all the day, and then found that I had walked back to where I started from.'"

He looked up at the scientist. Receiving no response, he proceeded with the reading:

"'Kingston—King's Stone. H.C. again. Fair bonza.' That's all, except—"

An exclamation from Dr. Manson interrupted him. "Read that over again, Jim," he asked. Merry did so.

The face of Manson brightened, and the wrinkles and the crinkles disappeared. "Yes, that's it," he ejaculated. "That, I think, will be it." He spoke no more than a score of words to Merry. The sergeant nodded quick and definite agreement. "It is a working hypothesis to begin with," he agreed.

"Now let us see if the clothes can tell us anything else." The doctor picked up a shirt as he spoke, and looked it over. "Open front, and no makers' name. There wouldn't be; this kind of shirt is sold in thousands. No laundry marks. Washed in the hotel laundries, of course. Nothing much in it at all."

The vests and pants conveyed no more information to the scientist than did the shirt. There was left the outer garments. Dr. Manson picked up the jacket.

The cloth was a dark russet-brown worsted, of good quality, and with a faint and thin red stripe, widely spaced. Manson pulled a chair towards him, and slipped the jacket over its back. He frowned at the appearance as it hung. "The man did not strike me as being of so broad a build as that, Merry," he commented.

Merry chuckled. "Possibly not," he responded. "Mebbe he was a fashionable gent when he was alive. Look at the shoulders from the inside of the jacket and see if there is not a disparity."

Dr. Manson held up the coat and inspected the interior. "You are certainly right there, Jim," he agreed.

"Shoulders are padded to give the effect from the outside of broadness," the sergeant explained. "All handsome men are broad-shouldered, so I'm told," he added.

"Not *all*, I fear." The doctor looked pointedly at the broad figure of the deputy scientist.

"But this jacket, I do think, is a little on the ultra-broad side in the shoulders, Harry," was the final decision of Merry.

Placing the jacket back on the chair, Dr. Manson turned his attention to the waistcoat, examining it thoroughly. It did not, apparently, return any dividend for the examination, for, without speaking, he replaced it on the table.

It was when he proceeded to conduct a similar examination of the trousers that he betrayed the first sign of interest. He had stretched them full length on the table, legs together, so that the right-hand side was uppermost, displaying the slit giving access to the hip pocket. The cloth there lay in a baggy fold, as though stretched by holding regularly some bulky object. Slipping a hand into the pocket, the scientist found it considerably deeper than is usual. Also, it was of a less width than is customary. He clicked his tongue. "This is beginning to get intriguing," he said. "What manner of man is he, Jim, who has his suits made with a revolver hip pocket?"

He pulled out the lining of the pocket and, taking a sheet of litmus paper, rubbed it several times along the lining material. It came away with a greyish-black discoloration. The scientist examined it through a lens. He called the laboratory assistant. "Have this tested, Wilkins," he ordered. It would have been noticeable to a chemist that he gave no indication of what had to be tested. That was Dr. Manson's way. He held that if a person knew for what he was to look he would test only for that reaction, and give a 'yes' or 'no' as the case may be, thereby quite possibly missing something else for which no test had been made. But the same research man, knowing nothing of the circumstances, would have to begin his tests from zero, and was not likely, therefore, to miss anything.

Further examination of the pocket lining disclosed a small stain in the cloth, and this was repeated in almost the same position on the opposite side. After a close inspection of the stain through a lens, Dr. Manson switched on a small electric iron. When it had gathered, in his opinion, sufficient heat, he tore from his table-pad a piece of blotting-paper and, laying it over the stain on the lining, pressed the iron against it for a few seconds. The result was seen on its removal; the stain had transferred some of its content to the blotting paper.

Sergeant Merry bent over it. Little inspection was needed to arrive at the substance.

"And what manner of a man is he who not only carried a revolver in his pocket, but kept it well oiled?" he demanded.

"Quite," responded the doctor. "This case gets more and more interesting. I think we had better investigate further, and see whether the suit can give us anything more," he added.

Merry nodded, and from a cupboard produced a Soderman.

Now, the Soderman is one of the aids to criminal investigation that the lament of thousands and thousands of housewives provided—about the only one. The housewife now, and in the past, filled her house with carpets. Carpets have to be kept clean. First, the housewife of the older days used a brush to get rid of the dust in the carpets. Then, because she complained that in the sweeping the dust was simply transferred from the carpet to the furniture, walls, crevices and articles of adornment, whence it later fell back on the carpet again, science devised a carpet-sweeper, which collected the dust into a box cavity as it swept. This was all very well, until the housewife realized that the only dust that the sweeper gathered was that on the *surface* of the carpet. In time the carpet became impregnated with dust that had sunk into the pile. At this, an American gentleman devised, for her delectation, a machine in which, by means of a dynamo worked by electricity, so strong a suction could be caused that the dust was actually sucked up from the very bottom of the pile of the carpet, and at the same time it was deposited in a bag in the inside of the machine, whereby it stood no earthly chance of returning to its haunt in the carpet. The contraption became known as a vacuum cleaner.

It was a long time before science, as applied to crime, realized that the same kind of machine on a smaller scale could collect the dust from the clothes of a man; and before it realized that, whereas dead men tell no tales, dead dust from their clothes, or from other things, can unfold, in certain circumstances, a very enlightening story. So a Mr. Harry Soderman, who was a Doctor of Science, and an investigator into crime, made a miniature carpet-sweeper, and with it detectives have since swept up the dust in clothes and other things. His vacuum, however, was worked either by running the thing over the clothes, creating its own suction, or by being held on a certain spot, while a second operator worked a pump, like blowing up a bicycle tyre in reverse. Dr. Manson had improved on the Soderman by fitting a motor to it, so that it worked exactly on clothes as did the vacuum cleaner of the recently acquired Mrs. Merry. It was this Soderman that Merry now produced, and switched into an electric point. He opened the container, and fitted behind the muzzle a small parchment bag.

"I think we will take the shoulders first," said Manson.

The nozzle was pushed over the part of the garment indicated, and it sucked up the dust thickly engrained in the cloth. Merry detached the paper bag, sealed and labelled it, and fitted another bag. "Where next?" he asked.

"The interior of the jacket side-pockets, I think," replied Manson; and two separate bags were fitted, and sealed and labelled. Before the Soderman was replaced in the cupboard, some half a dozen bags of dust had been accumulated.

"Going to examine it now, Harry?" the sergeant asked.

"We may as well," was the reply. He pulled a microscope towards him and fitted on an objective and eyepiece. Taking the envelope labelled 'Shoulders', he opened it, and gently tapped some of the contents on to a piece of white glazed paper. After closely scrutinizing the medley he transferred a small portion of it to a glass slide. Guarding it with a cover slip, he proceeded to inspect it through the microscope. Merry followed him at the eyepiece.

"What do you make of it?" the scientist asked.

"Soot, a few fragments of fluff, plain dust, fragments of limestone, and . . . what is the other stuff, Harry?" asked Merry.

Manson shook his head. "That is precisely what I want to know," he said.

"Crystals, anyway," was the reply. "But hanged if I can place them."

"There seems to be only a minor proportion, Jim, but all the same we ought to find out what the stuff is. Let's try the inside pocket collection."

He turned to the laboratory assistant, who was hovering round. "Yes, Wilkins, what is it?" he asked.

"Undoubtedly metal rubbings, Doctor," was the reply of the man who had tested the litmus paper discoloration.

"Which is just what I thought," was the reply, as the scientist turned again to the table.

The new exhibits provoked an exclamation from the scientist. "Upon my soul, Jim, the stuff seems to be in the majority here, together with tobacco dust and more fluff."

A thought struck him. Transferring another portion of the dust from the envelope to a watch-glass, he poured on it a few drops of alcohol, very gently swilling it from side to side. Then, extracting the moistened dust from the now slightly discoloured liquid, he placed them on to another slide, which he fitted on the stage of the microscope. The fragments were now revealed to be crystals of a reddish colour. Finally, Dr. Manson opened the envelope marked 'Right-hand pocket of jacket', and tipped some of the contents into a small porcelain bowl, letting a little distilled water drop on them. On being stirred with a glass rod, and the crystals being broken up, a definite red-coloured tinge resulted.

From the bookcase the scientist lifted down a formidable tome on Geology. He carried it to a chair and for five minutes read diligently. He took down the volume of the *Encyclopedia Britannica* marked 'A', and continued his reading at a certain section. His next move was to take up a book of wireless and cable forms, and on one of them write out a message.

Criminal Investigation Department Melbourne Australia Stop Wanted name of man beginning with letter L who sailed for England probably March Stop Urgent Stop Habitually carried revolver Stop Resident in Melbourne Stop Here on holiday Stop Manson Scotland Yard End message.

He rang the bell and gave the message to the constable who answered the call. "Have this sent by wireless, urgent, at once," he ordered.

The telephone bell shrilled out a call. Manson lifted the receiver. The voice of the assistant commissioner came over the wire. "That you, Doctor? If you can spare a few minutes, I would like to see you here," he said.

"I'll be there in a minute or two, A.C."

TO THE READER

This is Clue Number Two in the riddle—the reason for Dr. Manson's definite decision that the dead man had come from Australia to England. Observation and a little reference to geology should give you the answer.

Chapter Eight
FOUR CIGARETTES

IN THE WINTER of 1921-2 those Bohemians who eked out a precarious, though an exuberantly gay, existence in the *pieds-à-terres* around Cheyne Walk, Chelsea, organized at a celebrated London venue a ball of the Arts. All those who dabbled in Art—and there are some queer branches of Art—made the night festive with their presence; and so, too, did those who were not of the Arts; and wore large black bows and velvet smoking-jackets in proof of it! Beneath the giant replica of Bacchus, the Bacchanalians made merry with song and dance and the nectar of their god. At six o'clock ante meridian, on a cold and frosty morning, the revels ended.

At seven-thirty on that same frosty morning the life of one of the queens of the Arts also ended. She had been one of the pivots round which the revels had sparkled. She, as the saying goes, had been the life and the soul of the party. Back in her flat, she had repaired to her virginal couch and there, at midday, her maid had found her, the breath gone from the body of her. And, said the doctor who was hurried, unnecessarily, to her side, it had been gone for four and a half hours at least. The doctor lifted the closed eyelids and looked underneath. What he saw made a post-mortem necessary. The inquest demonstrated that her body was choc-a-bloc with cocaine; that her life and soul of the party was purely an artificial exuberance, followed, inevitably, by depression at her own company, until another dose of the stuff sent her soaring off again. The verdict was that she, a dope addict, met her death by an overdose of drugs, there being no evidence to show whether it was accidental or suicidal.

A few weeks later an actress of great promise, young and beautiful, and of greater popularity even than her promise, left the theatre at eleven-thirty o'clock, and attended a lively party at a hotel. In the middle of the following afternoon she, too, was dead. And she, again, was riddled with the drug.

These were the first intimations to the police of the extent to which drugging and doping had developed in the capital of the world; and investigations, demanded by the populace and Parliament, got under way to ferret out the dope-mongers.

The police made curious discoveries. They found, for instance, that ships came grandly up the Thames and passed slowly to the Port of London. They found that, casually, little boats would leave a wharf and, rowed by river men, would cross to the other side. There is not, of course, anything illegal in this. But the police of the river came to realization that the crossings coincided remarkably with the passing of the big ships, and they watched and waited. They found that in the crossing the boatmen paused for one of their number to lean over the gunwale, screened from the shore by the length of the boat, which was to the blind side, and lift from the water one or more waterproof silken packets, floating invisible from the shore. They found that the packets, thus dropped and retrieved, contained opium powder worth a small fortune.

They searched backwards. The ships had come through the Suez. Their last call had been Port Said, in Egypt, where the growing of opium is prohibited. They found that field after field of grain or sugarcane which blossomed in the irrigated soil of Upper Egypt was a snare and a delusion. The grain went back, and the sugar-cane went back, only a small depth; it screened the fields of white poppies *(papaver somniferum)*, the growing of which is forbidden by statute.

They searched forwards, and found strange comings and goings in the heart of the West End of London. They found men and women who betrayed an earnest desire to inspect the beauty of, and the inscription on, the statue to the memory of Nurse Cavell, which same stands facing Trafalgar Square from the triangle of Charing Cross Road. What is more, so much did the beauty of the statue impress them, apparently, that they were impelled to visit it every other day. Puzzled at this, the police apprehended the visitors, and found on them packets of cocaine, opium, heroin, and other drugs. Then they knew that the statue was the clearing-house of drugs, and the Mecca of addicts.

Gradually the police tracked down the traffickers; men went to gaol, and when they came out went to deportation, and within a couple of years the trade had been reduced to little more than the legitimate sale of drugs for medicinal purposes, for opium forms the base of nearly forty of the greatest healing preparations in the Pharmacy.

But now the menace had sprung up again. The illicit drug trade was once more rearing its ugly and deadly head. One addict had, under the influence of the drug, committed manslaughter. There were others. When the assistant commissioner at the Scotland Yard conference between Dr. Manson and Inspector Carruthers had said to the doctor, "Can you spare the time from the other matters?" and had added, for the benefit of the inspector, "Dr. Manson is pretty well occupied at the moment with a matter of some importance", the matter was the tracking down of this new rising of drugs. And his call to the scientist, as the wireless message to Australia was being written out, had reference, also, to this matter of some importance.

Dr. Manson walked into the assistant commissioner's room in answer to the summons. Superintendent Jones and Inspector Kenway were already there. He sat down in one of the armchairs which stood on the thick carpet in front of the desks of the commissioner and the assistant commissioner. "Something happened, A.C.?" he asked.

Sir Edward nodded. "Drugs again, Doctor," he answered, curtly. "Do you know young Cartwright?"

"The financier's son?" asked the scientist.

"The same. He has been taken to hospital, nearly raving mad. The doctor thought he had had a stroke, or something. Looked him over and found that it was abstinence from drugs. He had been ill and had not been able to get out to obtain his supply. Cartwright came to me. I sent Jones to the hospital. They had quietened him down with a shot. Tell him, Jones."

The superintendent heaved himself forward with many squeaks from the protesting chair. "Frightened life out'r him," he announced. "Sight o' Yard made 'im think he was goin' to die . . . asked him where he got the stuff . . . wouldn't say.

. . . Said then I'd have to put him in police hospital . . . put him under 'rest . . . unlawfully obtainin' drugs contrary to Order. . . . Caved in. . . . Said he went to Palatviate . . . supply appeared on side o' plate with coffee."

"What!" Manson looked up sharply. "Put there by the waiter?"

"Sez he dunno. Only knows it appears there—always. Sez he always meant to watch for it. But somethin' always attracted his 'tention. When he turned round there was the stuff."

"Why was it not there this time?"

"Would 'ave been if he'd gone. Couldn't . . . been ill . . . just at end of supply."

Doctor Manson studied the problem for a minute or two, his eyes still on the fat superintendent. Then: "This is a queer business, Jones," he said. "Do I understand that he just walks into the place, sits down and has a dinner, and the drug just falls like manna from heaven to the Israelites?"

"Not quite that, Doctor. . . . 'Parently always goes to one table . . . the big guest one. And asks for coffee, usin' the phrase 'Not black, but milky.' Then the stuff comes."

"How about payment?"

"Cartwright says that after receiving the stuff you go to the cloak-room and there hand over five pounds to a chappie who says, 'They serve good coffee here, sir, don't they?'"

"But, for the Lord's sake, Jones," burst out the assistant commissioner, "do I understand that anyone sitting at that table asking for coffee not black but milky receives a packet of dope for five pounds?"

"So I understand, A.C.," said Jones.

"Bear in mind, A.C., that the person disposing of the stuff only knows that he is receiving the right password, and from the right table. Because we know from Cartwright the formula it doesn't mean that anybody, and all and sundry, know it. Each person is, of course, bound to secrecy. And the penalty for breaking secrecy is, of course, the stopping of their supply of the drug."

"Then you think we may set a trap?"

"On that I would not like to venture an opinion, A.C. The people in this business are pretty cute. But it is worth trying. Not with a policeman, though. I'll get Wilkins in my laboratory to go there. And I'll be in the place myself. This distracting the attention of the customer is a pretty smart device—like the patter of the conjuror—and I can watch Wilkins while he is watching."

"Supposing something *does* happen, Doctor? How do we meet that?"

The scientist sat silent, turning this aspect of the problem in his mind.

"If I might butt in, Mr. Assistant Commissioner," suggested Inspector Kenway.

"Yes, Kenway?"

"I am a frequent visitor to the Palatviate. Go there with my wife. My presence would not be anything unusual, and would not arouse any suspicion. Suppose I had a table near the entrance?"

"The very thing, Kenway." Manson greeted the suggestion with a sigh of satisfaction. "It could not be better. Where is this big table, Jones?" he asked, turning to the superintendent.

"Dunno, Doctor. Never been there."

"I expect it's the one on the ground floor, which runs alongside the arena," said Kenway.

"Then if I had a *fauteuil* table at the front of the balcony, I could overlook without any undue interest being noticed?" he asked.

"I think so, Doctor."

"Very well, Kenway. Then book me a table. Better use the name Henry. If you cannot get it for tonight, book it for tomorrow. You have a table near the entrance. Now, listen. If I see anything at all suspicious, I will leave the table and walk to the cloakroom. You follow. We meet and enter into conversation as strangers. What happens afterwards must depend on circumstances. Is that clear?"

"Quite clear, Doctor. I'll let you know if I can get a table."

The superintendent and Kenway rose and left. Dr. Manson at a sign from the A.C. remained. The A.C. passed over his cigarette-case and the two lit up. "This is a rotten business, Harry, this damned drug racket again. Do you think anything will come of the plan?"

"Hard to say, Edward. But if it does, we shall pull in only the lesser fry—the go-between. We shall not get the real criminals, the men who are getting the stuff into the country. The only chance we have of getting near those is if one of the go-betweens can be induced to talk. And they aren't likely to do that, I'm afraid."

"No. I agree there. . . . How is that village affair going, Harry?"

"Thames Pagnall? I'm still collecting facts." The wrinkles ploughed their way across his forehead and the crinkles crept from the corners of his eyes. "There are one or two queer features about it. I am hoping to get some news of the man's identity before long, and that may give a definite starting point."

A knock at the door interrupted the talk. A sergeant entered. He tendered a large square envelope to Dr. Manson. "It is marked 'Urgent', sir, or I would not have disturbed you," he apologized.

Dr. Manson glanced at the envelope. "Cable and Wireless" was written across it in blue script lettering. He extracted the message, read it slowly, and then handed it over to the assistant commissioner. Sir Edward read it aloud:

"Manson Scotland Yard Stop Eliseus Leland former officer Criminal Investigation here sailed England February twenty-eight Stop No other letter Ell known to have sailed Stop Anything wrong Stop Jarvis Melbourne CID Stop."

Sir Edward eyed the scientist in inquiry. Dr. Manson detailed the discoveries which had led him to radio the Australian police.

"And you think that he is the man?" Sir Edward asked.

"I have very little doubt about it, but I shall make legally sure, of course." He pulled a sheet of notepaper towards him and wrote out a further wireless message.

Jarvis Melbourne CID Australia Stop Radio Leland finger-print code Stop Reply you after check Stop Manson Scotland Yard

* * * * *

Dr. Manson, a distinguished figure in evening clothes, wandered into the Palatviate at eight-thirty o'clock and was shown to the table booked for him in the name of Henry. A waiter took his order and vanished. He looked around and saw Inspector Kenway at his table for two. With him was Mrs. Kenway, who had been a detective-inspector's daughter, and was now the wife of another.

It was a remarkable place, this Palatviate. In the years agone, before music-halls became theatres of variety, or vaudeville houses, they had, below the stage, a long table at which sat a chairman, and to which was invited such patrons as would see that the chairman was consistently supplied with his favourite beverage. The ordinary patrons sat in the stalls, the pit and the gallery. The programme bill announced to the world that the charge for admission was "Sixpence, twopence of which is returned in refreshment." And at a convenient interval, usually when the artists had gone once round, and were getting up their strength for the second effort, attendants brought round glass or pewter mugs filled with beer—one for each customer. That was the twopennorth of refreshment.

The only difference between those old music-halls and the Palatviate was that the latter was a trifle more on the garish side, the chairman had become a compère, and the price of admission had risen to a guinea, about half a crown's worth of which was returned in refreshment. In other words, the fee of £1 1s. included dinner, or supper, and the entertainment. The refreshment was not served during a convenient interval, but went on all the time. There wasn't a stage; instead, in a circular arena, in the centre of the floor, a cabaret show ran its whirl of song and dance by half-naked girls, its jugglery and card manipulating, the while the audience ate the concoctions of French chefs in stalls, pit and gallery, raised in tiers above the arena, until the place looked like what the Coliseum of Rome must have appeared when, with the gladiators below, the Roman populace ate their *offula*. (Generations later an Earl of Sandwich also ate the Romans' *offula* at the card table, so that he need not break off his gambling; we called them sandwiches after him!)

Dr. Manson, one eye on the fish course and the other on the course of events going on below him, saw Wilkins eat his way through his meal to the sweets. He saw the waiter remove his plate. He saw Wilkins turn towards him, and knew that he had asked for coffee, "Not black, but milky." The waiter returned with the coffee. Though he kept his eyes on the table and on all who approached it, or left it, the scientist saw nothing more. No stranger spoke to Wilkins; no stranger even approached him. Wilkins drank his coffee slowly; but made no move and no sign to his chief who was, he knew, above him. No drug appeared.

"Cleverer than I thought," said Manson to himself. "They have rumbled that things are not exactly what they seem."

He lay back in resignation and let his gaze wander idly over the scene below him. It was a colourful spectacle; white arms and bare shoulders shining above evening frocks which out-coloured the rainbow, and contrasting with their attendant swains in the unchanging black and white which is the heritage, and the law, of the Englishman in his gaiety. It was the kind of leisured spectacle that can be seen nowhere but in London, in Paris, and in New York (and, once upon a time, maybe, in Budapest). Laughter came in joyous ripplings, rising and falling like waves on the restless seas. Manson, from behind the fragrant smoke of his cigar, watched it enharmonically.

It was that germ of observation ever active in his analytical mind, suddenly springing into activity, that jerked the scientist violently into suspicion. Unconsciously, his eyes had been following a tall figure of a man in well-fitting evening clothes, a white gardenia in his buttonhole, who meandered charmingly round a circle of acquaintances at other tables, pausing to chat, or bandy a jest here and there, before flitting on his gay way elsewhere. There was nothing unusual in this; there were others, men and women, making a butterfly round of friends. But a similarity of formality in the peregrinations of the gardenia man was unconsciously exciting the quiescent mind of Manson. Once, twice, three times, he noted idly, the wanderer pause at a table, greet an acquaintance and, after a moment or two, produce his cigarette-case and proffer the contents. The offer was accepted, and a cigarette taken. Thrice he noted it placed beside the plate by the recipient, apparently until the tit-bit on the plate, or the cigarette already being smoked, was finished. "I'll smoke it later," muttered Manson mentally to himself, with a smile, in mimicry of the phrase that was undoubtedly being spoken in the distance.

When the wanderer stopped at a fourth table, the doctor found himself *waiting* for the formula. Not until it occurred did realization break on him that his mind was sending him a warning. When that brain of his told him to look for a thing, it was always a warning that it was working in his unconsciousness.

With an exclamation he rose to his feet and pushed a way towards the entrance. Inspector Kenway seeing the move, slipped through the door. The pair met in the cloakroom.

"What is it, Doctor?" asked the inspector.

"Wait," was the reply.

They stood together chatting, as were others around them. Manson's eyes stared at the doorway; he touched the inspector on the arm as two men entered, one with a gardenia in his buttonhole.

As they drew level, the doctor stepped in front of them. "May I have a word with you gentlemen?" he asked.

The couple eyed him in some perplexity. "Well?" inquired the elder.

"We are detective-inspectors of Scotland Yard, gentlemen, and we would like to see your cigarette-cases." He held out a hand.

The men stared. "You must be crazy, sir," was the retort. "I have no intention of taking part in any kind of a practical joke."

"Nevertheless, I am sure you would prefer to humour us here than, say, at Bow Street police-station," suggested Manson.

The two men looked at each other, and then, with a shrug of the shoulders, the elder of the pair drew out his case and handed it over. Manson opened it. He inspected the paper-covered cylinders, looking carefully at the ends of each. Then with his pocket-knife he slit the length of paper of one of them, and opened out the tobacco. He sniffed the weed. In turn, each of the cigarettes was similarly treated. Four cigarettes lay ruined in the case.

"Satisfied, sir?" the gardenia-decorated gentleman asked. Perhaps you will now allow us to rejoin our friends."

Dr. Manson looked up with a disarming smile. He deposited the mixture of paper and tobacco in a cigarette-end bowl on a ledge, and, closing the case, handed it back to the owner.

"Now, will you oblige me by letting me see the other case?" he asked.

"The other case?" was the answer. "How many cases do you suppose I carry around with me, sir? I have no other case."

"The one which you carry in a most unusual place, I mean— in the right-hand waistcoat pocket." He held out his hand for the second time.

The man made no move, and the scientist nodded to Kenway. The inspector moved to the side of the man. The action seemed to decide him, for Gardenia, with a shrug, extracted the second case, and handed it across. Once again the doctor opened the case, and again inspected the contents of six cigarettes. He passed his fingers along the first of the cylinders, feeling the contents. Quietly, he handed the open case to Kenway to hold; and with his knife slit the cigarette and opened it out. Running through its centre for some inch and a half was a paper tube. Dr. Manson opened an end of the tube and tapped it over the opened case in the hand of the inspector. A little cascade of white powder settled itself in a tiny heap. Taking a crystal or two on a finger, the scientist touched it with his tongue. He turned to the second of the men.

"Now I will have from you the cigarette which this man gave you in the restaurant a few minutes ago," he said.

Silently, the man produced his case and handed it over.

Manson extracted a cigarette, felt its length, and nodded to Kenway. The inspector addressed the two men. "I am going to take both of you into custody on a charge of being in possession of certain scheduled drugs, you not being persons authorized to possess or deal in such drugs under the Dangerous Drugs Act," he announced.

"Get a constable to take charge of them, Kenway," said Manson, "and we will get three more in the bag. I can identify them in the restaurant. I watched him hand each of them a cigarette without realizing what it meant."

Half an hour later five men were in custody.

The news was conveyed to the assistant commissioner next morning.

"That means that we have broken up the new distribution centre, Doctor," he said. "And that's good. But will they talk?"

"I doubt it, A.C. Still, there is no harm in trying. The four of them will want their drugs pretty badly before long. They may say something in order to get it."

CHAPTER NINE
SECOND FITTING

A WIRELESS MESSAGE on the desk of Dr. Manson next morning solved the identity of the dead man on the green. It read, when set out in its correct order, as follows.

```
I R      II    I R 11    I R      I R      I R
- - —;   -- 6; - - — 6;  - — 6;   - — 6;   - — 6.
I R      II    I R 10    I Ra     I Rr     I Rt
```

The scientist walked with it to the Fingerprint Branch. Inspector Baxter looked up from his desk. "Who's this?" he asked, taking the code.

"Exactly what I want to know, Baxter."

"Umph!" Baxter rose and crossed the room.

Three minutes was sufficient to find the answer. "It's that body of yours, Doctor," he said. "That all right?"

"It is what I expected, Baxter, if that is what you mean," was the reply, as Manson left the room.

He wandered to the office of Superintendent Jones, ponderingly, the wrinkles on his forehead and the crinkles in the corner of his eyes. The superintendent eyed him inquiringly. "In trouble," he said. "Kin see that . . . want somethin', eh?"

Dr. Manson nodded. "My village body was an Australian member of the C.I.D. in Melbourne, Jones," he said. "Can you tell me why anybody in Thames Pagnall should want to go killing a Melbourne detective over here on holiday?"

"Know nothin' about the place, Doctor. . . . Better ask that local inspector. . . . Only one reason why man should kill him as I kin see."

"And that is—what?"

"Cos if he didn't he'd be pinched."

Dr. Manson started in surprise, and looked hard at the fat superintendent. "Do you know something which I should know, Jones?" he asked, for the lack of imagination of the bulky super was a joke in the Yard. Jones was the man who ferreted out every possible fact that there was to be obtained—for others to use their imagination in assessing the values.

"Nothin', Doctor. Mind you, I'm only s'misin', and you don't have s'mises."

"No Australian suspects or inquiries over here?

"Not any I know of."

The scientist wandered out, and in the Special Branch. "Any Australian gentry in the news?" he asked the inspector in charge.

A shake of the head answered him. "Not that we are aware of, Doctor. Why?"

"My village corpse was an Australian detective, and I wondered was there anyone over here who might have had interest in his demise."

"Sorry, know of nobody. But I'll have the lads scout round for you."

Inspector Carruthers, in Thames Pagnall, answered the scientist's telephone call. "Come along here, Carruthers," the voice said. "I think we should have another round-the-table talk." He rang off, and dialled the number of the chief constable.

"I'll be there with Carruthers," said that chief.

The conference was held in the room of the assistant commissioner. Dr. Manson opened it. He looked at the chief constable and Inspector Carruthers. "Is there any Australian living in Thames Pagnall or district, or any person who has visited Australia?" he asked.

"Well, there's me, Doctor," said the chief constable.

"Anybody else you know, Carruthers?" asked Manson.

Carruthers shook an emphatic head. "Nobody, Doctor, I'm sure of that. I know all the people there pretty well. They've mostly been there for years and years, except one or two—Mr. Bosanquet, for instance—"

"What about him? Who is he?"

"Oh, he comes from Oxford. He was an undergrad there twenty years ago. I looked him up in the University book. Just to make sure after the death, you know. Anyway, why do you want to know that?"

"Because I have identified our body," replied Manson, slowly. "His name is Eliseus Leland, and he is, or was, a member of the C.I.D. in Melbourne. He was obviously, from his diary and journeyings, paying his first visit to England, where he knew nobody. Why should a stranger shoot him on a village green?"

"You mean that it might have been an Australian over here?" asked Carruthers.

"It would be a fair inference that his enemy would be somebody he had shopped over there," put in the chief constable.

"Or somebody he could have shopped over here," put in the assistant commissioner.

"Well, Mr. A.C., and you, Doctor, I know of no Australian our way. But I'll have a search round among the residents," promised Inspector Carruthers.

"But without any publicity, Inspector," warned the A.C.

And I will see if Melbourne can help us further," said the scientist. He wrote another message for wireless transmission:

Jarvis Melbourne CID Stop Leland shot dead here Stop No reason known Stop Help wanted Stop Had he any special assignment or known enemy likely to murder Stop Do you know a Kathleen Smith Stop Manson Scotland Yard End message.

"Now we had better, I think, review the case in the light of any discoveries either of you may have made," said the assistant commissioner. "What have you to say, Doctor?"

Manson pondered for a moment, gathering his thoughts into sequence. "Well, I have now been through Leland's diary," he said, "and there are one or two points which have interested me. I emphasize, firstly, the phrase *'T.P. Saturday'*. A rather queer note, do you not think?"

"In what connection, Doctor?" asked the A.C.

"The man had been sightseeing for some time. Yet I find no date for any particular place, only for *'T.P.'* Why should he especially want to recall that Saturday was a day on which he simply *must* pay a visit to *'T.P.'* when, apparently, it did not matter on which day he paid visits to other places?"

The scientist paused.

"Unless it was not a sightseeing visit, and Saturday was the only day that would do for what he wanted," he added slowly.

"It's a bit curious, put like that, I must admit." The comment came from Inspector Carruthers.

"Perhaps he didn't want to miss the place, Doctor," suggested the chief constable.

"But why, Colonel?" asked Manson. "What the deuce is there in Thames Pagnall to see? And you must not overlook the fact, as shown by his diary, that he had been twice on the doorstep— at Hampton Court, and hadn't worried about stepping over to this place that he was so keen to see as to give it pride of place in his diary.

"Or had he?" he added, suddenly, speaking more to himself than to the company.

"What did you say?" asked the chief constable.

The wrinkles and the crinkles were back on the scholarly face, and for a moment he stared, as though uncomprehendingly, at the chief constable. "Now, I wonder?" he said. He turned to the three men. "Suppose he *had* been in Thames Pagnall before, A.C.?" he went on. "And suppose something that he saw there made it necessary for him to pay another visit—"

"But you said just now, Doctor, that there was nothing there for him to see," protested Carruthers.

"I meant in the sightseeing line, Carruthers," Manson retorted. "But if there chanced to be something that was not sightseeing, but more serious? Let me go into this. Don't speak for a few moments." He produced the diary and studied it, going slowly, once, twice, three times, over the entries.

He looked up once to ask Inspector Carruthers if he had arrived at any conclusion as to what the initials S.F. represented. The inspector shook his head. "I cannot connect them with any spots round about the place, Doctor," he said.

The scientist returned to his cogitations. It was a couple of minutes before he looked up. The audience waited. He met their looks with a quiet gaze.

"I think we may be getting into shallower water, A.C.," he said. He laid the diary on the table. "The entries in this on examination along my new lines of thought seem to have an odd sequence. On June 11 he was in H.C., which I think we may take as being Hampton Court. On June 12 he was at Kingston. Then, the following day, June 13, he was again in Hampton Court. Now, the vital entry concerning S.F. follows that. *"Saw S.F. today. Strange. Must look into it. May be interesting."* June 13 was a Saturday. Then follows the entry *"T.P. Saturday"*, under the date June 21—that is the following Saturday, from seeing the interesting S.F. You follow me so far?"

A chorus of "yes" acknowledged the interest.

"Now, we have been assuming that S.F. was a place such as H.C. Suppose it was nothing of the kind. Suppose that, while in H.C., on June 13, he walked across to Thames Pagnall, *and there saw S.F.* In what direction does that take us?"

The assistant commissioner broke in with an exclamation. "You mean, Doctor, that S.F. may be an individual?" he asked.

"That is the idea in my mind."

"Which is the reason, Doctor, you asked me if there was an Australian in the district, or anyone who had been in Australia?" commented Carruthers.

Dr. Manson inclined his head in agreement. "I should doubt whether he would find anyone so interesting, except some person known to him in Australia," he said. He paused to collect his interrupted thoughts, and then continued.

"Now, supposing that he had seen the mysterious S.F. in Thames Pagnall on Saturday, the 13th, why should he make a special journey again to the place on the following Saturday— the 21st, and mark it in his diary in order to jog his memory?" The scientist looked round the company. "Why not the following Monday, Tuesday, Wednesday, or any other day? Why next Saturday?"

"Perhaps he was not free on any other day, and Saturday was his next clear date," suggested the chief constable.

"But his diary is quite clear of any other engagement," protested Manson. "T.P. is the only date reserved."

He paused for any further suggestion. None was forthcoming; and he leaned forward, addressing the inspector. "Is there a cricket match on the green every Saturday?" he asked, quietly.

"Yes, Doctor. Either the first or the second team is pla—"

He stopped in the middle of the word, as realization of the implication in the question struck his consciousness. "My! You mean that he saw S.F. on the cricket pitch?" he almost shouted.

"That seems a reasonable way to look at it, Inspector. I am not stating it as a fact; but it is distinctly interesting to note, in passing, that he lets a whole week go by before investigating S.F. who is so 'interesting' and there are matches in Thames Pagnall *only on each Saturday*."

"It seems pretty good circumstantial evidence, Doctor," commented the assistant commissioner.

"Now let us see if there is any direct evidence which might tend to support that view," said the Doctor. "Is there anything in fact—fact, mark you—possessed by us which associates such a possibility with his death?"

The chief constable and Inspector Carruthers considered the point for a few moments, but without result. They shook their heads.

"I think I see what you are getting at, Doctor," from the A.C. "His position on the green, I think. But you develop the thesis in your own way."

Manson gave the Yard chief an appreciative glance and smile. "That is, indeed, the association, A.C.," he replied. "The man moved a deck-chair apart from the crowd and sat in it. I think the reason may have been to obtain an uninterrupted view. And he sat in the chair, and he was shot. Now, what was he viewing? What was he there to watch? He was looking at the pitch. *He was watching the players. If he went there to look at the mysterious S.F. he was looking at the match.* Now, that seems to me to be a matter of some significance."

"Was there any player, or players, in that match whose initials were S.F., or just plain F.?" asked the assistant commissioner, quietly.

In the pause that followed the question all eyes turned on the inspector. Carruthers looked a little startled at the suggestion, but ran over the teams in his mind. "Yes, Doctor, there are four that I know of," he said. "There's the squire, Major ffolkes; his Christian name is Samuel, which gives us S.F. Then there is the Maplecot Sebastian Ferris. Bill Farquhar is another 'F', but he hasn't got an 'S' to his name, and there is Sid French, a bowler."

"Hmm"—from the assistant commissioner. "Is the man Ferris you have just mentioned the Ferris who possessed a .22 rifle, Inspector?"

"Yes, sir, the same."

The A.C. pursed his lips, and looked significantly at the scientist. Dr. Manson nodded and turned to the inspector. "I don't doubt your word, Carruthers, that the rifle he possesses had not been fired recently, and could not have been fired because of its condition, but I should like to have a look at it, personally, in order to set my mind completely at rest. I have, I confess, a penchant for satisfying myself at first hand."

"I will get it for you, Doctor," the inspector promised.

"And we must look into these four gentlemen who have the misfortune to be named with the initial 'F'," added Manson.

"Yes, because, as I see it," put in the chief constable, suddenly seized with a brainwave, "if it was, by any chance, one of these 'F's', then he was on the green and could have robbed the body, as the Doctor here says somebody did."

Dr. Manson nodded, but in an abstracted way. "Yes," he said, half to himself, "that is rather a complication."

"In what way?" asked the assistant commissioner. But the scientist made no answer. Instead, he rose.

"I do not think we can go much further at the moment," he said. "But when the points I have raised have been looked into, I should like us to have another little chat together to consider other circumnavigations. That is what I meant by complications. Should these ideas lead us to anything, then the further ideas to which I have referred will not arise. If we fall down on these, the others will certainly come in for comment." He turned to Carruthers. "I am coming down to the village later on, Inspector," he announced. "If you see me there forget that you have ever known me, unless I speak to you first. It's a little idea I have," he added, seeing the inspector's look of surprise.

"Then you can drop in for tea, Doctor," said Colonel Mainforce. "And what about you, A.C.? It will give you a breath of fresh air, and I reckon you Londoners need it. Besides, you ought to see the scene of the foul crime," he added, jestingly. "Tell you what: bring a rod down and have half an hour with the evening rise among the trout in my pool. And you, Doctor."

"Can't refuse that, Colonel. And I am sure that the Doctor cannot. All right, we'll turn up about five o'clock."

* * * * *

Dr. Manson stepped off the train at Thames Pagnall and, rod in its canvas case, and a box of flies poking out of his pocket, wandered across a field footpath to the police-station, some quarter of a mile away. There, he left his encumbrances; and turning at right angles, wandered another quarter of a mile into the village proper. For Thames Pagnall is a series of three centres of social and communal life. One clusters itself round the station, the second hugs the village shops. The third—which was the original—anchors round the cricket green like ships lying at peace round a harbour.

It was to the second of these communities that the scientist made his way. An idea had occurred to his mind, and he was now about to experiment with it. The village was a necessary beginning. The suggestion that Leland had previously visited Thames Pagnall and there seen the mysterious S.F. was nothing more than conjecture; Manson was not content to leave it at that. If he could prove that such a visit had been paid, then he would be out of the dungeon of possibility and into the freedom of absolute fact.

One feature of the dead man's belongings had struck him as incongruous; and anything out of the ordinary, where sudden death was concerned, always caused him to walk warily. 'I have a very suspicious mind' was one of his sayings, frequently quoted. It was, in fact, a well-worn cliché in the Yard. The incongruity in this case was Leland's tobacco. The man had a pouch practically empty, and he had an ounce of tobacco in a packet in his pocket. Now, a confirmed pipe-smoker does not keep tobacco in his pocket; it dries very quickly, and not only does it then powder, but it loses much of its flavour and attractiveness in smoking. In the cool depths of a rubber-lined pouch its moisture and quality are retained. Why, then, was Leland carrying it in a packet in his pocket, with his pouch nearly empty? The only reason that seemed to Manson to be feasible was that he had only shortly before purchased the packet in order to replenish his depleted store.

"Suppose," argued the doctor, "he had proceeded to Thames Pagnall by train after buying the tobacco. His natural reaction would be to pack the weed into his pouch. Similarly in case of entrance by bus. Inspector Carruthers was quite certain that he had used neither of these means of transport. Was there any other method of arriving there which left him no opportunity of transferring the tobacco from the packet to his pouch?" Having reached that stage in his reasoning the doctor came to the opinion that there were two possibilities—he had either purchased the tobacco in the village, or—the second, he decided, could wait until he had exhausted the first. It was no use trying to cross a stile until you came to it.

He walked through the main street of the village, lying back from the river that had given the place its name. He passed old, timbered houses which had been standing there in those days when Sweet Nell was queening it over the duchesses; and were as firm and steadfast today as they were in the time of Charles—a marked contrast to the 1922 jerry-built brick houses adjacent, now nearly falling to pieces. At last the doctor reached the compact shopping centre. He tried his luck at a couple of sweet shops, which also catered for the smoker, but without result. "Broadway Mixture, sir? No, I'm sorry, there's no call for that kind round here, sir."

It was not until he had walked to the end of the street, and back again, that he noticed the little shop lying below street level, and almost hidden between two pretty and venerable cottages. Its old window contained a heterogeneous collation of books with lurid covers, women's articles of toilet, dummy tobacco packets, pencils, ink-bottles, and advertisements for women helps, prams, bicycles and all the fun of the fair, all jumbled together higgledy-piggledy, like an inarticulate Tower of Babel. "This looks a likely place," he said to himself, and dropping down the three brick steps, he lowered his head and passed through the 200-year-old low doorway.

From round the sacking curtain screening the passage between shop and living-room, a woman appeared at his entrance. She wore a smile of invitation—in addition, of course, to the normal garb of woman—and Manson summed it up as a permanently cultivated smile which went on as soon as the curtain was parted. "Yes, sir?" she asked.

"You wouldn't have any Broadway Mixture, I suppose?" he asked.

The woman's smile gave place to a gloomy despondency. "There, now, isn't that a pity," she made answer. "I'm *that* sorry.

There isn't a bit left, m'dear. If only you'd a' come last week, ducks, I'd got a bit. Pity you didn't come then, m'dear."

"You sold it, I gather?" said Manson, with a grin at the flood of endearment.

"Yes, m'dear. I only had two packets of it left, what I'd got for a gentleman when he was on holiday. He left before he'd bought all of 'em, ducks. Then I had two left. It *is* a pity you didn't come last week now, m'dear."

"Sold it last Saturday, did you?" asked Manson.

"Yes, m'dear. I think it was last Saturday. Gentleman come in just like you and says he wants some bacca, and then he sees the packets in the glass case"—she pointed behind her at the showcase behind the counter—"and he says, 'I see you've got Broadway Mixture. I'll have an ounce of that.'" The woman stopped and thought. "Oh! I'm *that* sorry, ducks. That was the Saturday afore last Saturday. Then last Saturday he come in and said as how he'd have the other ounce. Yes, that's it, m'dear."

"Did you know him?" asked Manson.

"Oh no, ducks. I never see him afore. Nice gennelman he was, too. Stopped talking to me, just like you're a-doing, ducks."

"And what did he talk about?"

"Oh, he was a friend of the vicar's, m'dear. Came from America, he did. Stayed here weeks and weeks with the vicar, he did."

"Have you not heard that the police are asking for any news of a stranger being in the village on that Saturday you are talking about? Why haven't you told them about the man buying tobacco in your shop?"

"The perlice, ducks? No, I don't know anything about the perlice. I don't go out much. The shop and the kiddies keeps me busy."

Manson regained the street, and walked slowly along, his eyes searching the business premises as he walked. Presently he reached an opening which widened inside into a yard. Garages ran along the three sides, except for one small break which seemed to be the workshop of the garage owner. Various car parts, tyres and other accessories filled the large window which gave light to the workshop. The scientist noted it gravely. He turned in at the door and approached the owner.

"I have reason to believe that a man may have left a bicycle with you some time last Saturday," he said.

"I dare say, sir," was the reply. The man looked inquiringly at his questioner. "Quite a number of people left bicycles here on that day. There was a cricket match on the go."

"Quite so. But I should think it more than likely that this particular cycle was not claimed."

The man put down the tool he had been using, took a key from a nail and led the way into the yard. He unlocked a garage door and opened it. "If it wasn't claimed, sir, then it's still in here," he said. The two men entered. In one corner stood a cycle resting against the wall. "That will be the one, sir?" asked the man.

"I do not know," the scientist answered. "But I should think it most probable." He approached the machine and examined it. It bore, however, no marks by which it could be identified. The tool-bag was empty, and the slit in which it is customary to insert the owner's visiting card, by way of identification, was also empty.

From a pocket, Dr. Manson produced his wallet, and from the wallet he extracted one of his professional cards, handing it to the garage owner. The man eyed the name and the rank of his visitor in perturbation. "Now," said Manson, "can I rely on you to lock this garage, and keep it locked until a detective comes along to conduct an official examination of this machine? It may prove of very great importance."

"Certainly, I'll do that, Inspector. You can have the key yourself, if you like."

"No, I prefer to leave it in your charge."

* * * * *

"So that, Carruthers, is how Leland came into the village to his death," explained Manson. It was a quarter of an hour later, and the doctor, in the police-station, had explained his suspicions, and their realization, to the chief constable and the inspec-

tor. "And I dare say that your men, Colonel, will be able to identify one or two fingerprints on the machine as those of Leland's."

(As a matter of interest the task was a simple one. A dozen or
so prints on the handlebars and the crossbar were easily recog-
nizable as those of the fingers of the right hand of the dead man.)

"But what the deuce made you inquire at the shop in the first
place, Doctor?" asked the chief constable.

Manson explained the process of his reasoning over the tobacco packet. "The village shops were worth trying, I thought,"
he said. "It was a piece of exceedingly good fortune that the
woman remembered the man coming in the previous Saturday. That makes it certain, I think, that my reasoning of S.F.
is correct, and that when Leland was in Thames Pagnall on the
13th he saw S.F. and that his subsequent visit, on the day of his
death, was to obtain further information of S.F. or to see him
again, and, perhaps, confront him. You will remember that he
states in the diary only that he *saw* S.F.; there is no suggestion
there that he *spoke* to him, and there is no suggestion that S.F.
had seen him.

"A further circumstance seems to me to strengthen this inference. On his first visit to the shop he merely bought tobacco.
On the second occasion—after he had seen S.F. in the meantime—he was asking questions about the houses, and who lived
in them, and so on. He was feeling his way into S.F. That must
be obvious."

The chief constable chuckled. "And all that, I take it, Doctor,
comes through that very suspicious mind which I hear you've
got."

"I fear, Colonel, that it does," replied Manson. "And now that
we have settled our doubts about Leland, how have you progressed, Inspector, with those four gentlemen whose names
begin with an 'F'?"

Inspector Carruthers grunted. His face lost that buoyant look
which the doctor's story had engendered. "I am afraid. Doctor,
that I have some bad news for you there," he announced.

"That will not be any new experience for me, Inspector," was
the response. "What particular bad news is it?"

"None of them could have done it, Doctor. It is impossible."

Dr. Manson digested the statement. "Let me hear the proof," he said at last. "One at a time, if you don't mind, Carruthers."

"Right. We'll take the squire first. That's Major ffolkes. If Dr. Lumley is correct about the time of death, about half past four o'clock, then the major cannot have fired the shot."

"Why not, Inspector?"

The chief constable chortled the answer before the inspector had time to reply. "Because the old war-horse was batting, I reckon," he said.

Carruthers nodded. "That's so, sir," he agreed. He explained to Dr. Manson. "You see, the major went in to bat in his usual position, which is first wicket down. And he wasn't bowled until ten minutes past five."

"I think you will find that Dr. Lumley gave the time limits for the death as between four-thirty and five-thirty, Inspector," the doctor replied. "Have you ascertained definitely that the major could not have been in a position in which he could have fired a shot between five-ten and five-thirty?"

"Absolutely, Doctor," from the inspector. "For one thing, wild horses and his worst enemy wouldn't have dragged him from that match in the state it was when he came out. They wanted only four runs to win. Very keen on the village cricket is the old major. Until the match was safe he was dancing round the scorers like a cat on hot bricks. Hundreds of people will testify to that. And he was roaring: 'Don't hit that one, George!' and 'Run like hell, you two!' and things like that. No, the major didn't do it. And he isn't S.F."

"All right, Carruthers. We will accept the major's alibi. Now what about Bill Farquhar? What part did *he* play?"

"Bill Farquhar? He was the Maplecot scorer, Doctor. He didn't do it. Bill wouldn't have left his book to the care of the Thames Pagnall scorer not for all the tea in China. Why, he would have his eye glued to the Thames Pagnall man all the time to see that he didn't sneak a run on to his side's total. Cripes, Doctor, you don't know these two teams. They've got a more suspicious mind between them than you have where their cricket is concerned."

A roar of laughter from the chief constable was echoed by an appreciative chuckle from the scientist. "All right, Inspector. I'll have to concede Farquhar. Now we are left with Ferris and French. I think Ferris was the gentleman with the gun. And you were going to get the gun for me."

"I've got it. Doctor, in the next room. But I'm afraid that we shall have to wipe out both men in one go."

"Because?" queried Manson.

"Because they were a fielder and a bowler in the Maplecot side. *And Maplecot were fielding.* From four o'clock until the last wicket fell at half past five, Sid French was bowling. He took the last wicket—at least the man was given out stumped off his bowling. And Ferris was fielding at short slip. If he had been off the field he'd dern sure have been missed, and the Maplecot folk would have raised Hades with the game in the state it was."

There was silence.

"Then that disposes of that," said Manson, at last. "But I'll have a look at the gun just the same." The inspector fetched it. The doctor took no more than a couple of minutes to reach his conclusions. "You are right enough here, Carruthers," he announced. "This weapon could certainly not have been fired without exploding in the marksman's face."

"So we are back exactly where we started," grunted the chief constable. He looked out of the window, and into the village street. "And here's the assistant commissioner. Come along and we'll have that cup of tea we promised him."

"Put my rod in the car," Manson reminded him.

Colonel Mainforce lived in an old manor house, some three miles out of Thames Pagnall. His father had lived there; and so had his grandfather and great-grandfather, and the father of his great-grand-father. And there had been Mainforces in that house, or rather in the house which had stood on the site the present manor house now stood, before the Conqueror came to this country for our good, or, as he said on landing, 'for all your goods' (whereupon a cynic, who was blessed with considerable foresight, and who was standing by, commented, "He should have added 'and chattels'.") The Mainforce of that day must have ranged himself on the side of the invader, since his family still held the land and possessions, and the fortune that attended on them. And generation after generation of them went soldiering for their country, and for their king (when there was no longer a Lord Protector to be served.) There were some 200 acres of the Manor—woodlands, bracken-covered game covers, among which rabbits abounded, and, in the middle of it, a large lake, fed by a stream which had its rising in a spring some three miles away.

There was a story of great friendship beneath the waters of that lake.

When, after the war of 1914-18, the peace depression was at its deepest, Colonel Mainforce bethought himself of a plan to aid the men who had fought under him on the fields of France. He engaged two hundred of them to dig the lake in order that they might have work and wages. For those who came from a distance, wooden huts were erected on the estate. In these they lived. And they dug, and dug, and dug, until three acres of land lay deep. The task brought work, salvation and the return of their self-respect to the men; it brought a sizable piece of water to the colonel. When, after it had been plastered and prepared, the stream was loosed into it, the water held. The narrow necks of the stream at its entrance and exit were securely held with small-gauge iron netting. The colonel sent post-haste to New Zealand for two thousand young rainbow trout. Carefully, the contents of the tanks were loosed into the lake. They had lived and bred; and since then had furnished the colonel and his friends with some of the best trout-fishing in the county, if not, indeed, in the country.

It was to this lake that, after they had refreshed themselves with tea, the party proceeded. The colonel, the assistant commissioner and Dr. Manson carried rods and landing-nets; the inspector, to whom flies and the other concomitants of the angler were still a mystery, went as spectator. The evening rise was just beginning, and now and then, ripples disturbed the surface of the water, as a fish came up along the edges of the weeds and snapped a fly whose flight had landed him on the water. The ripples widened in ever-growing rings and dispersed, only again to appear in another part as another fish rose at another spot.

The doctor, an expert fly-man, after a few moments of watching the natural flies skimming the surface, put up a red spinner. From behind the shelter of a bush he sent his line through the air, to straighten out at a distance of some forty feet. The fly landed, light as a feather, at a spot where a line of clear water lay between two banks of reeds. There was a plop, a ring of movement in the water, and a tightening of the line. Ten minutes later the doctor had landed his first fish—a handsomely spotted three-pound trout.

For an hour the men moved separately round the lake, whisking lines through the air, and, when the fly had dried from its contact with the water, dropping it once again, cunningly, in such spots as a natural fly would drop as, spent by its flight, it came to rest, exhausted. The sun, now a ball of yellow, as it sank lower, turned the surface of the water into liquid gold, across which the shadows of the trees threw russet streaks, and the bushes a mixture of green and russet. There is no more beautiful sight in Nature than the setting sun, at the close of a hot summer day, reflected in the waters of a pool in Surrey.

Round the lake went the fishermen, converging step by step on the entry flow of the feeding stream. They met, and pooled the contents of their creels. Ten brace of handsome, speckled forms was the result.

"I know of no more appetising meal than a dish of freshly caught trout cooked at once," said the chief constable. "You will all stay and have a bite?" he asked.

Not until the catch, served up in golden-brown breadcrumbed cutlets, had been disposed of, and the company had adjourned to the library for coffee, was a return made to the original reason for the gathering. The chief constable provided the atmosphere. "Now, I have Benedictine, Cointreau, Crème de Menthe or Chartreuse," he announced. "Take your choice." The liqueurs assembled in their vari-colours on the table beside the coffee, Colonel Mainforce sent a box of his cigars perambulating round, and with the weeds sending a comfortable and fragrant aroma round the room, he spoke.

"As I said some time ago, we seem to be just where we started, Doctor, eh?"

"Oh no, Colonel." Dr. Manson shook his head emphatically. "Oh dear, no. We have progressed considerably."

"Progressed?" from the chief constable.

"Most certainly," from Dr. Manson.

"Hmm! How have we done that, Doctor?"

"Every step we make nearer to the person we want must be a progression, Colonel. Now, let us consider how we have progressed today. This morning we had at least five suspects—"

"Five, Doctor?"

"Certainly. Four men who were either S.F.s or just plain F.s. In today's work we have wiped out four of the five. That, surely, is progression. I know of only one sure and certain method of solving mysteries when there is an entire absence of clues. That method is the process of elimination. It is quite simple. You bunch all the people who could, by any conceivable means, have done it, and then you pursue your investigation of them, and, one by one, cancel out those who are innocent, though having a seeming opportunity. The one who cannot be eliminated—he is the gentleman we want. There is no doubt whatever about it. It is as certain as a game of chance."

"Game of chance certain?" echoed the assistant commissioner.

"Most decidedly. I have never been able to subscribe to the argument that gambling and chance are hazards," insisted the scientist. "They are certainties. I know of no greater certainty than that of winning money on horse-racing, or on the spin of a coin, or, say, cards."

The chief constable scratched his head in bewilderment. "That, Doctor, is surely against the general belief?"

"Merely because general belief does not take the trouble to complete its thinking," was the reply. "It has a careless mind. I have a tidy mind—"

"and a dashed suspicious one," put in the A.C. with a chuckle. "But go on, Doctor. This argument is getting decidedly interesting. How, for instance, do you make betting on horses a certainty?"

"Perfectly simple, A.C. Suppose you set out to win money by backing, shall we say, favourites. You back the favourites in each race on Monday. They lose. You back the favourites to cover your lost stakes and show a profit on Tuesday. Again they lose." Dr. Manson paused, and looked round the company. "Have you ever known a week or a fortnight or a month go by, gentlemen, in which one favourite has not won his race?"

"Never," replied the Chief Constable, who was a knowledgeable man on racing, and a frequent attender at meetings.

"Never! Very well then, Colonel. If you back the favourites to cover all previous losses and show a profit, there is nothing more certain under the sun than that, when a favourite wins, you are in pocket. Where is the chance? Where is the gamble? As I say, it is a certainty."

"But, dern it, Doctor, suppose you did back, as you say, all the favourites, and they lost steadily for a month. You'd never have enough money to cover the losses and leave a profit. It wouldn't work."

"What has that to do with it?" asked the scientist. "Chance, or the law of averages, has nothing whatever to do with how much money you have in your pockets. Chance is limitless and timeless. What, for instance, are the odds of a tossed penny coming down heads ten times in succession?"

"Pretty hefty, I should say," put in Inspector Carruthers.

"There you go again," retorted Dr. Manson. "Completely careless thinking. The chances of a penny coming down heads ten times in succession are *even*. There are two sides to a penny—head and tail. Every time you toss it is even money which side turns up. That same loose thinking says that, by the law of averages, if a black card wins at *Trente et quarante* twenty times in succession, red *must* turn up soon. And I have seen in casinos stakes gambled upon this. Certainly, by the law of average, there must be at some time twenty corresponding red turns-up. The thing that everybody seems to overlook is that the law of average does not work for a week or just a month. The law of averages operates between Creation and Eternity, not just for next Tuesday. Red can turn up twenty million times in succession and still leave the law of averages undisturbed, because some time within the next twenty million years or so black can turn up an equal number of times. All this is why I said that the process of detection by elimination is as certain as a game of chance."

The scientist took a gulp of coffee, and chuckled. "Do you know where I learned that chance was a certainty—the greatest certainty in the world?" he asked.

Interested "Nos" ran round the company. "Where *did* you learn it, Doctor?" asked the A.C.

"The first time that I played in the Casino at Monte Carlo, gentlemen," was the reply. "And that," he added, reminiscently, "is a good few years ago. That is where I learned that chance is a certainty. I watched a rather well-known gambler lose nearly twenty thousand pounds in a day. And I knew that one man, at least, had realized before me how great a certainty is the game of chance. Also, I saw how he had circumvented it, to such good effect that it brought him double figures in millions as a fortune."

"And that man was—whom?" asked the assistant commissioner. He was listening, like the others, with marked interest to the reminiscence.

"The man was François Blanc, who owned the Casino," replied Manson. "Years before, he had been brought to the verge of ruin by a gambler named Garcia. He had to hurry to Paris and borrow a large sum of money to tide him over the crisis. And a nice job he had to get the money, too. He had watched the play of the gambler; he had watched his croupiers. He had suspicions that they might be wangling the tables. He mentally apologized to them later. For he quickly saw the loophole in his tables. He made provision for it—in a new rule of play. And never again did Monsieur Blanc find himself in any danger of losing his motto, spoken by himself to an old uncle of mine. . . ."

"The motto?" The query came from the chief constable.

"Rouge gagne quelqefois, Noir gagne souvent, mais Blanc gagne toujours." (Red wins sometimes, black wins often, but Blanc—white—always wins.)

A ripple of laughter greeted the *bon mot*. "And what was the rule which circumvented chance?" asked the assistant commissioner.

"François Blanc *instituted a maximum to stakes*," said Manson, quietly. "That did the trick. I smile when I am told that Monte Carlo is a place of chance. It is not a place of chance. François Blanc took the chance out of it. When a player, in his doubling, or progressive increase of stakes, in order to take advantage of chance, reaches the maximum stake and loses, then he is finished. And so is chance. He was a wily old man was François Blanc.

"However, all this is by way of digression. We have rather strayed from the point, which is that we are not where we started—because of the elimination of the cricketing gentlemen whose names began with the letter F. I said, you will remember, that we had progressed, because we had eliminated four people who could have been suspect. I also said that I know of only one successful method of solving the mystery of whodunit, as the detective writers put it; and that was by bunching all the possible suspects together and eliminating them one by one. The one whom you cannot eliminate is the person you want. He may not appear to be; he may have seemed the most innocent of them all. But if he cannot be eliminated *by hard fact*, then he is guilty. I am not going to say that you can prove him guilty, but he *is* guilty."

The scientist leaned back in his chair and watched a smoke-ring from his cigar growing larger and larger in circumference as it rose until, at last, it dispersed itself in a whiff of blue-grey smoke. "Do you know," he said, "I sometimes think that a great deal of any success that has come my way is due to my reversal of the ordinary forms of detection."

"Such as?" asked the assistant commissioner.

"Well, it seems to me that I take the easy way of detection. I can think of nothing more difficult for a detective officer to do—as he mostly does do—than to look round the scene of any crime for the perpetrator. Out of a company he devotes himself to finding one particular man or woman, whom he doesn't know, and to whom he has no guide. It is a tremendous task. And he sometimes fails. That he succeeds at all is remarkable. Now, I work in just the opposite way. I do not believe—not in detection—that dictum of the law that a man is innocent until he is proved guilty. When I start on any investigation, I assume that every living soul connected with it in any way whatever *may* be guilty until I have proved he or she innocent."

A ripple of laughter interrupted his discourse. Dr. Manson pointed his cigar at them collectively. "You may laugh," he admonished. "But let me demonstrate the value of my argument. There was some years ago, you remember, a very sticky piece of crime, which was pretty deeply investigated, and never solved. At least it was not solved until the person concerned, lying on his deathbed, and seeking the good wishes of the Hereafter, confessed his sin, and repented of it. You remember it, A.C.?"

Sir Edward nodded. "I remember it perfectly, Doctor," he agreed, quietly.

"Now that person was so little suspected that he was never even questioned. He had, seemingly, to have everything to lose and nothing whatever to gain by the crime. Yet his confession gave detailed points which, had they been at all investigated at the time, could not have failed to have been brought out by any competent detective-inspector. He was not questioned because he was so palpably innocent, gentlemen.

"He could not have escaped *my* net. I say that, not boastingly, but because it just could not have happened. He would have been one of my bunch of people in that case who would have had to be eliminated. *He could not have been eliminated, and all the others could have been.* Ergo: I should have known him for the guilty person.

"Now, that is exactly the position we have here today. Everyone who is concerned with the Thames Pagnall affair in any way is in my scheme of investigation, a possibly guilty person until I have eliminated them one by one. So far we have set four people free. That means to say, I am four stages nearer the guilty one. Do you call that 'back where we started'?"

Inspector Carruthers scratched his head at this piece of introspective reasoning. It was, he said, a bit beyond him. And where did they start searching now for the wanted man?

"I reckon I can answer that quite easily," put in the assistant commissioner. "The Doctor will rustle up another bunch of folk and start eliminating them."

Dr. Manson grinned delightedly. "That is the very thing I *am* going to do, Sir Edward," he said. "And we may as well start now."

CHAPTER TEN
ELIMINATION NO. 2

"As WE HAVE so far failed to find or even suspect who fired the shot, we might, I think, attack the case from another angle," said Dr. Manson, in the process of finding his other bunch of people and eliminating them.

"That being?" asked the assistant commissioner.

"The person who took the wallet from the person of Leland. I said once before that he was most likely the murderer, but that is not definite. He might have been no more than an accomplice. Should that be the case, then, if we can track him down, we should be able to get a line on his principal, for people can only be accomplices to someone they either know personally or in whose affairs they are closely involved.

"In order to have purloined the wallet (and anything else that may have been taken, but of which we have not, as yet, any evidence) the person or persons must have had access to the body; and they must have had access in such a way that no suspicion has been aroused in us who are investigating the case. That is, I think, obvious. For nobody has been found who saw anybody with the dead man. That statement is of course, erroneous."

"Erroneous, Doctor?" said Inspector Carruthers.

"Certainly erroneous. And also a case of very careless think-ing, typical of the state of intellect of the average person today. I told you that the dead man had been robbed. You asked three or four people had they seen anyone approach the chair in which the man was sitting. Each one replied, I think, that they had not seen anyone approach the man. Is not that so?"

The inspector nodded.

"Yet every single one of them had seen someone approach the man and the chair in circumstances which would have given either one of them an admirable opportunity of taking the wallet, unnoticed."

"The devil they did!" The chief constable sat up with a jerk.

"The devil of it *is* that they did, Colonel," retorted Manson. "Mr. Bosanquet said, for instance, that he saw nobody go near the man. Yet he walked across to Crombie to tell him about his fowls—and Crombie was standing by the chair. He had had the man and the entire green to himself. Crombie swore at the in-quest that he had seen nobody by the man. Yet he left Bosa-nquet there with the body while he himself raised the alarm at the public-house. Bosanquet was alone with the body for at least five minutes. Moreover, he admits that he slipped a hand inside the dead man's clothes and decided that there was no heartbeat. What does he do then? He sends Crombie off to the public-house, leaving himself with the opportunity of quietly searching the entire stock of the pockets of Leland and in per-fect security, too.

"These are two persons to be eliminated, or not, as the case may be. But there are others. Major ffolkes was by the body. So was Constable Lambert. And there were one or two other per-sons who slipped their hands into his clothes and might well have taken something unnoticed."

"Who are they, Doctor?" asked the startled A.C.

"One was Dr. Lumley, and the other was Inspector Carru-thers here."

"M—m—m—me?" gasped the astounded inspector.

"Of course, Inspector. Who are you to make me deviate from my rule that everybody on the spot is guilty until I have proved them not guilty? Let me state a case. You are being blackmailed. You know that the blackmailer has a document of yours which he keeps on his person for safety. Then, one day, you are called to a man found dead on the green at Thames Pagnall. You whip off his hat, and you recognize him as your blackmailer. You know that any search of his body will reveal the document concerning yourself. So, under the guise of feeling for any injury, and to ascertain whether the man is really dead, you extract his wallet. What is wrong with an hypothesis like that? Well, there you are. We now have five more people to eliminate, each of whom was by the body at one time or another. Where do we start?"

The astounded inspector was the first to speak. "I think I can eliminate Constable Lambert, Doctor," he said. "He could not know that the man was on the green, because he had only a few moments before coming into the police-station from Cobham, where I had sent him on official business in the morning. I saw him step off the Cobham bus outside the police-station. He entered, and had been there only a minute or so when I received news of the man on the green and packed him off to see what it was all about."

"Add to that, Inspector, the fact that when he reached the scene, the major, Bosanquet and Crombie were all there, as well as a ring of spectators," said the chief constable. "I don't see how he could have got away with anything."

"Does Lambert play cricket with the club at all?" asked Manson.

"No, Doctor," replied the inspector.

"Then I think we may as well be quit of him," was the reply. "For I am quite certain that Leland saw someone at the match on the previous Saturday, and that was why he came again this Saturday."

"And what do we do about Carruthers?" asked the chief constable. "Regularly *sprawled* over the man, did Carruthers."

"Perhaps we might write off Carruthers also," decided Manson. "Had he known that the man was there, he would not have sent Lambert to him, knowing that Lambert might search the man and obtain the thing that he (the inspector) wanted. Or had he done so, and later found that Leland was associated with him, he would have demanded from Lambert anything that had been found on the body. Then there was, of course, quite a company of people on the scene when the inspector arrived. I think we can acquit the inspector. He is eliminated."

Inspector Carruthers wiped a heated brow in relief.

"So that we are now left with Dr. Lumley, George Crombie, Major ffolkes and Mr. Bosanquet," said the assistant commissioner.

"I thought we had eliminated the major, A.C.?" protested the chief constable.

"Only as the murderer, Colonel," was the reply. "He may yet be an accomplice, according to the doctor's argufying."

"If you acquit me, Doctor, because there was a crowd there when I arrived, then you have to acquit Dr. Lumley. He came after me, and I watched him make his examination. Had he removed anything from the body, I should have seen it," said Carruthers.

"Now we have Major ffolkes, Crombie and Bosanquet. Which of them do we start with, Doctor?"

The scientist frowned at the question. "Of Crombie I know nothing," he said. "He seems a simple soul to me. But Bosanquet worries me somewhat."

The wrinkles were on the scholarly forehead of Dr. Manson, and the crinkles in the corners of his eyes. And the fingers of him were playing a tattoo on an arm of his chair. The assistant commissioner caught the warning signs. He shifted back in his seat, preparing his mind for the reasoned argument he knew was coming, and seeking to see in it what the doctor saw. "And why does Bosanquet worry you, Doctor?" he asked.

"Because there are several points in his story which do not, to my tidy mind, fall into cohesion," was the reply. "And because Bosanquet, all the afternoon, was *behind* Leland."

"On the other hand, Doctor, there were about fifty people also behind Leland. Why pick on Bosanquet?" asked the chief constable.

"They had not the same peculiarities, Colonel," was the reply.

"Such as?"

"It was rather a remarkable thing that he should have gone on to the green at all, was it not? The man was entertaining a party to the cricket. They had been sitting on the front lawn of his house all afternoon. Mrs. Bosanquet had prepared tea. One would have supposed that the host would have remained with his guests. Instead, he was inspecting his fowl-house, finding that the fowl were out, and then walking over the green to Crombie to tell him the tale."

"He might have seen the fowl perambulating the garden and then, of course, he knew that Crombie would be collecting the chairs, and so would be on the green," said Inspector Carruthers.

"And he would know, would he not, Carruthers, that Crombie would have to pass his gate with the handcart load of chairs on the way to the store—because I noticed that the only bridge over the dyke separating the green from the road was just below the Bosanquet bungalow. Why leave his guests and go across the green? This, by itself, however, is not entirely a suspicious action. But, viewed with others, it becomes so in my mind."

"The others being?" from the assistant commissioner.

"Let me refer you to Bosanquet's statement at the inquest. I can, I think, remember the wording of it pretty accurately. He is describing how he felt the man's heart and found that he was dead. He continued:

"'I thought it best that Crombie should raise the alarm, while I remained to see that the body was not disturbed in any way.

"'*Coroner:* Had you recognized the man at all?

"'*Bosanquet:* I had not then even seen his face, sir. . . . His hat was over his eyes. . . . When I found he was dead I felt sure that the body should be left until the police arrived. Had the man been still alive, I would have endeavoured to render him assistance, which would doubtless have meant disturbing his position in the chair.'"

Dr. Manson ceased speaking and looked round his circle of listeners. He smiled a little as he saw behind their interest expressions of inquiry. "It does not convey anything to you?"

he inquired. "Now, it conveys quite a lot to me, I having, as you have heard, a very suspicious mind. Here we have a man who leaves his guests and walks across a green to a workman who has, in any case, within a few minutes, to pass his door. He finds the workman in trouble over a man lying in a chair. 'I can't make him move,' says the workman. What does Bosanquet do? The man has a hat over his eyes. He is lying back in his chair. Does Mr. Bosanquet do what you, or I, would have done—take off his hat and have a look at him to see if he is ill, or if he is conscious, but unable to speak? He does not. He slips a hand into the man's waistcoat and says to Crombie: 'By Jove, he's dead! You nip off and tell the squire, and I will stay here with the body of a man I don't know and haven't troubled to look at. *It must not be disturbed*.'"

"Gee whiz, Doctor! I get the point," broke in the assistant commissioner.

The doctor acknowledged the comment with a nod, and then continued his hypothesis. "Now, what are the circumstances in which any ordinary person understands that a body should be left undisturbed until the police arrive, Chief Constable? If you saw a man fall down in a fit, or if you saw that a man suddenly laid back in his chair and died, would you raise an alarm and leave the body undisturbed until you could get the police?"

"No. I do not think that I should do so, Doctor," replied the colonel. "I should, I suppose, lay the body down and possibly try artificial respiration."

"Of course you would. In what circumstances would you stand back and leave the body exactly as it was until the police arrived and made an examination?"

"You mean, Doctor"—and the words came slowly from the chief constable—"you mean that the only occasions on which a body would be left undisturbed in such circumstances is *when the person is known to have died a violent death*?"

Dr. Manson nodded. "Of course I mean that, Colonel," he agreed. "Take the explanation given on the green by Crombie to the inspector, of the scene when Bosanquet arrived, and was told that the gentleman could not be awakened. Mr. Bosanquet said: *'Perhaps he's fainted with the heat and excitement. Let me see him.'* Again I say that I would have expected any ordinary person at once to have whipped off the man's hat and attempted to render some assistance. He might have loosened his collar, which is a thing most people know should be done in the case of fainting from the heat, and he might have said we had better give him some air. But no. Mr. Bosanquet, without more ado, slips a hand inside the man's waistcoat, and says he's dead. *'Perhaps he's fainted with the heat and the excitement,'* Bosanquet had said. If that was so, why on earth should he say that the body should be left undisturbed? *But if he knew that the man had met a violent death, then, indeed, he would follow such a course."*

"Then you think, Doctor, that Bosanquet is the man?" asked the assistant commissioner.

"I do not think anything of the kind, Sir Edward. I am merely, as is my custom, pointing out curious circumstances, because I do not like curious circumstances in connection with violent deaths, any more than I like coincidences in connection with violent deaths. It may be that Mr. Bosanquet is an unusual person; but, if so, I want that to be proved to my satisfaction, and to the satisfaction of Justice.

"Let us go on with the curiosities. Crombie is an aged man, very wobbly on his pins. Yet, when Bosanquet finds that this man is dead, and must not be disturbed, and that the alarm must be raised quickly, does he run as fast as he can to tell his friends the cricketers? No. Instead, he sends Crombie hobbling at a mile an hour for help, and remains himself with the body. Had I, now, knowing that the man had been killed, wanted to retrieve anything from the body, I should have done exactly what Bosanquet did. Instead of waiting until Crombie came past my house with his barrow, leaving the body on the green for anybody to discover, I should have walked out to Crombie when the green was still clear except for him and the dead man, I should have told him at once, what I knew already, that the man was dead, and have sent him off to raise the alarm, leaving me free without interference, or spectators, to take just what I wanted at my leisure. That is what I would have done. The point we have to decide is did Bosanquet do it, or didn't he?"

"Heavens, Doctor! You do see things, don't you?" ejaculated the inspector.

"There is still one other point which, taken in conjunction with the others, can also be counted as a curiosity in Mr. Bosanquet."

"And what would that be?"

"His recollection of the shots fired, if they were shots, or the backfires, if they were backfires. Bosanquet said at first that he had heard a shot, and he gave the time as about a quarter to five o'clock. Then he changed his mind and said that it was a backfire that he heard. The change of opinion, you will notice, was after he had talked the matter over with Mr. Catling. When I asked if he knew the sound of a shot, he said he knew nothing at all about shots and had never shot anything in his life. Now, is it not a little curious that he, knowing nothing whatever about shots, as soon as he hears an explosion says, 'That was a shot, that was'? The more so as he possesses a car, and, I have no doubt, is perfectly familiar with the noise of a car backfiring. The average motorist's reaction on hearing such an explosion coming from down the road is that the noise comes from the backfire of a car. Why should a man who doesn't know anything about a shot, and does know about motor-cars, assume that the explosion was not a backfire, but the report of a gun?

"Now, again, all the people who were with the Bosanquets were together on the front lawn. Everyone except Mr. Bosanquet heard two shots or backfires. But he heard only one. Why did he hear only one, and the others with him hear two? There may be nothing in this, of course. He may have been a little preoccupied at the time, though it was no more than a minute after the first explosion. But, on the other hand, taken in conjunction with all the other things I have mentioned, there may be a good deal in it."

There was a silence as the scientist finished his summing-up of the position, and sat back in his chair. It was broken by the assistant commissioner. "Well, Mr. Chief Constable, what do you say to all that?" he asked.

"That we will have to get busy on Bosanquet," was the reply. "Though, mark you, I've known the man for years, and he's as nice a fellow as ever I've met. I can't picture him in the role of a killer or as an accomplice of a killer. Mind you, I reckon the doctor has made out a good case for inquiry, and I admit that up to now the inquiry into him has been no more than superficial. But I do wish we had some idea of motive on which to work. As I say, I have known him for years, and he was at Oxford a little after me. Why does he want to go killing an Australian he has never likely seen, since Leland only reached this country a few weeks ago. And what connection have the initials S.F. with Albert Bosanquet?"

"Are you sure that he has never been in Australia, Colonel?" Manson awaited the reply with some interest.

"Positive, Doctor. Whenever I have mentioned that place or New Zealand, where, as you know, I have fished, he always expressed envy of people who have travelled. He knew that I had been in India, and told me once that he had always wanted to see India."

"The point of that being, Colonel?" asked the A.C.

"That he would have to call in India to get here from Australia."

"Unless he went from Australia on the Pacific route, and came across America from San Francisco," suggested Dr. Manson.

"Which he didn't do, Doctor, because he was for ever saying he would have to try to find time to pay a visit to the States."

"Do you know all this of your own knowledge, Colonel, or is it what you have gathered in the course of talks with Bosanquet?"

"Well, if you put it that way, Doctor, it is from talks with him and with mutual acquaintances."

"Then, of course, Colonel, it is like what the soldier told the girl—it is not evidence. Get me evidence. As for the motive, we really want to know what S.F. was to Leland. Perhaps I can get evidence on that. May I use the telephone?"

"Go right ahead, Doctor."

The scientist dialled Whitehall 1212, and asked for the laboratory. A voice responded. "That you, Merry?" he inquired.

"Manson here. Will you get this message radioed to Australia. Ready?

"Jervis CID Melbourne Stop Leland diary states quotes saw SF today Stop Must look into this Stop End quotes Do you know anybody SF having association Leland any time Stop Radio reply details Stop Manson Scotland Yard End message.

"That may bring some results," said Manson as he replaced the receiver. "Perhaps we had better not proceed with any inquiries until I have a reply to it. We might, go barging up an inconvenient pole. And now. Colonel, much as I dislike to leave your very pleasant hospitality, I think I shall have to be returning. If you can drop us down in your car, Inspector?"

The party broke up. Inspector Carruthers drove the assistant commissioner and Dr. Manson back into the village of Thames Pagnall. They stopped at the police-station. "The next train isn't for half an hour, Doctor," he explained. "Perhaps you would like to wait in my house. It's more comfy than the police-station."

"Better if we had one for the road, or rather rail, in the pub over there," suggested the A.C.; and the men walked down the road to the 'Green Man'.

Old Gaffer Baldwin saw them approaching, and his grin displayed his one remaining tooth.

"Evening, Gaffer," greeted the inspector.

"A pint, thankin' yer," was the reply.

The inspector laughed. He gave the outside potman the order: "Four pints, please, George."

"This that magpie fellow, Inspector?" asked the assistant commissioner.

Carruthers nodded.

"What's his name? Baldwin, isn't it?"

"Yes, A.C., but he's always called just plain Gaffer."

The A.C. looked at the old man. "Seen any more magpies lately, Gaffer?" he asked, jocularly.

"Wot's he a-sayin' of?" asked Gaffer.

"He says have you had any more presentiments?"

"*Wot!* . . . No, that I ain't. But I don't mind a-tryin' of a pint on't. Though I reckons as 'ow it won't be as good as beer." Baldwin emptied his pot at a gulp.

The A.C. chuckled. He bent close to Gaffer's ears and bellowed: "I didn't say have a drink. I said have you had any more presentiments?"

Gaffer planked his mug down on the bench. His eyes roved the heavens as for enlightenment.

The inspector giggled. Dr. Manson cupped his hands. "Seen that magpie of yours again, Gaffer?" he asked.

"Ah!" The oldest inhabitant pushed his mug forward for a refill. The magpie was still a good selling line. He turned to the inspector.

"Yer minds that there dog of old Beasley's, 'spector?" he asked. "That there one he sez is a collie, wot ain't no collie 'cordin' to my reckonin'?"

"I know it, Gaffer. What about it?"

"He wer a-'owlin' summat turr'ble las' night, he wer."

"Well, Gaffer, they will howl sometimes, you know," rejoined the inspector. "It's no use a policeman talking to it."

"All down River Road, he wer. And 'owling half'n'our. When I 'ears 'im, I sez to meself, 'Gaffer—'"

"Oh, crumbs! Is he at it again?" moaned the chief constable, amid a guffaw of laughter.

"I sez to meself," went on Gaffer, "'You mark me words. Summat's goin' to 'appen.' And I tells old Bill Jennings as 'ow he'd better get his spade ready." Gaffer made another insinuating movement of his mug.

"Bill Jennings?" muttered the chief constable. "Who the devil is Bill Jennings?"

"The gravedigger," said the inspector.

"Oh lor," from the assistant commissioner. "Is this ruddy place hag-ridden?"

"He'll be hearing a robin singing in the church next," opined the inspector.

"For the love of Mike, don't *you* start, Carruthers. What the heck does a robin do?"

"According to local tradition, sir, if anybody in the place is going to die, a robin flies into the church here, perches on the altar and starts to sing."

"Well, for crying out loud! You'd better have Lambert take that rifle of Ferris's and shoot the damned thing before it can get its voice going, Carruthers. We don't want any more deaths round here. We haven't solved the one we've got yet," enjoined Colonel Mainforce.

The party drained their mugs and broke up, the A.C. and Manson towards the railway station, and the chief constable back to his manor house.

CHAPTER ELEVEN
DISCOVERY AT WAPPING

THREE MILES TO the south-west of Cirencester, in the county of Gloucestershire, you may come upon Trewsbury Mead. And there, if you follow the edge of a meadow, pass a line of straggling bushes, and, paying no heed to a dead tree, follow your nose, you will arrive at a large ash tree. Cut in the bark, on one side of the trunk of the tree, are the initials 'T.H.'

Down by the side of the tree is a well, almost enclosed by thorn bushes. There is no water in the well; it is, in fact, nearly filled with stones. But at that well, nearly one thousand five hundred years ago, Roman legionaries drew water to slake their thirst; and Roman mothers and children carried in jars from it the water required for the camp on the adjacent heights.

This well is, or was, the fountain from which grew the River Thames; the 'T.H' on the bark of the ash signifies Thames Head. Take no notice of those who will have you believe that Seven Springs, in the Cotswold Hills, South of Cheltenham, is the rising of the great river. Earliest engravings of Thames Head show a fountain of water, like a burst main, swelling into a lake, with its banks lined with tall bushes. What matters that the well be dry today? It gave birth to Father Thames, and has passed. The murmuring waters remember.

From Gloucestershire, the Thames flows to the sea—through places that have written the Pageant of our History; through places the names of which strike the ear like the sound of rippling music—Nuneham, Shillingford (Shellingford, if you prefer the spelling that way), Ashton Keynes, and Mapledurham, where the Royalists fortified the great house for Charles I in the Civil War. It flows on past Runneymede, and its waters saw John acknowledge the Magna Carta with a cross in the place in which a king who could have written his name would have signed 'John R.'; past Hampton Court, where a cardinal, who was for a time greater than a King, was rowed in his barge; past Royal Richmond, with its king and duchesses, who shared him with an orange girl; and on to Vauxhall, lapping the sprawling, depressing streets which once were the Gardens of Vauxhall, resort of roysterers, dandies, and ladies of the court, with entertainment which Pepys found 'mighty divertising'; with its lovers' boxes in which, seeing but unseen, they could indulge their courtship to the strains of the band. (The boxes live still in the phrase: "He's in the wrong box".)

It was Swinburne who said that 'rivers grow weary on their journey to the sea'. But not the Thames, wandering joyously through flowery meadows, dancing over foaming weirs, eddying round still backwaters and singing past the rows of white and green houseboats on the reach of Thames Pagnall, and the stretch of Maidenhead, while gramophone and radio send it rollicking on its way, its waters crossed, at eventide, with the shafts of colour cast by fairy lamps from the water-borne homes. Venice has been less beautiful than the Thames-side on a June night.

True, Father Thames grows more staid, and a little weary, when it approaches The Pool, where the luxury pleasure-craft make way for the dirty little ships that have ploughed their way from the corners of the Seven Seas to the drab surroundings of commerce; where the only lights are the riding lights of those same ships. It flows yellow and sombrely past Execution Dock, remembering its three tides that had by law to engulf hanging pirates before their bodies might be taken from the chains that held them.

And so on to Wapping, where, the day after the conference at Thames Pagnall, Chief Detective-Inspector Manson and Sergeant Merry were wandering along the busily drab High Street. They had turned from the Commercial Road into Nightingale Lane, which had not been a lane this hundred years, and had never heard a nightingale for double that space of time, and had wheeled into the direction of Wapping.

The story of Wapping is writ in the name itself—*wapp*, a ship's rope. The ropemakers flourished there, as did the farrier-smiths in Hammersmith; and ships journeyed there not only to discharge cargoes, but to fit up with ropes, blocks and pulleys, boats, oars, and other nautical necessities. Warehouses, today, line its land-side, the Wapping High Street, ships' chandlers set between them; busy little boats dart out from the Wapping Stairs, over which Bloody Jeffreys looked from the windows of the 'Red Cow' alehouse, as the people's representatives broke in and seized him from behind, and took him the short river journey to the Tower. That was in 1688. And now, two hundred and fifty years later, Authority, in the persons of Dr. Manson and Merry, were once again at Wapping on the tracks of enemies of Law and Order, and of the State.

The pair had journeyed to The Pool to undertake the questioning of two seamen held in the local lock-up. Wapping is the headquarters of the River Police. The previous night, Superintendent Lawrence, commanding the river patrols, was drifting down-stream with the engines of the police launch silent, when the erratic wanderings of a small ship's dinghy excited the comment of his sergeant. The police craft drew into the shadow of a convenient barge tied to a wharf, and a watch was kept on the boat through night-glasses.

The reason for the presence of the police launch on the water was, of itself, interesting. A ship from the East had berthed in The Pool during that late afternoon—a small vessel of some 5000 tons. Since it was known that drugs were being smuggled into the country via boats conducting trade with the East, close watch had been maintained from the shore and from the river for any evidence of drugs. None had been found, but the superintendent held the opinion that should there be any attempt to get drugs ashore, supposing that there were any on board to get ashore, such an attempt would not be made until after darkness had set in. Accordingly, the launch had made its way to a spot from where it would be possible to keep an eye on any movement from the river side, while detective officers took charge of any such attempt on the landward side.

To dispose of any suspicions any intending culprit might have, the police craft put out from the station, passed the newly berthed vessel with hardly a glance, and proceeded upstream as though on patrol. Once out of sight, however, it had been put about, and allowed to drift back under the shadow of buildings on either side of The Pool.

The ruse had, apparently, succeeded, for within a very short space of time two seamen swarmed over the side of the vessel and dropped into the dinghy tied alongside. There was not, of course, anything suspicious in this; a dinghy was invariably kept tied there for that very purpose. But what was suspicious was that the men, without any apparent reason, and without the customary use of oars for the purpose, pushed the boat round to the port side of the ship, aft, and then spent some minutes leaning over one side. Finally, and still without any noise, the boat was pushed off, and one of the occupants, taking an oar, levered it from the stern, thus paddling the boat noiselessly in the direction of the opposite shore. This, the officers decided, was definitely suspicious, for why should a seaman navigate a boat in that fashion when he could the more easily *row* across The Pool to the King's Stairs on the Rotherhithe side of the river? Only the necessity for silent movement could make such a means of locomotion feasible.

Superintendent Lawrence sent the police launch out from its hiding-place, pointed its bows down-stream and began to go down with the now fastly ebbing tide. Before the seamen were aware of its presence a searchlight beam was switched full on their craft, and a hail ordered them to heave-to. They did so, as a matter of Hobson's choice, and were searched. Nothing was found on them, or in their boat. But a lynx-eyed policeman saw the little float bobbing in the water, and pulled up a waterproof silk-wrapped envelope with two pounds of opium safe and dry inside it.

The men vehemently denied any knowledge of the parcel. Nor could any of Dr. Manson's questioning on the following day associate them with the opium. Their nefarious departure from the ship, they averred, was due solely to the fact that they were taking French leave, after the captain and the chief officer had retired to their respective cabins. With that, and the parcel of opium, the police had to be content.

It was unfortunate that the silk which had encased the opium had, by an oversight, been destroyed; for, as Dr. Manson pointed out, inspection through a microscope or by infra-red photography might have shown the fingerprints of one, or both, of them; and that would have been conclusive evidence of their guilt.

The first stages of the questioning by the scientist had been interrupted by loud clanging as a fire-engine tore past the police-station. A second and a third followed. The scientist looked inquiringly at the local inspector.

"Fire in a chemical place just round the corner, sir. Not very serious, I gather. Some room on a top floor," the inspector replied. "What do you think of the men?" he added.

"That you will have to let them go, Inspector. You haven't a ghost of a chance of proving that they lifted the parcel from under the stern of the ship where they had conveniently sunk it, waiting the opportunity. And if you cannot prove that, how can you prove that they dropped it overboard again in mid-stream, where you found it? You and I know, of course, that they did so. But they will tell the magistrate, at a pinch, that it is a well-known habit of drug smugglers to drop such packets in such a way into the river to be picked up by the drug-smugglers' agents. They will stick to their own story, and you haven't a come-back of any kind. The only satisfaction you get out of the affair is that you have a nice sizable parcel of opium, and they haven't."

"I expected you to say that, Doctor," was the reply. "All right, I'll let them go. Thank you and Sergeant Merry for coming down.

Better luck next time." He accompanied them to the door, and saw them on their way out.

"The superintendent's trouble, Jim, was that he left it too long," said Dr. Manson. "Had he cut them off ahead as soon he realized that they had lifted something from the water under the ship's stern we would have had them. His headlight would have been ahead of them instead of across the boat and leaving one side in a convenient shadow, to slip something overboard. It is, of course, easy to talk after the event in such cases, and he might have been close enough for them to have spotted the police launch was on their track—I don't know. Anyway, we've lost them."

He paused at a corner flanked on one side by a school and on the other by two churches. "This is, I think, Red Lion Street," he said. "We can cut through here and come out on a bus or tram route."

The pair turned into the street and walked alongside the recreation ground, only to find that the junction of Red Lion Street and Tench Street was obstructed by hosepipes crossing from a main on the right side of the former road. Their pause to glance down the byway at the engines, now silent, was observed by a uniformed inspector. He hurried up behind them. "Sorry, gentlemen, but I must ask you to pass along," he said; and then caught a glimpse of the scientist's face. "Oh, sorry, Doctor. I did not know that it was you. Do you want to go along to the scene?"

Manson smiled. "No, I don't think so, Inspector, thank you," he said. "We were on our way to a bus route, and fires are not, I fear, my line of country."

"No, Doctor. But I think corpses are."

"Corpses?" Dr. Manson looked quickly at the inspector. "What do you mean by that?"

"The firemen have telephoned that there is a body in the burned-out room and I am just going along to have a look at it. If you—"

"Then I think we will accompany you, Inspector. Bodies, as you have rightly said, are very much in my line."

The three men walked down the street and up to a doorway through which a narrow stairway was visible. Dr. Manson crossed the road, and inspected the premises from the outside. It was a four-storey, double-fronted building, some hundred years old. The ground floor was obviously a warehouse for ships' stores, with the offices on the right of the entrance. The first and second storeys were, apparently, offices. The top floor, it could be plainly seen, was the scene of the fire, for an escape ladder was still resting on the sill of a window on the left-hand side of the building. The scientist, rejoining the other two at the doorway, consulted the name-board of the tenants. The top floor was, it appeared, rented to the firm of Bickerstaffe and Company, manufacturing chemists, and Mr. W. B. Bernstein, a shipping agent. The doctor looked at the inspector, and nodded at the board.

"The fire was in Bickerstaffe's, Doctor," he explained. He led the way into the building, where they were joined by a brass-helmeted fire officer carrying an electric torch, and they started to mount the staircase. They were half-way up when the doctor stopped and sniffed. The inspector looked inquiringly, but the scientist made no reply. Instead, he resumed the climb. But as they turned the corner to the last flight the inspector himself sniffed. "Queer kind of smell, is it not, Doctor?" he asked.

"I do not think so, Inspector. Not queer," was the reply. "It might be a bit queer to smell it here, mind you. . . ."

"Two of our chaps who came up to the room were gassed," the fire brigade officer said. "We wouldn't have known it if the fellow up the escape hadn't have been looking in the broken window and noticed them stagger and fall. We couldn't get in the place for some time, and then we found the body under a bench below a window on the other side of the room. I reckon he was gassed."

"Not gassed, Officer." Dr. Manson sniffed again. "Not gassed. Chloroformed."

"Is that what it is?" ejaculated the inspector. "I was thinking that the smell reminded me of a hospital."

A few more steps and the procession of men entered the room. And a curious room it was, thought the scientist. Its only furniture was a chair and a table. A long wooden bench ran along the inner side and held a number of articles at which the doctor glanced with marked interest. A stranger entering the room would have put the place down as a laboratory, until he had given it a second inspection, when he would have realized that though there were various scientific oddments scattered around, they did not represent even the barest requirements of a laboratory. For a moment, the scientist, after his formal glance round, ignored the room. Instead, he turned his attention to the occupant. The man lay, as the fire officer had said, alongside the bench and half underneath it, as though he had fallen along-side while working, and his body, possibly in a death agony, had rolled over.

He was a man of between forty and fifty years of age, with jet-black hair. His clothes were such as befitted an ordinary artisan-class worker. A suit of brown worsted, shirt and collar matching each other, and of the mass-produced five-shillings-and-sixpence quality. And strong, black shoes. The body was lying on its back, with eyes closed, and was relaxed as though in sleep. Dr. Manson bent over it. There was no apparent sign of injury and the body showed no evidence of having been in con-tact with the flames. The face, however, and other parts of the exposed skin, had a cyanotic coloration, and the lips, also, were blue-tinged. Dr. Manson lifted the eyelids in turn. Each showed wide dilation.

"Chloroform poisoning, evidently," commented Merry. The scientist nodded. "I agree, Merry," he said, "and this is, appar-ently, the source of the poisoning." He turned over with a move-ment of a foot a large fragment of glass—one of a number which were scattered over the floor of the room, in close proximity, chiefly, to the doorway. On it was a label—"Chloroform".

"It looks as though he had been carrying the bottle from the bench to somewhere else in the room, sir, and dropped it," haz-arded the inspector.

"Possibly," agreed the doctor, non-committally.

"Would the contents of the bottle overcome him?"

"The contents of the bottle, or rather jar, would have over-come half Wapping, Inspector," replied Manson.

"Then, possibly, the man was dashing to the window for air when he fell, overcome by the fumes, eh?"

"Possibly, again, Inspector. But I should have thought, in-stead, he might have been safer had he gone out of the door near where he seems to have dropped it. Still, we do not know the circumstances."

"And, speaking of doors, Doctor, have you noticed this one?" asked Merry. He nodded towards it standing against a wall, where it had been placed by the firemen after they had broken it down in order to gain entry to the room. "Wouldn't have thought that the contents of this room were so valuable as to need all that."

The reason for Sergeant Merry's attention was evident when the four men gathered in front of the door. It had no fewer than three fastenings—and all three were of the type known as mor-tice locks. Now, a mortice lock is burglar-proof, so far as any lock can be burglar-proof. Whereas the iron holder into which the bolt of an ordinary lock slides can be freed of its holding screws by strong and continuous pressure, or by a levering of the door, a mortice bolt fits into the heart of the door lintel, and only violent battering, entailing very considerable noise, could smash the bolt through the wood and release the fastening. The firemen had been able to get admittance only by breaking the door off its hinges with the aid of axes, and then sliding the bolts out of the lintel cavities.

Dr. Manson turned to the fire brigade officer. "I suppose you did not interfere with this door at all after you had forced it?" he asked.

"No, sir. We forced the hinges, as you can see, pulled it from the fastenings, and stood it where you now see it."

"You notice, Inspector, that the bolts of the locks are pro-truding, so that the door must have been secure at the time of this man's accident."

"I *had* noticed the fact, Doctor," replied the inspector.

"And does it convey anything to you that may be regarded as sub-normal?"

"That the man required secrecy in the room." He looked round the place, and added: "Secrecy for which I see no immediate necessity."

"But do you see any keys in the locks?" the scientist inquired, quietly. "That is what strikes me as sub-normal. There are bolts on the inside of the door which would have made certain the privacy you think he desired. *Why turn all three locks?* Perhaps you would be good enough to ascertain whether there are any keys in the pockets of the body, and Merry and I will look round the room on the same errand."

Five minutes of thorough searching, however, failed to reveal any keys, either on the dead man or in the two or three drawers fitted to the bench. The inspector stared at the scientist. A wary alertness had crept into his mien. "But that must mean, Doctor, that the room was locked from the outside," he said.

"Which is precisely what I was trying to convey to you, Inspector," was the reply.

"And when he dropped the bottle of chloroform he was unable to get the door open, and was rendered unconscious by inhaling the fumes before he could reach the window?"

"It might be that he was killed by the inhalation of the fumes, Inspector. But I should like to know where you think he was carrying the bottle when he dropped it. The bottle was obviously along with the other bottles and jars at the end of the bench. There is a table opposite the bench on the other side of the room, as you see, but there is nothing at all between the bench and table and the door near where the bottle was dropped. Nor is there anything at the end of the room to which the bottle could be taken and rested upon. As to the theory that he was overcome by the fumes before he could reach the window—do you know anything of the effects of the inhaling of chloroform vapour, Inspector?"

"No, I have no first-hand knowledge, Doctor."

"Well, I can tell you something about it. How long would it take you to step from the spot in this room where the remains of the smashed bottle are lying and across to the window?"

"I should say about three seconds."

"I should have given the same measure of time myself. Now, chloroform vapour, when exposed in a concentrated form, is speedily fatal to life. By that I mean when taken through a mask. If it is diluted with a certain amount of air—as it would be when dropped in this room—it produces insensibility with entire loss of muscular power in from two to ten minutes. Suppose we take the minimum period of two minutes. What was there to prevent this man, when he had dropped the bottle, taking a three-second journey to the window and sticking his head out in the open air?"

"I don't know, Doctor. I see no reason why he did not. Only, he didn't."

"I can conceive of a very good reason why he was prevented from carrying out that course of action—and that is that he was unconscious before the bottle was dropped."

"Unconscious before he dropped it, Doctor?" The inspector looked up in puzzlement.

"I said unconscious *before* it was dropped, Inspector—which is not quite the same thing. My reading of the signs I have observed in this room suggests to me that the man now dead was rendered unconscious at the spot where we found him, and that the companion who was with him at the time, for some reason which we have yet to discover, left him there, took up the bottle of chloroform, walked with it to the door, opened the door, and from the safety of outside, dashed it to the floor, saw it smash, and then closed and locked the door and made his way out of the building, having previously arranged some contraption to set the room on fire at some time posterior to his departure."

"Arranged the fire, Doctor?"

"Certainly. The seat of the blaze is over there in the corner of the room, and near that part of the bench on which are bottles of ether and chloroform." The scientist crossed the room and, bending down, picked up a piece of some material about half an inch in length and an inch in width. "This, inspector, is a piece of celluloid film, and it is, as you see, burned. I have no doubt that the fire was started deliberately, by allowing some light to come into contact with the film—probably the old trick of a small length of candle. Except for the short space of time which elapsed between the fire starting and the brigade being summoned, and their subsequent quick extinguishing of the fire, I am quite certain that the flames would have spread to this wooden bench, and would quickly have reached and burst these bottles. The result would have been a conflagration in which the building would have been destroyed—and so would the body of this man."

The inspector stared, aghast. "Good God, Doctor!" he ejaculated. "But what is the reason?"

"That we have yet to ascertain. But possibly some of the contents of this room may assist us in that. I am more than a little interested in the set-out of this bench." He walked across and stood looking down at it. Standing waist-high, the bench had a surface of enamel-ware. In the centre had been sunk a porcelain sink, with two taps fixed above it. Racks at the back contained a number of chemist's jars and test tubes. But it was the impedimenta on the bench to which Dr. Manson particularly directed his attention. On the left side of the sink stood a Bunsen burner with, over it on a stand, a large beaker. A little coloured liquid remained in the bottom of the beaker. From the beaker's corked neck, two glass tubes emerged. One ran through a water-jacket, the entrance tube to which was connected with a tap over the sink, and the second to the runaway in the sink. The second of the glass tubes merging from the beaker neck was connected to a smaller flask. A tap in the glass tube, between the two beakers, connected them up.

"Very interesting, indeed," commented the scientist. He called to the Deputy Scientist of the Yard. "Would there be among those jars and bottles in the corner of the bench one containing acetic anhydride, Merry?" he asked.

The sergeant passed his gaze over the collection of chemicals. "There is, Doctor," he announced. He eyed the filters, and a second Bunsen on the right of the sink, and added: "There are also bottles of ammonia and two Winchester jars of chloroform and ether."

The scientist eyed his colleague, and smiled. "There would have to be if we are thinking correctly, Merry," he remarked.

The inspector had listened to this conversation with growing concern. He now sought enlightenment. "Chemistry is a closed book to me, Doctor," he announced. "I'm only a police officer. I gather there is something which interests you scientific gentlemen in these things; but what I should like to know is whether they have any bearing on my job, which is to find out how this fellow came to be here dead?"

"Inspector"—the scientist's voice struck a hard and a grim note—"these things will be found, I think, to have a very marked bearing on your job. Let me demonstrate to you exactly for what these things have been used." He moved to the left side of the sink, and motioned the inspector to stand beside him. "Now, Inspector, there is only one purpose I can visualize for which such a set-up as this is required, and only one, mark you."

"And what would that be, sir?"

"The obtaining of heroin from morphine, Inspector." He tapped the beaker, still on the Bunsen burner. "I put into this beaker a quantity of morphine, and sufficient anhydrous alcohol to dissolve the morphine, and then bring it to the boil by means of the gas jet. You follow me? . . . Now I pour acetic anhydride into this small beaker, or flask"—he indicated the smaller of the beakers with the tap between it and the larger one—"and I let a few drops at a time through the tap until I have the correct quantity. I need not worry you with the chemical details. Now I pass the contents of the beaker through cold water. Heroin, Inspector, is not soluble in water. All the other contents of the beaker are. So the heroin is precipitated, or left in the bottom, and is separated from the water by filtration."

"Well, I'm blest! And you find all this out just by looking at these glass things?" The Inspector beamed his admiration.

Dr. Manson smiled. "There is not, I fear, much credit in that, Inspector," he said. "Any analytical chemist would have spotted it. But perhaps he would not have reached the same opinion as myself as regards these other contraptions. They are, as you see, filtration requirements. There is a beaker here over a Bunsen obviously used for heating, and I notice that there is no hot water, or method of heating liquid except by this Bunsen burner. The necessity for the array was not apparent to me at first. But I think that Sergeant Merry realized it when, in reply to my question whether there was acetic anhydride on the bench, he said that there was also chloroform and ammonia. You see, Inspector, whereas chloroform is not required to extract heroin from morphine and narcotine, and is, therefore, not necessary in this room for that purpose, there is one allied reaction for which both those things are demanded, and in order to carry out that reaction warm water is required also—hence this second beaker."

"And what is that, Doctor?"

"The extraction of morphine from pure opium, Inspector. You extract juice from the dried opium by means of warm water. You filter the juice and add an equal amount of alcohol to the clear liquid. When you then pour on ammonia, the morphine and narcotine present are precipitated in solid form. You have to separate them by filtration, dry them, and then wash them in the very necessary chloroform. The chloroform dissolves the narcotine and leaves the morphine on the filter.

"Thus, Inspector, this room has been producing heroin for addicts in this country, and has been producing it from poppy opium. You know the only reason for which illicit heroin is circulated. I have no doubt whatever that the opium which has been smuggled by seamen to this port has been brought to this room, and here has been changed into morphine and heroin, and found its way to the dope peddlers in the West End of London. We have just left Superintendent Lawrence, who is engaged on an investigation into the illicit drug importations. I think you would do well to acquaint him with what has been happening here, and you might say, I think, that I have been here with you. Which reminds me, I assume you do not know this dead man?"

The inspector shook his head.

"You will, of course, have to get him identified. And we want to know something about the proprietor of this firm. I think we can take it for granted that he, or they, will not be returning.

Your fingerprint people may possibly get something on which you can work.

"One more thing: there will have to be a post-mortem on this man. If you will be so good as to telephone me at the Yard when you know the surgeon, I would like to have a talk with him. I suggest to the superintendent that if he can procure a pathologist it might be an advantage over the ordinary man."

Thus fortified with the inspector's assurance, Dr. Manson and Merry left the scene, and continued their broken journey back to Scotland Yard. The scientist exhibited a certain despondency as he reviewed their morning's adventures. "I don't think, Jim, that we can leave this business to the people down here," he opined. "I feel that we should let the assistant commissioner know, and that Superintendent Jones and Inspector Kenway really should take over—yes, I'll suggest that. It is more than a Wapping investigation."

Sir Edward Allen's views coincided with those of the scientist investigator. "I'll get in touch with Wapping, Doctor," he confided, "and Superintendent Jones must take over."

The fat superintendent came to the room in answer to a message. He sat solidly in his chair and listened to Dr. Manson's story. After a moment or two's thought, he heaved himself forward, to the accompaniment of sundry grunts. "Think . . . it's . . . good . . . break, Doctor . . . eh?"

"Not the death of this man, or the discovery of the outfit, Jones," was the reply. "That is dead, and could easily be handled by Wapping. The big break is in the fact that we know, now, the source, or one of the chief sources, of the supply of heroin getting into the hands of addicts. It is not being imported. It is extracted here. It is a home product. The direction in which we should exercise our activities is in finding where the stuff is being extracted now that the Tench Street laboratory can no longer be used."

"You mean that the dead man is not the chemist?" asked the assistant commissioner.

"Not on your life he isn't, Sir Edward," was the reply. "His hands were not those of a chemist. I think it elementary deduction that something occurred in that room today which made it necessary to dispose of the man, and very quickly. It had to be done there, since the time was broad daylight. The operator is not going out of the game just because he had to discard Tench Street. It is far too lucrative a business for that. Have you any idea, Sir Edward, what is the percentage of profit on the illicit sale of drugs?"

"I have no actual knowledge, no, Doctor—except that it is exceptionally high."

"It is colossal. I can give you rough figures. Firstly, you must know that the stuff supplied to addicts is not by any means pure heroin. It is always adulterated with either chalk or sodium bicarbonate, the price of which need not be considered. Occasionally salicin is used, but even this is cheap enough for the cost to be ignored. Now, a sample weighing 5 cgm. and containing 20 per cent of heroin is sold for about 1s. 6d. The price of a kilogramme of this powder is, therefore, £2,500, and the price of the pure heroin contained in it is £12,250 per kilogramme. The price of heroin, about 80 per cent pure, at the factory has varied from about £40 to a little more than £100 during the past ten years. And these people, in addition, are extracting their own heroin from opium, and the cheaper opium at that. Oh no, Sir Edward, I am quite sure that the Tench Street chemistry firm is not the end of the manufacture, but merely an unfortunate pause in it, so far as they are concerned. I think you must get the local police to inform you of all chemistry and chemical firms outside those well known in the trade; and I suggest that a visit be paid to them unexpectedly. Sergeant Merry ought to be one of the visitors; he knows for what to look."

"And what remains at Wapping, Doctor?" asked the assistant commissioner.

"The local people are trying to identify the man. They stand more chance of that among the people round there than do the Yard. They will send you his prints. They are also inquiring into the head, or reputed head, of the firm. Someone must have seen him. And the local surgeon will communicate the results of the post-mortem to me."

"That seems all we can do at the moment. Dr. Jones and Kenway will take over at this end. And call upon Sergeant Merry when you want any assistance, Jones," he added, turning to the superintendent.

Dr. Manson returned to his laboratory to find Sergeant Merry looking thoughtfully at a slip of paper on the desk. He looked up at the entry of the scientist. He passed the paper over with a grunt. "This is a nice how-de-do, Doctor," he said.

The scientist stared at the words on the radioed message:

Manson Scotland Yard Stop Inquiries Leland Stop Last five years career charge dope running Melbourne Stop Initials Ess Eff presumed here to be Snowy Freud head dope gang Stop Vanished four years ago Stop Fellowes High Commissioner's Office knows all story Stop Jervis CID Melbourne End message.

Dr. Manson digested the message. Then, turning on his heel, and still holding the paper, he retraced his steps to the room of the assistant commissioner. Without speaking, he put the message in front of Sir Edward.

The C.I.D. chief read it. He looked up at his friend and colleague, and there was comprehension in the eyes of him. "We are in something big, Harry, by the look of it," he said. "And you were right again, as usual. Do you know anything of Freud?"

"A little, Edward. But only what I have read and heard. He organized dope in the Chinese quarter of Melbourne and Sydney, if I remember rightly. There were two gang-men in Melbourne at the time, the other being a man named Morgan. I will walk round to Fellowes, and see what he knows."

CHAPTER TWELVE
MR. BOSANQUET

MR. ALFRED BOSANQUET was a man of fifty-six years of age. His birth certificate said so. He showed it to Inspector Carruthers when that officer of the law called upon him to chat over the difficulties which, he explained, he was experiencing in the death of the visitor to the cricket match of which Mr. Bosanquet was so honoured a supporter; and did Mr. Bosanquet think he could assist any further by recalling whether he had noticed anything at all suspicious during the time that he had been watching the match, with his friends, from his front lawn.

No. Mr. Bosanquet did not think he could help any further at all. He had already told the police and the coroner all he could tell. The entire business was very annoying to him. He wished, now, that he had never gone over to old Crombie at all. He realized that it had placed him in an unfortunate position, since he was alone with the dead man for some minutes. It was all the fault of his confounded fowls. Had they not broken out of their pen he would never have wanted Crombie, and accordingly would not have gone to look for him. He had a damned good mind to get rid of the confounded fowls.

Inspector Carruthers agreed that fowls were a nuisance. He himself kept a few Rhode Island Reds, and when he came to count up, first the initial cost and then the cost of the food, the eggs obtained were, he thought, pretty high priced, and could be bought more cheaply at the village stores. Apart from which, fowls were a tie on his wife and himself, who could not go away for a weekend lest the birds should starve to death. But that was by-the-by. He had, as a detective officer, to investigate the death of the man who had perished on the green, and that meant, as Mr. Bosanquet would realize, being a man of importance, and a man of the world, investigating everybody who had been near the man at any time, or who might have seen him. Such a man included, of course, Mr. Bosanquet. They all, in Thames Pagnall, of course, knew Mr. Bosanquet since he had come to the village—how long ago would that be?

"Four years," replied Mr. Bosanquet.

"And before that?" asked the inspector, apologetically.

"London—a flat in Maida Vale; and before that Wadham College, Oxford University."

"You were born abroad, were you not?" hazarded the inspector.

"British, Inspector," was the heated reply. It was then that he produced the birth certificate. Carruthers perused the document. It announced that Alfred Bosanquet had been born at Chelmsford on April 10, 1882, the son of Frederick William Bosanquet, gentleman of that parish, and of Mary Elizabeth, his wife, *née* Parson. The inspector handed it back.

"School?" he asked.

"Prep. school and Charterhouse," replied Bosanquet. "And then Oxford, and since then in business. I am a self-made man, Inspector," he announced. "I started as a small importer of merchandise, made myself markets, and I have made a pile. I'm still making it, though sometimes it's a worry fighting our import quotas."

"I've been told so by gentlemen in the City," agreed the inspector. "Don't know anything about it myself. I never had the brains to go into business," he added, in a libellous insinuation against the force. "Now, what is worrying us, Mr. Bosanquet, is how the man came to be where he was found. We have discovered that he was there because he had seen someone in Thames Pagnall whom he thought he knew, and had apparently come down to see him again. You were sitting behind him all the time, and we were hoping that you could remember whether anyone approached him. The chief constable says you were watching the match, and must have been doing so through the back of him, so to speak." The inspector stopped and waited for the answer.

"I did not see anyone go near him, Inspector. I did not even notice him."

"There you are, sir," said the inspector with a nicety of surprise. "That's what the chief constable said. He said: 'Carruthers, Mr. Bosanquet will think that he did not see anyone. He'll probably think that he did not even see the man himself. Yet he must have seen him, unconsciously. He *must* have seen him right in front of the pitch. And he may have seen the man who went near him in exactly the same way. You must try to get into his subconscious mind.' That is what the colonel said, Mr. Bosanquet," the inspector concluded.

Mr. Bosanquet looked as though he wished it was the inspector who was subconscious, not his own mind. But he made the effort.

"Did you, for instance, see Crombie go near the man?" the inspector asked.

"No, not consciously, or unconsciously," was the reply. "I should think that Crombie would be more likely to approach the 'Green Man' than the deck-chair, if I know him."

"Perhaps one of the fieldsmen stood near him at some time, and spoke to him. He was watching the match, sir. Would you remember seeing something like that?"

"Preposterous, Inspector! Why the devil should fieldsmen be posted near where he was sitting? A skipper would be crazy to put a man there—and on the boundary, too."

The inspector tried again. "Well, perhaps a man obstructed your view by walking past you on the green. He would, of course, pass the deck-chair."

"No. It's no go. I'd have noticed anybody, consciously, in that case, Inspector. The two of them would certainly have obstructed my view, and I should have called out to them."

"And you didn't shoot the man?" the inspector inquired, humourously.

"Me? In front of my guests? Ha! Ha! Likely, isn't it?"

"Just my joke, Mr. Bosanquet," apologized the inspector. "That reminds me, sir. Were your guests with you all the time? I mean one wasn't missing for any period, I suppose?"

"Nary a one. We sat there from start to finish of the match except for lunch, and we were all together at that meal. We did not even leave the lawn for tea. Mrs. Bosanquet and Miss Malcolm brought that out to us in our chairs."

"When you went across to the man we know that he was dead. The doctor agrees that he must have died somewhere between four-thirty and five-thirty o'clock. Crombie was there before you. Was Crombie in any way peculiar when you approached him? I mean to say, supposing he had killed the man, or knew something about it, was there anything about him that seemed to you suspicious?"

"No, Inspector. He was a bit annoyed because the man was holding him up from getting the chairs away; and the sooner he got 'em away the sooner he could get down to the 'Green Man', you understand. As for Crombie killing him, I don't reckon that old George knows the first thing about guns. No, I still think that Leland was shot from the road by accident."

The inspector, during the conversation, had put down the purport of the interview, with, here and there, verbatim notes of the more important pieces of the replies. He now read over the essential features, and Mr. Bosanquet signed the book. The inspector rose. "Well, I think that's all there is to it, Mr. Bosanquet," he said. "Many thanks for trying to help."

"That's all right, Inspector. It's a duty, you know. I'll show you out."

The inspector's next call was on Mr. Donald Watkins. Mr Watkins was an artist—and a very good artist. He was also a cricketer; and a very bad cricketer. Which was the reason why, despite all his assistance, financially and artistically, to the Thames Pagnall cricket club, he was never permitted to turn out in flannels for them. Once, when a 'butter-fingers' seemed to be only a small debit in a substantial credit account, they had given him a place in the team as a gesture, a reply to a very handsome donation of a large caricature of the members of the first eleven for the club-house. He managed to get two men run out, and, at a vital stage in the game knocked over a fieldsman who was as safe a catch as any team could hope for, just when the ball was entering his hands. Thames Pagnall lost the match. Mr. Watkins' assistance was limited, now, to watching each match and offering advice to the committee about the players who should be dropped.

But Mr. Watkins, keenly as he had watched this particular match, was unable to help the inspector. "I can't really say that I saw anybody go up to the man, Carruthers," he said. "I did notice him there, because, now I come to think of it, I saw him lean forward when the men entered the field." He paused, wrinkled his forehead, and then looked up. "Well, now, damme, thinking it over, I seem to recollect that there *was* someone with him, or just passing him—I don't know which. He was, of course, some distance away, about a hundred yards, as you know, but . . . yes, I remember he did lean forward in his chair and look towards the tent as they came out. Mind you, there's nothing in that. I do the same thing myself. Generally want to see if there are any new faces in the team."

"You didn't recognize who the person was you think you saw with him?"

"Lord, no! I wasn't looking at him, you know. Only just noticed that there was somebody else. And I hadn't got my glasses on. Perhaps Miss Malcolm saw him. She was looking for her nephew, who was supposed to be playing."

"You were, of course, at Mr. Bosanquet's at the time, Mr. Watkins?"

"Right. We were all there, as usual. It's a better position than my own bit of front, and, of course, better company than watching by myself."

"And you were all there from the start?"

"Sure."

"And all the time? So that you would have noticed anything unusual?"

"Except for the spot of lunch during the interval, yes, we were there all the time. Except Mrs. Bosanquet and Miss Malcolm. They went in to get the tea ready at a quarter to five."

"Nobody even went on the green to see how the score was going? I notice that the scoreboard faces the tent. You see, I'm trying to exclude anyone who might have gone on the green."

The artist chuckled. "No reason for us to go across the green to look at the score, Inspector. Whenever there is a change, the board is always first turned towards old Bossy. He's the club's chief financial prop, you understand."

"How do you think the man was shot, Mr. Watkins?"

"Well, so far as I can see, it must have been done from the road, Inspector. I reckon you're making too much fuss in thinking the fellow was deliberately killed. I reckon it was an accident shot, and the chap with the gun is too scared to come forward and say so."

"You think that the explosions you heard were shots, and not backfires, eh?"

"Wouldn't like to say, but they might well have been. Not expecting to hear shots fired at a match, not even between Thames Pagnall and Maplecot." He chuckled. "I reckon one would take sounds like that to have been backfires. We get plenty of backfires along that road, you know."

Mr. Catling could give no more help than Mr. Watkins. In fact, he could give less. Told of the artist's fleeting impression of having seen someone near the dead man, he expressed himself as doubtful of that vision. "We were all there, Inspector," he said, "and looking for the team to come out. I don't remember seeing anyone near the chair. I do faintly remember seeing the bloke himself, as planking his carcase in our line of view, and wondered that Crombie let him sit there. I reckon old Watkins has been imagining things. He had to go for his spectacles, I remember. I doubt if he would have seen anyone plainly. He's a bit short-sighted and wouldn't get what he would call perspective."

"He went away, you say?"

Mr. Catling laughed. "Oh, don't try to hang poor old Watkins," he joked. "That was before lunch and just about the start of the match. And he wasn't gone more than a couple of minutes. He's only three doors down from 'Green Shutters', you know."

"He seems to think that Miss Malcolm may have seen the other person, Mr. Catling. She was, he says, by his side and was looking in the same direction. I suppose she hasn't said anything to you about it?"

"No, Inspector; and I think she would have done had she seen anyone. We have, naturally, talked the death over, since it must have taken place in front of our eyes."

"I'll have a word with her about it, Mr. Catling."

"You'll have to wait a few hours, I'm afraid, Inspector. She's in town at the moment. We have a bit of a party at the 'Olive Grove' to-night. Making a night of it, you know. Birthday celebration. Anyway, I'll ask her, and give you a ring in the morning."

"Thanks very much. I suppose you haven't thought any more about those explosions? Do you think they were shots, or backfires?"

"Don't know what to think, Inspector. They may have been shots, of course. When you aren't listening for anything you don't take particular notice, you know. I suppose that the natural inclination on hearing noises like that from the direction of the roadway, is to put them down as backfires. That's as far as I can say."

With this inconclusive result of his inquiries, the inspector returned to the police-station. He sat down at his desk and prepared to write out his official report for the chief constable. Inspector Carruthers was a worried man. A doubt was taking root in his mind: a doubt as to whether Leland had been murdered at all; a doubt as to the omnipotence of Chief Detective Inspector Dr. Manson, of Scotland Yard. The doctor had, notoriously, a suspicious mind. The inspector began to wonder whether it was not *too* suspicious a mind. He sat twiddling his fountain-pen between his fingers, as he cogitated whether he should express this opinion to Colonel Mainforce in his report.

As though by the process of telepathy, Sergeant Wharton entered. "Oh, Inspector, Dr. Manson sent a man down for the photographs taken of the body on the green. He said that he had arranged with you to have them. I gave them to the messenger. I hope I did right?"

"Quite right, Sergeant, thanks. . . . Wonder what he wants with those," he said to himself as the door closed behind Wharton.

"He's seen the green and reconstructed the crime with Lambert. S'funny."

He turned again to his report. *I incline to the opinion that the man Leland was not deliberately shot*, he wrote. *I have carefully examined all the people suggested. . . .*

* * * * *

Dr. Manson received the photographic prints in his laboratory. With the aid of the deputy scientist he laid them out, side by side, on the large table that occupied the centre of the room.

The cine ten-millimetre films had each been enlarged up to a picture measuring ten inches by eight inches, and since all the shots from the four positions had been printed, they numbered forty-eight pictures. "And very well taken they are, Jim," the scientist acknowledged to Sergeant Merry. "Perfect exposures and sharp in every detail. We could not have done better ourselves. Now it is our task to see whether they can tell us anything more than we already know. Suppose we begin with the front view?"

Sergeant Merry brought forward the twelve snaps which Mr. Bosanquet's camera had taken from exactly face to face with the dead man, and the pair stared at them intently. They showed Leland lying easily in his chair, the body at an angle of some forty-five degrees. The face was, of course, covered by the tilted hat. The hands, which in the case of a person resting in that position would normally be crossed over the stomach, were lying alongside the thighs. Apart from that there seemed nothing in the photographs to distinguish them from snapshots of a man sleeping quietly in the sun. Dr. Manson laid them aside for the time being.

The prints taken from the left-hand side of the dead man were next considered. There appeared to be two sets of "shots"; the first obliquely from an angle of about seventy degrees from the central front of the chair, and the latter square to the side of the chair. They, again, had been given perfect focus and exposure. This, together with the fact that bright sunlight had been pouring down on the subject at the time the pictures were taken, had resulted in well-defined lines—and shadows.

It was the shadow along the body of the man that appeared chiefly to attract the attention of Dr. Manson. This appeared as a thin line of black, marking, of course, the projection of the top of the body from the background of the chair—in other words, the thickness of the man's body. The scientist measured the width of the thickness with a micrometer gauge. It scaled a fraction over a millimetre.

"Now this, Merry, may give us something," the scientist suggested. "Where is the corresponding picture taken from the opposite side—the right side?"

Sergeant Merry sought it out and produced it. A similar black shadow ran along the figure equally with the former. Using again the micrometer scale, the scientist, after a careful re-check, gave the thickness as one and a quarter millimetres.

"So that, Doctor, we get the strange result that on the side on which the sun would be shining, and therefore casting less shadow, the shadow is, nevertheless, thicker than on the shaded side, where one would expect to find it thicker," said Merry.

Dr. Manson looked sharply up. "On the side on which the sun is shining, Jim?" he asked,

"Of course, Doctor. According to the position of the road in the picture background, the body was lying obliquely to it, and the road runs south-west to the coast. Therefore, the body is lying almost west to east. Now, at six-thirty o'clock, when we know the pictures were taken, the sun would be due west. Therefore the shadow on the right side of the body should be less than on the left side of the body. We have just the opposite."

The scientist consulted the pictures again. He walked across to the map drawers and produced an ordnance map of Surrey. His next task was to check the geographical run of the road where it passed through Thames Pagnall. "I think, Jim, you are as near right as makes no matter," he said. "Now, where does that lead us?"

"To a certainty that the man was not lying squarely on his back, but was definitely leaning to one side—the right side."

"We must, I think, Merry, concede that. And it gives us a somewhat interesting calculation, Jim, does it not?"

"Such as?"

"Well, take the possible angle of the sun's rays at six-thirty o'clock, at which they would strike the body. That should give us a rough estimate of the thickness of the shadow which should appear on the left side of a man of his build—he was about your size, Jim. It should be, roughly, twice the thickness of the shadow on the sunny side. Having calculated that, we can, I think, calculate at what angle out of the straight the body must have been in order to give us a shadow on the sunny side nearly a millimetre thicker than on the shadow side."

The two men settled down to an independent working of the calculation. Some minutes passed before each looked expectantly at the other. The results, checked, showed only an infinitesimal difference.

Dr. Manson's face, usually in repose, was now alert. His eyes, deep sunk in the broad forehead, seemed to have come forward in their sockets. The wrinkles had gone from the brow, and the crinkles from the eyes of him. Merry saw and knew the signs, as would, also, the scientist's colleagues at the Yard, had they been present; the doctor was seeing an idea working out. He took from his pocket his notebook. He opened it at a page on which he had entered the calculations made at the cricket green experiment with Constable Lambert in the deck-chair. A porcelain tile resting on the top edges kept the book open at the pages.

"Now, before we go any further, Jim," he suggested, we must make certain that the two photographs we are taking are exact as to scaling of the chair and the man." With a gauge he obtained the distance from the head of the chair in one picture to the lower extremity of the model's feet. This was checked against the same objectives in the second picture. There was a difference of no more than three millimetres in the depth and two in the width, ensuring a somewhat complicated readjustment of the earlier calculations. Satisfied, at last, that the figures represented the narrowest margin of error, the two scientists entered upon the next progression.

"Now, Jim, assuming that we have here the correct position of the figure of Leland in the chair, what effect would it have on the angles which we obtained by our experiment at Thames Pagnall, and which are entered in my note-book, and, I expect, in your dossier? We had better, I think, arrive at individual conclusions to avoid any semblance of error."

In a silence that was pregnant with expectation, the two men worked with pencil and paper. Two minutes . . . three . . . four . . . five passed. Sergeant Merry laid down his pencil and waited. The scientist, after a final check of his figures, looked up. "Well?" he asked.

"I make it thirty-five feet ten inches, Harry," replied Merry.

"I work it at thirty-six feet one inch," countered Manson. "We must, of course, allow a margin each way, since our earlier calculations are, of necessity, arbitrary. Suppose we say that the difference is not less than thirty-three feet and not more than forty feet. It should be somewhere within those figures."

"Agreed," Merry nodded affirmatively.

The two men, scholars both, mathematicians, and hunters of men, looked at each other—a long look; and in it was the perfect understanding that had made them the successful trackers of those men upon whom the hands of the Law waited to fall.

* * * * *

Detective-Inspector Kenway strode down the Embankment to Blackfriars Bridge. He turned off at Tudor Street, and turned again at Temple Avenue. Half-way down the latter thoroughfare is a block of buildings; on the ground floor, left-hand side, was a doorway which bore the intimation, "Bosanquet and Co. Importers". In the office of the porter, or rather commissionaire, Inspector Kenway found Edward Marshall. Which, said Kenway to himself, was a bit of luck. For Marshall was an ex-detective sergeant of the Yard, retired, who, like so many of his colleagues, and like so many old soldiers, had joined the Corps of Commissionaires, that body of men, all of unimpeachable character, who take charge of offices, banks and other business premises where honesty, smartness and intelligence are necessary.

Marshall had been a sergeant when Kenway had joined the Force as a constable. He was prepared to tell the inspector anything he knew which could be helpful, and there was still sufficient of the policeman in him not to ask any questions, Mr. Bosanquet, he said, was not a particularly inviting man to know. He was brusque, sarcastic in his comments, and not at all generous when services were rendered by the porters or the commissionaire himself.

The premises of the firm, said Marshall, consisted of the ante-room in which were a manager and a typist, and two inner rooms, one of which was the private office of Mr. Bosanquet, and the other a mixture of file room, store-room and home for samples of the goods which the firm imported.

The Inspector inquired about the importing.

"Oh yes, Inspector, he's got quite a good business, I should think. There is a fair mail each day."

"What does he import, Marshall?"

"Well, that's rather a problem, Inspector," the commissionaire answered. "I should say nearly everything. He has an agency for briar pipes—thousands have come in—then he's in with seeds and nuts for oil from South America. He gets glass from Vienna, and electrical stuff from Germany. Then, there's chemicals, too. At the moment we have a good line in Japanese toys, or rather toys from Japan," Marshall said with a smile; "and also some clockwork toys from Germany."

"He doesn't have them all sent here, surely?"

"Oh, lord, no! He has a warehouse in the Docks—the King George Dock."

"Does he ever go abroad?"

"Not that I know of. If he does it must only be over the Channel, for he's never away more than a day or two."

"Any women in his life?"

"Only one of the typists, I think. But nobody ever turns up here."

"Any foreign visitors?"

"I don't recall any, except one or two persons from foreign firms with London offices."

"How long has he been here?"

"Now, lemme see." The commissionaire waxed reminiscent. "It's just about four and a half years," he said after a few moments' thought. "That's when they started."

Inspector Kenway walked thoughtfully away. "Seems all square and above board," he said to himself. "Genuine business and so on. Suppose I'd better have a look at the warehouse. The doctor will be sure to ask if I've seen it." He set off for Dockland.

The warehouse of Bosanquet and Co. was easily found. It occupied a place at the dockside and consisted of a large, barn-like premises with double gates and a wicket-gate. The latter led into a wooden partitioned compartment of the warehouse serving as offices. Porters were, at the moment of the inspector's visit, wheeling numerous large packing-cases into the warehouse. The inspector stole a glance inside. Cases and bags, apparently toys, half-filled the premises.

It is not generally known that the Port of London Authority has its own police force, numbering about eight hundred men. They have power over seven thousand acres of docks and forty-five lineal miles of quays. Inspector Kenway sought the help of the senior officer of the Dockland police.

"Bosanquet and Co.'?" that official echoed. "Oh yes, quite a good firm. Only a small concern, you know. But there is no complaint against them. They import from the East and the Middle East, mostly. Bosanquet himself? Doesn't often come down here. When he does it's in a Rolls-Royce. He drives himself. Seems pretty affable, and generous to the men in the warehouse."

* * * * *

Detective-Sergeant Willoughby walked languidly along Pall Mall, turned into the doorway of the Oxford and Cambridge University Club, and gravitated to the library. There, he took a volume down from a shelf, and ran a finger down the columns of several pages. Reaching one line, he read it through once or twice, finally copying the entry into his note-book. He replaced the book, but selected in its place a volume of the London telephone directory, A to K. From this he copied out a telephone number.

The number he dialled out in a telephone-box in the hall. A high-pitched voice demanded the reason.

"That you, Stinky? . . . Pongo here. . . . What? . . . No, I haven't arrested anybody today. But I might have had you last night for playing poker in the 'Rubicon'. Poker is a game of chance, and illegal. Tell the 'Rubicon' to stick to bridge. Now listen, Stinky. You were up at Wadham in '04, weren't you?"

"You know damn' well I was, Pongo. . . ."

"Did you know a chap named Bosanquet?"

"Bosanquet? . . . Did I know a cove named Bosanquet? . . . Like hell I did. Why, the blister nearly got me sent down . . . and you dashed well ask me if I knew him. What d'ye want *him* for? If you're pinching him I'll come and lend you a hand."

"I'm not pinching him, Stinky. The way your mind runs to arresting people will land you in clink yourself one of these days, for slander."

"Then what *do* you want him for?"

"I don't want him at all. He's merely cropped up in one of my inquiries, and I thought I'd like to know all about him."

"Oh, that's easy. He came up from Charterhouse. Pater was something big down Chelmsford way. How I knew him was through his mother, who was a friend of my blinkin' rich aunt. Name of Parson."

"What church?"

"Church? What the devil are you burbling about? I said Parson."

"I know. I said what church was he at?"

"Heaven give me bloomin' patience! I didn't say he was a parson, Pongo. I said she was a Parson."

"What! A woman parson?"

"You burbling badcock! Heaven give me strength. . . . I never said she was a parson. What I said was that she was *a* Parson."

"That's what I said. Where was she a parson?"

"In her own house, you dimwit."

"What? A parson in her own house! Do you mean they had a private chapel?"

A bellowing roar came through the earpiece. Willoughby jumped a foot into the air, and held the receiver at arm's length. A voice came through as though from a mighty distance. "Listen, you half mental blatherskite. I said his mother was a friend of my rich aunt, and her maiden name was Parson. *Now* do you understand?"

"Then why the devil didn't you say so at first? Babbling about a church and a chapel!"

"Damn it!" The roar came again. "I never said a ruddy word about a church."

"Well, forget it. Do you know what became of him?"

"He went down in . . . lemme see . . . yes ... it would be '06. Back to the ancestral fold, I gather. I saw him about a year later in London, and he looked pretty prosperous. Never seen or heard of him since. I thought he'd died."

"Well, he hasn't. He's a City merchant."

"Merchant? What's happened to the family spondulicks, then?"

"No idea. Only know he's a merchant."

"Dem it. I'd never have believed it if it wasn't you tellin' me. Anything else you want to know, Pongo?"

"No thanks, Stinky. Much obliged."

"Pleased, old chappie. If you're seeing the Big Cop, give him my regards, and tell him I'll shin up his personal lamp-post next Boat Race night."

* * * * *

At 11.55 p.m., the 'Olive Grove' night-club, situated in the heart of the West End of London, was at the acme of its synonym for riotous enjoyment! The revels were in full swing. Perhaps you have not had the felicity of being admitted to membership of a London nightclub. If not, you are fortunate. Your stomach is the gainer, and your purse is immeasurably the greater gainer. But, in order that you may be able to visualize the hilarious scene in the 'Olive Grove' at this five minutes to the witching hour, we will attempt to present a picture of it as seen through the eyes of Inspector Carruthers, when he stepped through the doorway.

Firstly, then, the 'Olive Grove' was no more than a couple of cellars running underneath two shops from which baby linen and other adornments could be purchased during the daytime. Had the cellars been fitted out with tables and waitresses, and opened up as tea-rooms, the company of women now assembled in the 'Olive Grove' would have flounced their way back into the street disdainfully, saying, "How perfectly *putrid*, dear. A *cellar*. Yes, really, a shop cellar."

But, with the brick walls hung with draftings, rudely daubed with what the artist fondly assumed in his futuristic mind to be an olive grove, and the tea turned into champagne, at four times the wine merchant's price, the fair sex pursued every conceivable course, short of selling themselves—and quite a number did even that—to become accredited with a membership card.

The cellars of the 'Olive Grove' were low. In addition to the draping on the walls, the iron stanchions here and there, and which supported the roof, were hidden behind three-ply wood olive trees, and round each, and between this south of France bogus grove, were the tables. The centre space of the floor was clear—for about a dozen yards square. It was also laid with pine wood. It was, in fact, the dance floor; perhaps the walking-round floor would be a more apt description. A band blared forth dance—sorry, swing—music, on the understanding, apparently, that the more blare it made, and the less melody, the better band it was, with a considerable higher rate of payment than a less noisy and more musically inclined orchestra.

Amid these surroundings a concourse of people with nothing better to do than sit in dim lights from 11 p.m. to 4 a.m., roaring loudly at infantile jokes for want of something better at which to laugh, guzzle champagne at several pounds a bottle, and make whoopee, because it is the etiquette in the silly circles in which they revolve to visit the 'Olive Grove' and make whoopee. Of all the resorts of boredom in Europe—and we have seen most of them—a London night-club is the most boring.

Once a night—at twelve-fifteen o'clock—the 'Olive Grove' cabaret made its appearance on the floor. Half a dozen half-sozzled girls, all dead tired from dancing all the evening on the stage of a theatre, and as much naked as they were sozzled, kicked their legs a few times in the air. Nobody noticed them unduly, and, dispirited and tired, they at last vanished. A singer or two, a raconteur, the chorus again in a finale—and then the customers settled back to their task of drinking the hours away.

This, then, was the scene when Inspector Carruthers, resplendent in an evening suit which carried a slight aroma of mothballs, stepped through the doorway. He stood for a moment peering into the half-gloom of the smoke-filled interior, and then, skirting the dance floor, sat at a table beneath one of the three-ply olive trees.

The manager, fetched by the doorman, had been chary of letting him in. "You are not, sir, a member, and you must know, as a police officer, that we cannot allow you in."

"I am not wishful of becoming a member. I do not want any of your poisonous drinks, and you should know as the manager—and, might I add, proprietor—of this club, that a police officer can demand entry at any time. I merely wish to see if two people I know are here, and if they are, to have a few words with one of them. The entrance is down the stairs, I believe." And the inspector stalked below.

The cabaret show, which began five minutes later, gave him the opportunity to take stock of the patrons. His glance round sought, and stayed at, a table round which six people were sitting. He noted their presence with satisfaction. One of them was Miss Malcolm, another Mr. Catling. His eyes counted six bottles of champagne, four on the table empty, and two in the ice-bucket. Six sixes are thirty-six, said the inspector to himself. That's thirty-six pounds in drinks. And Catling's doing the paying, he added, as he noticed the Thames Pagnall man giving orders to the waiter.

The inspector was devising ways and means of speaking to Miss Malcolm, when she herself settled the problem. She danced with one of the three men of the company; and in passing the inspector's table, caught sight of him.

"Good gracious, Inspector Carruthers, I never thought to see *you* in a midnight haunt of sin!" she announced, in astonishment.

Carruthers grinned sheepishly. "Even inspectors of police are human enough to want a night out, Miss Malcolm," he replied. "I don't very often come into the West End, and this is the first time I have ever wanted to see what the inside of the 'Olive Grove' looks like. I've a few friends who seem to spend all their nights here."

"You *do* surprise me. You'll be telling me, next, that you even dance the modern steps."

"My wife tells me that I achieve a certain modicum of success in them," was the answer.

"Then you must dance the one now beginning with me," she decided. She turned to her escort. "You dance with Myra, Johnny," she ordered.

They danced.

"You aren't by any chance going to raid us, are you, Inspector Carruthers?" the girl asked. "I mean to say, if you are I'm getting out now. Mother doesn't like me going to night-clubs at all, and if I was pinched and put in the dock at Marlborough Street—well, that would be the finish of me." She giggled.

The inspector shook his head. "No, Miss Malcolm. I'm just a private merry-maker—if you can call this merry-making. But I do want a talk with you."

"About?"

"About the day of the cricket match. It's rather urgent. I've seen everyone except you."

"But, Inspector, not tonight, please! I can't leave my party. Actually, I'm hostess with Mr. Catling. It can't be so important that a few hours can matter. Come round to my flat tomorrow— or rather today, now—and you can talk to me to your heart's content."

"Well . . . if I must." The inspector's voice was reluctant. "What time?"

"Let me see, now. I shall be asleep until mid-day, that's certain. Then I'll have to lunch. Say about two o'clock, Inspector."

"Very well, Miss Malcolm." He escorted her back to her table. Mr. Catling looked up as they approached—and stared. "Dash me, if it isn't Carruthers!" he said. "Didn't know you were a member of this place, Inspector."

"I'm a dark horse in many ways, Mr. Catling," was the reply. He bowed to the ladies, and left the club.

* * * * *

Now, all these wanderings of yesterday converged at ten o'clock next morning into a single entity in the room of the Assistant Commissioner (C), the 'C' standing for Criminal Investigation.

Criminal deduction is five per cent deduction and ninety-five per cent routine work. That is what the detective stories never tell you—or even allow you to guess. The amateur detective of the books listens to a few views of the police inspector, and then, fixing him with his gimlet eyes, or maybe with a piercing glance, tells him where he has gone wrong, and issues the name, or mebbe just a description, of the onewhodunit. That is not, however, the way it works out in Scotland Yard.

For instance, in the Gutteridge murder case of 1927-28, more than one thousand people were interviewed and nearly four months of inquiry and routine were occupied before Browne and Kennedy were put into the dock for the murder of P.C. Gutteridge. And never a day was there any let-up on the part of police all over the country. And the inquiries which led to the Thames Pagnall tragedy conference were the result of twenty-four hours of hard routine work by a dozen skilled man-hunters. Six men now sat in a room to review and dissect them.

Sir Edward Allen set the discussions going. "Now, Doctor," he said, pointing his monocle at the scientist. "Our last talk led to a line of investigation, and the most likely person—that is Mr. Bosanquet."

"Shall we say that we discussed whether Mr. Bosanquet could be eliminated, A.C.?" was the rejoinder. "It is not quite the same thing."

Superintendent Jones chuckled. "Don't see difference. . . . Doctor very particular, though," he said in his staccato explosions.

"Just as you like, Jones. The point is, Doctor, have you eliminated him?"

"No!" The reply came bluntly from Dr. Manson. "On the contrary, I regard such operations as Merry and I have carried out since our last meeting as even more closely demanding inquiries into Mr. Bosanquet. He is by no means eliminated."

"And what were the operations, Doctor?"

The scientist looked across at Merry. The deputy scientist took from a portfolio three photographic prints) and handed them over to his chief. Dr. Manson handed them to Inspector

Carruthers. "You identify these as photographs taken by your direction, Carruthers?" he asked.

The inspector nodded.

"Very well, let me draw your attention to them, gentlemen, and to a number of things which the photographs, under expert examination, show. Take the first of them—the view from the front . . ."

For a quarter of an hour the scientist, with micrometer gauge and pencil, demonstrated the mathematical calculations carried out by Sergeant Merry and himself. He spoke slowly and earnestly, waiting at each stage in order to assure himself that each member of the conference followed with exactness the various steps in his deduction. At the end, he sat back and jabbed his pocket lens at his colleagues. "That, to my mind, involved Bosanquet deeper than he was before, A.C.," he insisted. "It is possible that we may be a little out in our calculations, but the error can only be very slight, and does not, I am certain, affect the hypothesis."

The Assistant Commissioner nodded. "It looks like the real Manson reasoning and data to me," he remarked at length. "What does it lack in fact, Doctor?"

"Opportunity," replied Manson. "We have to find opportunity."

"Carruthers?" The A.C. looked across at that officer.

The inspector coloured. He cleared his throat with an embarrassed cough. "I don't like seeming to knock down the doctor's experiments, sir—"

"Never mind me, Carruthers," interrupted Manson. "All we want are the facts. We can all make mistakes, you know."

"Well, Doctor, it's the opportunity I can't get over. Bosanquet had no opportunity. I am sure of that. Between the time that the match began in the morning and up to his going over to Crombie, he was never away from his guests. They all say so. I've seen Mr. Catling. He says that he can vouch for the fact that Mr. Bosanquet was with them all, all the time. I've seen the artist johnny. He says the same. The only time he wasn't with Bosanquet was when he went back to his house for his spectacles, and that was before the match started. Mrs. Bosanquet was there. The only person I haven't seen is Miss Malcolm, and I'm having a word with her this afternoon. I make out that mebbe one of them might have been away and not seen Bosanquet leave the lawn of his house, but they couldn't all not have missed him. It's impossible. He didn't leave them at all. And where would he use a rifle from there without it being seen, or the sound being heard by the people all round him?"

"That, Inspector, if I may say so, is sound reasoning. Where the flaw is, I cannot yet see. We'll leave the matter there for the moment. What has Kenway to say?"

"Fortunately, Doctor, the commissionaire at the office building is an ex-sergeant of the Yard." He detailed the points gleaned from the man, and went on to describe the dockside warehouse. "Bosanquet has, apparently, a good business, Doctor, and has built it up in four or five years, or thereabouts."

"What about you, Willoughby?" asked the A.C.

"Checked him pretty thoroughly, sir," the sergeant responded. "I looked up the name in the Oxford University *Year Book*, and found that Alfred Bosanquet was at Wadham College. As it happens, a friend of mine was at Wadham at the same time, and I rang him up. He remembers Bosanquet; in fact he says that the man nearly got him sent down. Says he went up from Charterhouse—"

"Bosanquet told me that he was at Charterhouse," broke in Inspector Carruthers.

". . . And his father was a bigwig down Chelmsford way," went on Willoughby. "In fact, Stinky—that's my friend—said that he not only knew Bosanquet, but knew his mother, who was a friend of Stinky's aunt. I may say, though, that he was surprised to hear that Bosanquet was in business. Wanted to know what had become of the old man's money."

"So that, Willoughby, we can account for Bosanquet's life from the time that he was at Charterhouse until he left Oxford, in 1906; and from the time that we know he started up in business until now?"

"That's how I see it, sir."

The Assistant Commissioner studied the point for a moment or two. Then: "How does that fit in with the S.F. idea, Doctor?" he asked. "S.F. we are taking to be Snowy Freud, and Freud, we are led to understand, was an Australian gang leader. If it was S.F. that Leland came back to see at Thames Pagnall, then he couldn't be Bosanquet, could he?"

"It is difficult to see how he could be, A.C., on the stories we have heard this morning." The scientist turned to Carruthers. "You remarked just now, Inspector, that Bosanquet told you he was at Charterhouse. Why did he tell you that?"

"Because I asked him where he had been before he came to Thames Pagnall," was the reply. "He said London, and before that Oxford University. Then I made a plunge at Dr. Manson's 'S.F.' and suggested that he had been born abroad."

The scientist nodded approvingly. "And what did he say to that?" he asked.

"He produced his birth certificate. Sergeant Willoughby's friend was correct. It gave his birthplace as Chelmsford, and his mother's name was *née* Parson. I thought we'd check on that, and asked what school he had been at. He said Charterhouse. It all checks up with Willoughby, Doctor. I'm bound to say that he seemed quite open with me, and showed willingness to help. He said that he wished that he had never gone over to Crombie, and realized that being alone with the body had placed him in an unfortunate position. He stuck to his story of hearing a shot and said he thinks that Leland must have been shot from the road by accident."

Dr. Manson shook an impatient head. "You are giving a *précis* of the talk, Carruthers," he expostulated. "Have you the actual words he spoke and the actual replies to your questions?"

"Yes, Doctor." The inspector handed over his note-book. The scientist read through the recorded interview. At the end, he turned back a page and read several sections over again, before handing the book back to the inspector. He nodded to the assistant commissioner.

"And what about you, Jones?" asked Sir Edward.

"Checked up . . . man about town . . . coupla clubs . . . bachelor flat . . . Mayfair . . . spoken of as derned well off . . . good fellow. . . ." The fat superintendent lay back.

"There's one more thing I should point out, Mr. Assistant Commissioner," said Inspector Carruthers. "It rather supports Dr. Manson's earlier idea that Leland was watching somebody at cricket. Watkins thinks that there *was* someone with him on the green, or if he wasn't with him he was standing very close to him. He also said that when the teams first came out, Leland leaned forward as though looking for someone. He thinks that Miss Malcolm, who was with him—Watkins, I mean—and has better eyesight, since he had forgotten his glasses, may have seen the incident, too. They were both looking towards the tent."

"But that is very important indeed, Carruthers," broke in the A.C. "It may have been the man who shot him."

"And then he'd be a member of one of the teams, which was what the doctor first had in mind," added Carruthers. "We've only tried out those whose names began with 'F'. If it was Snowy Freud, he would probably have changed his name."

"He *has* changed his name, Carruthers," said Dr. Manson, quietly.

The company looked up, startled.

"Eh? What have you got hold of now, Doctor?" demanded the A.C.

"An idea, A.C.," was the reply, with equal quietness.

"Well, we've wiped out Bosanquet, then," the A.C. put in. "We've his complete life story."

Dr. Manson spoke again. "I think it vitally urgent that Carruthers should investigate further this mysterious person who has so suddenly appeared in the story, whom Leland leaned forward to see, and who was, supposedly, standing by, or near him."

The inspector nodded his head. "I am seeing Miss Malcolm this afternoon, Doctor," he added. "She may, as Mr. Watkins says, have seen more than he did."

The Assistant Commissioner stood up—and the conference ended.

TO THE READER

In Chapter Twelve, Clues Three, Four and Five presented themselves to Dr. Manson. They were found, subsequently, to be vital pointers to the murderer.

They are "on the table" for the reader.

Chapter Thirteen
TRAGEDY IN A MEWS

THE PIERCING SCREAM of the telephone brought to a violent end the trend of thought which Dr. Manson had, after long mental searching, just begun to pursue to what he hoped would be a satisfactory conclusion. He eyed the instrument in silent irascibility, and waited optimistically to see if the caller, receiving no answer, would conclude that the laboratory was entertaining no occupant.

The bell shrilled again. The scientist put out a hand and lifted the receiver. "Well, it's gone now, anyway"—referring to his line of thought. "Hallo," he called. The voice of Superintendent Jones answered.

"Doctor . . . got 'nother drug corpse . . . woman . . . girl, rather . . . dead in mews flat . . . dead hours. . . . You comin' down? . . . Landis Mews . . . that's in Bayswater . . . I'm stopping here."

"I'll be along at once, Jones."

A taxi-cab carried Dr. Manson along the Mall, through Hyde Park, and over to Landis Mews in Lancaster Gate. The fat superintendent was waiting in the cobbled yard. "Flat number five, it is, Doctor," he announced, and led the way.

Landis Mews was one of those queer London addresses that the modern miss of 1920 not only sported, but raved over. They earned for them among their male friends the nickname of 'fillies'. The reason is not far to seek. Now, the story of mewses is an interesting one, and one of evolution. In the good old days when men practiced falconry, a mews was a place where the hawks of the chase were mewed. When the birds were moulting, or were sick, they were taken to the mews to be nursed back to health. Well, hawking died—but the mewses didn't. Set, as they were, amid the houses of the 'hawkers', they became a very valuable adjunct for stabling the horses of the elite. So the mews became the coach-houses and the stables of the folk who sported carriages, and lived in the large blocks of houses amid which the mews existed. All over west London these mewses were scattered, but especially in Bayswater, when that now drab area was a fashionable address.

Then, the coming of a still newer toy—the automobile—swept away the horses. And the mews became deserted once again. But not for long. To meet the needs of the time, the stables of the horses, which had been the stable of the hawks, became the stables for the new conveyances. They aspired to the name of mews garages. Instead of the 'hiss-hiss-hiss' of the ostler grooming his horses, the mews re-echoed to the swish-swish-swish of water, washing down the road juggernaut. Then Bayswater went out of fashion. The car-owner moved to other places, and particularly in the country, where a garage could be built on to the end of his residence. The big houses fell empty, principally because there was no longer the income, due to taxation, to keep them going. So the mews fell empty, also. The grass grew between the stones in the cobbled yards, which had been cobbles when the hawks mewed in the mews. Until . . .

One day, an arty-crafty gentleman from Chelsea, for the sole reason of being accounted eccentric enough to get talked about, rented on lease one of the stables of the old mews, and converted it, or had it converted, into a flat. In the coach-house and stable he garaged his car. Now, above the stable there ran a loft in which, in the good old days, hay and straw were stored. Access to the loft lay by a narrow staircase inside a small door alongside the wide double-doors, and partitioned off inside from the horse stalls. This arty-crafty gentleman converted the loft into a *bijou* flat—and started the habit, which became distinctly the *mode*, of living in a mews. So much so that, today, a flat there costs as much to rent as a good-sized house.

It was a dwelling of this kind into which Dr. Manson followed the superintendent. Together they mounted the staircase, the rough, wooden affair of the old days, but now gaily painted red and yellow. They emerged into a narrow passage, dividing the long living-room from the bedroom and the kitchen on the other side of it. The superintendent led the way into the bedroom. It was a small, square compartment at the top end of the narrow passage, with a bathroom adjoining. The room was tastefully furnished with the modern low bed and furniture. The top clothes had been pulled from the bed, revealing the figure of a young woman.

Dr. Manson crossed the room and looked down on her. Had it not been that both he and the superintendent knew she was dead, she might have been mistaken for a sleeping beauty. The long, slim form was concealed only by a silken nightgown, and she lay easily and restfully, her face composed and peaceful. Dr. Manson put her age at about twenty-five or twenty-six. He bent down and lifted an eyelid, showing beneath a highly dilated pupil. "Heroin, of course," he said.

Superintendent Jones peeped into his note-book. "Doctor says poisoned by diamorphine hydrochloridum, and a lot of letters," he replied.

"Letters?" inquired Manson.

"Letters and numbers. C_{21}, H_{22}, O_5, N, Hcl H_2O."

"Oh, I see. That's how we scientists write heroin, Jones."

"The hell it is," said Jones. "Beats me why they can't write plain, ruddy English."

"Did the doctor say how long she had been dead?" asked Manson.

"He said about six hours—which would make it about six o'clock this morning."

"I see. And now, who is she, and who found her?"

"Name of Kathleen Malcolm, Doctor. Young woman independent means. Seems she has a daily woman come in about eleven o'clock to get her breakfast and to clean the place up. Woman came s'mornin', cooked meal . . . called girl . . . went on cleanin' . . . found breakfast cold . . . went into bedroom . . .

couldn't wake girl . . . felt her cold . . . and ran yelling for cop. Cop got police doctor. . . . There you are."

"Know who she is, apart from her name?"

"Not a derned thing. I've got the wagon comin' to take her to the mortuary."

A ring at the door below interrupted the conversation. Superintendent Jones plodded down the stairs. From above Dr. Manson heard an exclamation. "For the luv of Mike what do *you* want?"; and a moment or two later there appeared above the stairhead the face of Inspector Carruthers. He looked at the doctor in astonishment. "What the deuce are you doing here, Doctor?" he queried.

"We'd like to ask the same of you, Carruthers," replied the scientist. "Are you poaching on us?"

"I've an appointment here."

"With whom?"

"With Miss Malcolm." He gave a start. "This is her flat, isn't it?" Superintendent Jones was staring at the inspector, and the mouth of him was opening and shutting like a fish out of water. Dr. Manson, after the first start of surprise, spoke quietly and grimly. "Do I gather, Inspector, that this Miss Malcolm is the Thames Pagnall lady you were going to interview today?"

The inspector nodded. "But—" he began.

"Come and be introduced." The doctor led the way to the bedroom and ushered the inspector through the door. "Is that her?" he asked.

Carruthers looked, and his breath hissed shrilly through his lips. "That, Doctor, is the lady," he agreed. "What killed her?"

"Heroin." The scientist led the way into the living-room and appropriated a chair. "Now, Carruthers, let's have all you know," he invited.

"Well, Doctor, you remember when I checked up on Bosanquet and the others, I saw everyone except Miss Malcolm. You'll remember that Watkins suddenly recollected that he saw Leland lean forward and look at the team as it entered the field, and then thought that he saw someone with Leland?"

Dr. Manson nodded. "I remember perfectly," he said.

"Now, Watkins hadn't got his spectacles, and couldn't be sure about it, but he said that Miss Malcolm was with him, and was watching, too. I saw Mr. Catling after that and he couldn't help. When I said that I was going to see Miss Malcolm, Catling told me that l wouldn't be able to see her until the following morning, as they were all celebrating at the 'Olive Grove' Club that night, and she was in town. Now, I felt that we might want to get the point cleared up as soon as possible, so I went to the 'Olive Grove' last night. I danced with Miss Malcolm." The inspector detailed his talk, and the appointment made for the afternoon at the flat. "I came along earlier, hoping that she might be up," he explained.

"Did you know about this flat before?"

"I knew that she had a flat in town. She was a very independent young lady, and did not like being buried away in Thames Pagnall. She liked night life, and only came down to her parents during the weekend."

Dr. Manson sat back in the chair. Superintendent Jones, watching the closed eyes, with the crinkles in the corners, and the furrows lining his brow, kept silence. Something, he knew, was worrying the scientist. For the space of some two minutes Dr. Manson remained thus. Then the eyes opened, and rested on the face of Inspector Carruthers. "What kind of a woman was Miss Malcolm?" he asked. "Was she moody—you know what I mean: up in the air sometimes and down in the dumps at others?"

"No, Doctor. She was always about the same. Bright and breezy, if I might use that phrase of a woman. Always good company."

The doctor rose and left the room, to return a few moments later with the dead girl's handbag. Emptying the contents out on the table, he picked up each article, one by one, and examined each before dropping it back into the bag. "There's nothing here," he said, at the end. "We ought to search the place thoroughly."

"For what?" asked Jones.

"For heroin," was the reply. He went into the bedroom and rummaged through drawers and cabinets. Each box of powder

or salts he examined minutely, frequently testing the contents
with the tip of his tongue. But without success. Superintendent
Jones went through the bathroom, with equal lack of success.
Together the three men returned to the living-room. It was a
delightful room, furnished comfortably with a grey hair carpet,
two armchairs to match, and silk grey curtains edged and ap-
pliqued with Rust conventional designs. They found a match in
the cushions scattered on the chairs. Across one corner of the
room stood a baby Blüthner piano. A small marquesette writ-
ing-table rested beneath one of the two windows. A cupboard, a
gate-legged table and two small chairs in another corner made
the dining arrangements. Jones and Carruthers went over
them with a fine comb of investigation, while Dr. Manson examined the clothes which the dead girl had worn, and which
still lay across a chair in the bedroom. Her evening cloak was
felt carefully throughout its surface and inside lining and a few
fragments of dust gathered from the pocket were subjected to a
close scrutiny through a pocket lens. Similar examination was
carried out by the doctor of other clothes in the wardrobe, and
of the contents of the drawers which contained the girl's more
intimate garments. The result of all this was still blank.

Dr. Manson, defeated, made the next move. "Now, Jones, if
it can be managed I'd like an immediate post-mortem, and the
doctor's report as soon as he can write it. This is pretty urgent."
He turned to Inspector Carruthers. "And you, Inspector, had
better see Catling as quickly as you can. He must have taken the
girl home from the club. And let it be known that Watkins could
not distinguish anyone he thinks he saw at the match—in fact
that he doesn't know whether he really saw anyone, because he
was without his spectacles."

Kenway looked puzzled. "But why, Doctor?" he asked.

"Because we do not want Watkins to meet a sudden death,
too, Inspector. It looks odd to me that the person who might
have been able to tell us something about a mysterious figure
should be found poisoned on the very morning she was to talk
to us. I'm taking precautions. There may not be anything in it.
If so, we haven't lost anything. What we do not want to do is

to risk losing Mr. Watkins, who may remember something else presently. What about the 'Olive Grove', Jones?"

"Puttin' Kenway on it, Doctor."

"Right—and get a move on with that doctor."

It was evening before the report of the police-surgeon reached the scientist. Separated from the legal verbiage, decreed by red tape, it stated:

There was considerable dilation of the heart, oedema of the lungs and brain. There was some degenerative change in the kidneys not due, I think, to the action of the drug. I find that death was due to respiratory paralysis, consequent on an overdose of heroin.

Dr. Manson laid down the document and dialled on the telephone. "I have just received, Doctor, your p.m. report on the woman Malcolm. Can you give me any idea how large a dose of heroin was taken?"

A chuckle came back. "I rather guessed you would want to be asking me that, Dr. Manson," was the reply. "I have just completed an analysis. I think I am correct in saying that she took two-and-a-half grains of the drug—that is, of course, in round figures. It rather surprised me."

"It does me, Doctor. There was, of course, some kidney trouble?"

"Yes. That may, of course, explain so small a dose proving fatal."

"Quite so. Was it taken hypodermically?"

"No, Dr. Manson. I am of the opinion that it was swallowed."

"Swallowed!" Dr. Manson allowed an exclamation of surprise to escape him. "That, again, is interesting."

"I should have put it down to suicide had I been asked. One could hardly swallow two-and-a-half grains of heroin without knowing it. It would have, as you know, a very bitter taste."

Dr. Manson thanked the medico and rang off. He hurried to Superintendent Jones. The result of their short conclave sent a detective hurrying Bayswater way in a squad car. He was back within half an hour, and ushered into the superintendent's room a flustered woman.

"Mrs. Webster, isn't it?" asked Dr. Manson. "There is nothing to be alarmed about," he added, with a reassuring smile. "But there is one important question we want to ask you about Miss Malcolm."

"As nice a young lady as ever I worked for, gennelmen, and allus a kind word and a smile, and a bit extra if you did anything for her, and as happy as the day is long. I'd never 'ave thought—"

"Quite so. You went in each morning, I understand? Cooked a meal for her and generally kept the flat in the very clean and tidy appearance in which we found it?"

"I did me best, gennelmen. Such a kind young lady."

"Would I be correct in assuming, Mrs. Webster, that one of the first things you did on arriving at the flat was to wash up any articles of tableware left from a meal or a drink?"

"Yes, sir. I washed 'em up and left 'em to dry while I made tea and toast for breakfast."

"That was your invariable practice?"

"Beg pardon, sir?"

"You always did that?" interpreted the scientist.

"Yes, sir."

"Now, what did you wash up this morning, Mrs. Webster?"

The woman opened her mouth to reply, and then suddenly stopped as though paralysed. The look of surprise gave a comical appearance to her face. "Now I comes to think of it, sir, I didn't wash nuthin' up this morning," she replied. "There wasn't nuthin' in the sink."

"Nothing at all?" asked Manson. "Think very carefully, Mrs. Webster, because this is very important. What did you usually find waiting for you?"

"Well, sir, there was generally a cup and saucer, sometimes two. The young lady used to have a cup of cocoa or something at night, and there'd be a plate on which she had cut a sandwich. That's what there usually was."

"And there was no cup and no plate this morning?"

"No, I'm certain sure there wasn't. If there had a-been they'd be there now, because I'd have waited to put 'em away with the breakfast things, when I'd washed *them* up."

Manson stood up. "Thank you very much, Mrs. Webster. That has been a great help." He rang for a constable. "Take Mrs. Webster home again, officer," he said.

"Don't see point, Doctor. . . . May have washed 'em up herself," said Jones.

"Why?" snapped the scientist. "Why, on this night of all nights, should she do something that she had never done before? If she meant to commit suicide, what the deuce did it matter whether she washed up a cup or not? The thing is unusual, since she always left the crockery for the woman; and I do not trust unusual things in cases of unexplained death." He turned to the constable-secretary who had been taking shorthand notes of the interview with the woman. "Ask Sergeant Merry, in the laboratory, to come here."

The deputy scientist listened with lively interest to the story of Mrs. Webster. "Go down there, and have a good look round at the crockery, Merry. You know what to look for." He handed to Merry the copy of the interview which Mrs. Webster had read and signed. "And . . . Merry . . . call in on Prints on the way," he added.

"Had I better take the 'Box of Tricks', Doctor?"

The scientist nodded. "That's an idea, Merry," he agreed.

Merry returned within the hour. Dr. Manson and the superintendent were waiting in the laboratory. The deputy scientist opened the 'Box of Tricks', and lifted out two cups and a saucer, held securely in wooden frames for safe carrying. He placed them on the laboratory table. Dr. Manson eyed the fingerprints showing on their sides, outlined in black powder. A third cup followed—and a fourth. The sergeant proceeded to explain. "There was on the dining-room table, Doctor," he said, "a plate still containing toast, and a cup of coffee." He indicated the third cup. "I emptied out the coffee; I've got it in a bottle here. Then I tested the cup for prints. Two showed up." He pointed them out. "As I see it, they occur at the spots where they would be made by a person lifting the cup off a hook on the dresser." The sergeant produced the report of Mrs. Webster's interview. The bottom was now stained with a smudge. "Here is a print of one of Mrs. Webster's fingers—the first finger on the left hand. It compares with that on the side of this cup."

Dr. Manson extracted a lens from a waistcoat pocket and examined in silence the prints, comparing one with the other. "Undoubtedly," he said, and leaned back in his chair.

The sergeant produced a card. "This is from Prints," he said. "They are prints taken from the hands of the dead girl." He placed the card in front of the fourth cup.

Once again the scientist bent forward and made his comparisons. "These prints are undoubtedly those of the thumb and first finger of the right hand of Miss Malcolm," he said, and Merry nodded.

"Now we come to the first and second cups," continued Merry. "There were five cups and saucers hanging on the dresser, and the cup and saucer on the table. I powdered all those on the dresser one by one. On three of them were the prints of Mrs. Webster. I have left them for confirmatory evidence. The other two, and one saucer, are here. Have a look at them. There are no other marks whatever on the cups."

The scientist produced, again, his lens and pored over the prints, first on one cup, and then on the other. Finally he compared them again with those on the inside and underside of the saucer. He passed the glass over to the superintendent.

Jones studied the prints. "Look like man's to me, Doctor," he decided. "Too big for woman, except Mrs. Webster, and they aren't hers."

Dr. Manson nodded. "They are, I think, beyond question those of a man," he agreed. "And note the position." He walked to a cupboard and returned with a cup. Wiping it with a wet cloth at the sink, and then drying it, he indicated a line of hooks on a shelf over the sink. "If, after washing this cup I want to hang it, say, in its accustomed place, I take it so"—he held the cup between a first finger and thumb and slipped the handle over the hook. Then, holding it with a handkerchief, he unhooked and laid it on the table. With a sufflator from the 'Box of Tricks' he blew a little graphite powder over the surface. His fingerprints showed up at once, black against the white enamel. He placed the cup side by side with the cups in the wooden frames. "As near as makes no matter the prints appear in the same position, do they not?" he asked the company.

Merry nodded. The superintendent also nodded, as recognition broke, slowly, over him. "You mean that a man was in her flat, and that he washed up two cups and saucers, dried them and hung them on the dresser-hooks?"

"In the place where they would appear to be perfectly natural," put in Merry, "and would never, in the ordinary course of events, have been questioned. The man could not have known that the things were always left for the day-woman to wash up."

"Exactly. That is the lucky chance which sometimes aids us in investigation. Will there be anyone in Prints now, Jones?"

"Baxter should be there." He rang the house 'phone. "Baxter?" he queried to the answering voice. "Jones and Manson here. We're sending up a finger. We'd like to know the owner if we have him, and as soon as possible."

Merry departed with the cups.

"Carruthers said, did he not, Jones, that Catling took the girl to the 'Olive Grove', and was there with her?"

The superintendent grunted agreement.

"And she is his *fiancée*?"

Another grunt. "Hardly likely she'd let another man into her flat at that hour in the morning, except her *fiancé*," he put in.

The scientist nodded abstractedly. And, after a moment or two, "Do we know anything about Catling?" he asked.

"Only just the ordinary things, Doctor. Man about town, independent, clubman, and so on."

"Well, I hope Carruthers has been tactful with him. Better get Carruthers up here first thing in the morning."

The door opened. Inspector Baxter from the Fingerprint Branch entered. "We don't know the owner of the prints on the cups, Doctor," he announced.

"You don't? Well, that's a pity," rejoined the scientist, disappointedly.

"But we've got a copy"—with a chuckle.

"From?"

"Remember the Thames Pagnall affair? Inspector Carruthers sent us a print from the top bar of a deck-chair in which a man was found dead. It is the same print as these." The inspector placed the record card and the cups on the table.

The scientist made comparison, and expressed agreement. "Thanks, Baxter. That is a big step forward."

Superintendent Jones looked at his colleague. "Hell, Doctor!" he burst out. "Everythin' proving you right. The man who took the wallet from Leland, of course?"

"It might well be," replied Manson, non-committally.

"But who the hell is he?" said the harassed Jones.

Manson smiled. "I don't know, Super," he retorted. "Not yet," he added, and, after a pause, "not for certain."

It was at a conference in the room of the A.C. that Inspector Carruthers reported on his interview with Mr. Catling. Sir Edward had with him Superintendent Jones, Inspector Kenway, Sergeant Merry and the doctor. As Manson entered the room with Sir Edward, he whispered to that chief, receiving a nod in response. The A.C. greeted the local inspector with a smile. "It seems, Carruthers, that your confounded village is now mixed up with our drug investigation," he said pleasantly. "What had the girl's *fiancé* to say for himself?"

The inspector produced a sheet of blue foolscap paper, and spread it out in front of him. "First of all, sir," he said, addressing the assistant commissioner, "it seems to be correct that my place is mixed up with the drug business. Miss Malcolm was a drug addict."

"Was she indeed?" The scientist looked sharply at the inspector. "Who said that?"

"Mr. Catling, Doctor. When I left the Mews flat I motored straight back to Thames Pagnall and saw Catling. He had not heard of Miss Malcolm's death, and he was very much cut up about it when I told him. It was some minutes before I could question him. Then he asked what had caused her death. He did not seem surprised when I answered that it was due to an overdose of heroin.

"What did he say?" rapped out Dr. Manson.

The inspector consulted his book. "He said: 'I was afraid you were going to say that, Inspector. She was, alas, a drug addict. I had known for some time that she was sniffing heroin, and I had done my best to try to break her of the habit, but without success. I have tried to find out where she got her supply in order to stop it; but she wouldn't tell me, and though I watched her carefully, I could never find out.' He had told her," the inspector added, "that if she continued to take drugs, he would have to break off the engagement, and she then said that she would try to stop."

The inspector ceased his recital, and looked at the scientist.

"I see," said Dr. Manson. "And what did he have to say about last night?"

"He said that a party of six were attending a birthday celebration. He and she were the only members of the club, the others being their guests. They had intended to carry through to the closing of the club, but at three o'clock Miss Malcolm said that she felt very tired, and thought she had better go home. She left in a taxi at 3.15."

"What! Alone?"

"Yes," was the reply. "Catling explained that as he was the host to the party he could not very well leave them, particularly as they were not members of the club, and Miss Malcolm insisted that he should stay, and that she would be all right by herself. Mr. Catling, however, insisted on having a taxi-cab called, and putting her into it. He gave the driver the address and watched the cab down the street. Then he returned to his party."

"And what time did the party break up, Carruthers?"

"He said at four-fifteen o'clock. The four guests took a taxi, and he walked to a garage just off Piccadilly where he always parked his car, had it run out by the night attendant, and drove back to Thames Pagnall. He arrived there, he thinks, about five o'clock. He didn't notice the time, but drove back at his usual speed, which generally got him home about that time. I telephoned the garage, and they remembered him coming for the car. They charge so much an hour for garaging, and his docket is clocked on the time clock of the office as 4.25 a.m. That tallies with his leaving the club at 4.15 and walking to the garage."

"Have you checked up with the others?"

"With two of them. He gave me, at my request, their names and telephone numbers. They agreed that Miss Malcolm left about 3.15, and they parted with Mr. Catling outside the club at 4.15. They are sure of the time because the club closes at four o'clock."

"What check have you on the time at which Catling says he arrived back at Thames Pagnall, Inspector?" The inquiry came from the assistant commissioner.

"None, sir," was the reply. "He drove himself, and ran his car into his private garage. The time for the journey, however, would be about right. I have no reason to doubt his word, after his friends had corroborated his time of leaving."

"Then, Inspector, supposing that he did not drive straight home, but visited Miss Malcolm at her flat after he had left the club—it could be on his way, you know, if he went along the Bayswater Road, to take the Uxbridge Road through Ealing, Kew, Richmond and Kingston—then we have only his word for it that he has an alibi for five o'clock?"

The inspector looked puzzled. "I . . . I . . . suppose so, Doctor," he agreed. "But surely he would not go round to the flat at five o'clock in the morning."

"That is what we want to be sure of, Carruthers. Some man went there," said the scientist.

"I'll have a go at trying to confirm the time of his arrival, Doctor. Lambert may have been out on patrol somewhere near, and the neighbours may have heard the car, though they are not adjacent to the house." The inspector did not, however, look very cheerful at the prospect.

"I checked up with the club, Doctor," put in Inspector Kenway. "I saw the doorman who called the taxi. He remembers the time as 3.15. And he says that the club closed at four o'clock, and that it was 4.15 before the party had collected their wraps and left."

"He knew Miss Malcolm, did he?"

"Oh yes. And said he was surprised at her leaving so early, because she usually stayed until the close. I questioned him, and he said he thought she did look a little tired."

"Catling's prints should prove whether he did or did not go to the flat, shouldn't they, Doctor?" asked the A.C.

"Fingerprints?" said Carruthers, inquiry in his voice.

"Fingerprints," rejoined Dr. Manson; and detailed the results of Merry's investigation into the charwoman's story.

"And there is another thing which should interest you, Carruthers," he added. "The fingerprints are the same as that which you took from the top bar of the deck-chair on the green at Thames Pagnall. What do you say to that?"

The local inspector staggered at the news. "Do you mean, Doctor that the drug business you have been on and the Thames Pagnall death are linked?" he asked.

Dr. Manson inclined his head. "That is how it would appear, Inspector," he agreed.

"There is one point I would like to make," the assistant commissioner put in. "If Catling visited the girl in the flat after the night-club, he would go in his car, since he had to get home from there. Are there any other dwellers in the Mews, and might they have heard a car enter? Or leave?"

Superintendent Jones nodded. "Was goin' t-make same point 'self," he announced, regretfully. "First we've heard . . . any possible visitor. Taxicab feller lives top of Mews . . . has his cab in garage . . . have a word with him. . . . They tell me expert can tell make of car by sound of engine."

"Right, Jones. We'll leave that to you. Anything else you want to suggest, Doctor?" The Yard chief looked across at the scientist.

"Quite a lot, A.C.," responded Dr. Manson. He enumerated each word, putting an emphatic break between them. It was a psychological trait of the Yard's scientist investigator that when following closely a line of reasoning having a direct bearing on the case in hand his diction suddenly developed a startling clarity which gained in expressiveness from the quiet tones of his voice. The men at the Yard had learned to recognize in it a certainty of opinion. Superintendent Jones and Inspector Kenway looked up sharply as that tone now penetrated their ears. The doctor's eyes, they saw, were without crinkles, and the brow was furrowless.

"Quite a lot, A.C.," he repeated. "I am going to say, firstly, that Catling, in his statement, was committing what, in Churchillian parliamentary language, would be a terminological inexactitude. He has told us that Miss Malcolm was a drug addict. Had she been a drug addict, she would have been alive today."

"Your reasons, Doctor?" asked the A.C.

"Firstly, her appearance at the night-club when she left at 3.15. The doorkeeper said that she looked tired. It surprised him that she was going so early, because she usually stayed until the club closed. That is very strange conduct for a drug addict. *It is when an addict feels tired that he, or she, takes a shot of the drug, and is within a few minutes her own bright self again. Is that not so, A.C.?*"

Sir Edward, his eyes still on the scientist's face, nodded.

"Had she been an addict, so keen was she on always staying until the end of the festivities, that she would undoubtedly have taken a dose of the drug. She certainly would not have spoiled the party to which she was acting as hostess. Mrs. Webster, who only saw the girl in the mornings, in the flat, described her as always having a merry smile and as happy as the day was long— *at the time when any drug addict is at her very worst, from the after-effects of the drug*; the depression which follows the previous night's doping, and which is craving for another dose. Now, that is good deduction; but it is only deduction. Let me prove it by hard fact."

Dr. Manson paused, tantalizingly, while he selected a cigarette from his case, carefully tapped the end, and lighted it. He puffed a few rings towards the ceiling. Then he continued. "The surgeon who conducted the post-mortem on Miss Malcolm found all the symptoms of heroin poisoning, and he says that she died of respiratory paralysis, which is customary in such a death. The patient goes into a coma, with deep and stertorous breathing. The duration of the coma varies between a few hours and several days. In the absence of treatment death will ensue. The post-mortem showed heroin in the body. Now, the doctor, who knows me, had the sense to make an analysis of the liquid contents of the body. He says he found that, in round figures, it had originally contained just under two-and-a-half grains of heroin. And I am asked to believe that this caused the death of a heroin addict. Nonsense!"

"Exactly why, Doctor?"

The scientist eyed the assistant commissioner gravely. "The maximum medical dose of heroin, Sir Edward, is one-sixth of a grain," he replied. He emphasised the amount. "One-sixth of a grain. Heroin is excreted almost unchanged in the urine. Only a very small degree of tolerance is acquired, and then most of the drug is destroyed in the body. According to Faust, the acquisition of the drug habit is not due to the blunting of the tissues towards the action of the drug, but to a gradually increasing *power of the tissues to destroy the drug*. Further, to get the effect desired of the drug, the dose has to be rapidly increased. For instance, the official dose of morphine is one-third to one-eighth of a grain. It is difficult to find the toxic, or lethal, dose, for it varies considerably in different circumstances. But cases are known in which one grain has proved fatal. In the case of a morphine addict, however, fifteen grains of morphine a day are recorded by Smith as commonly taken. So you see the effect that addiction has in making the addict impervious to what would otherwise be a lethal dose.

"I have said that only a small degree of tolerance is required for heroin to be destroyed in the body. If Miss Malcolm had been an addict, *two-and-a-half grains of heroin would not have killed her*. Certainly it would not have killed her within a few hours of taking it. She might, possibly, have been found in a coma, and she might not have recovered, although that is doubtful. But several days would undoubtedly have passed before she died. I say emphatically, and the doctor will, I am quite sure, support me, that an addict of heroin could take very much more than two-and-a-half grains without feeling any undue effect.

"There is another point. Heroin is sometimes injected hypo-dermically. It is more often sniffed. The doctor states that *Miss Malcolm swallowed it*. I have never, in the whole course of my life, heard of a heroin addict swallowing the drug. It has an exceedingly bitter taste, which would revolt a person's throat. One last point. This girl is said to have been an addict. I searched her handbag, her clothes, her medical chest. I searched the entire flat. There was no trace of any heroin, or, indeed, of any drug, not even a soporific one. Nor could I find a receptacle which had ever held any such drug. I say that Catling lied when he said that Miss Malcolm was a drug addict whom he had been trying for months to break of the habit.

"Why should he lie?" The scientist glanced from one to another of the company, as though searching among than for an answer to his question. None was forthcoming. He supplied it himself. "One reason that occurs to me is because she is not an addict at all, but *some reason had to be supplied for her death from heroin poisoning*."

"Then how, Doctor, do you think she came to die?" The A.C. waited expectantly for the answer.

"Taking into account the discoveries we have made in the flat, I should say that her death was deliberately intended, and brought about. I should say that it had to be brought about in such a manner that persons involved must have an alibi. I should say that this bright girl, who always stayed to the end of any party, was drugged in the club sufficiently to make her feel sleepy and compel her to leave her companions and go home. That, I think, was the first stage.

"Then, she was visited at her home, by someone with whom she was on so familiar terms as to admit him to her flat in the early hours of the morning. We know that two cups and at least one saucer were used that morning. There is one drink which would disguise the bitterness of two-and-a-half grains of heroin. That drink is strong, black coffee. Incidentally, strong, black coffee is used to keep sleepy people awake."

"And you suggest—what?" Superintendent Jones queried.

"I suggest that the visitor introduced this dose of the drug into her coffee, and when the drug had acted on the already sleepy girl, he washed up the cups and saucers, dried them, and hung them up in their usual places on the dresser. I suggest that the idea was to kill the girl and have it appear that she had died from an overdose of the drug, self-administered. And to make that more certain it had to be stated that she was a drug addict. But he made two mistakes. All criminals make mistakes—thank goodness. He either forgot, or did not know, the drug tolerance of an addict, and, worse still from his point of view, *he forgot to leave a little heroin in her possession, to bolster up the theory that she took drugs.*"

Inspector Kenway was the first to venture an opinion. "Then, Doctor, since Catling is the man who says she was an addict, you infer that he is the man who murdered her?"

"I have not said so, Kenway, because I have no evidence to that effect. I have what I regard as reliable circumstantial evidence of the drugging. That is as far as I go. But it does, of course, place his alibi under suspicion. You have the solution in your own hands; we possess a fingerprint of the man who hung up the cups."

"My goodness, yes!" said the A.C.

"And Catling was in Thames Pagnall during that match," rapped out Inspector Carruthers. "And we have the same fingerprint there."

"Made while Catling was sitting on the lawn of a bungalow, and during the time that he can produce reliable witnesses to prove that he did not leave the lawn," put in the assistant commissioner.

"One of them the girl who has been murdered on the very morning she was to have given what might have been valuable evidence against the man who made that same fingerprint," put in Kenway again.

The company looked for enlightenment to the scientist.

He rose, and smiled on them.

"I have my views," he said.

CHAPTER FOURTEEN
SNOWY FREUD

From the pleasure centre of Melbourne, Australia, the streets run to the port on the River Yarra, two and a half miles from the sea itself. There is Flinders Street, there is Collins Street, there is Bourke Street, and there is also Little Bourke Street.

A queer thoroughfare is Little Bourke Street. Its houses are small and poor; and if you go through it at dusk of evening, a little frightening. For bright eyes peer out at you from inside dark doorways, and a curious sibulant murmuring comes to your ears. Stage folk from London who have played at the Theatre Royal in Melbourne will tell you all about Little Bourke Street, for the stage door of the theatre stood, and still stands, in it; and the shining eyes and the whispers like leaves falling from invisible trees were a nightly nightmare to them on their way homewards after the show.

For Little Bourke Street is the poorer Chinese quarter of the city.

The life of its denizens is little more than drudgery, opium and gambling. On a hot summer's night, should you pass along it, the chink of coins on the fan-tan tables will come to your ears. Quite illegal, of course, but a little of the drabness of the lives of these Chinese was relieved round the tables.

Now, in the 1920s, Little Bourke Street was a boundary line between the gang-land of Squizzy Morgan, Lord of Melbourne, and his rival in the underworld business. Really, Little Bourke Street belonged to Morgan, by right of conquest; but it was nothing unusual for the performances in the Theatre Royal to be enlivened by the sounds of an exchange of shots of the rival gangs; to the dismay of the audience, but more so of the artists, remembering that they had to traverse the street on their way from the theatre later on. The audience left *en masse* by the front door, which was round the corner from this little street.

However, Squizzy, always the gentleman, usually took the ladies of the chorus—and the principals—under his protection, and provided armed lieutenants at the two ends of the street, to see that the other crowd did not molest them. While grateful for this act of Raleigh gallantry, the ladies, nevertheless, had the uncomfortable feeling that the other crowd might, at any moment, come along and fight out the argument with Squizzy, with themselves between the two fires, so to speak.

He was a bit of a character, was Squizzy. A dapper man, short of stature, dressed like a fashion-plate, he entertained royally, and was hail-fellow-well-met in wealthy, and poorer, circles. He talked good English; he liked good music and good plays; and was prepared to pay good prices for them. But in his chosen profession, nothing was too big, or too small, to bring grist to Squizzy's mill; he would withdraw cash from a bank at which he had no account; if you left your Buick parked anywhere outside the orbit of an attendant, it was ten to one that when you returned, you would still find your car—but without wheels or tyres. Squizzy's gang would have whipped them off to his second-hand car accessories depot across the river—nor would you ever be able to recognize them. Equally, if your locomotion ran to a bicycle, Squizzy would find a use for the tyres of that, too.

However, this is digressing. Squizzy had a rival, and the two of them had an associate; and that associate was Snowy Freud. The parents misguided enough to bring him into the world, and then rear him, had christened him William. The underworld called him Snowy, because he dealt in drugs. A chemist deals in drugs; and nobody calls a chemist 'Snowy'. The explanation is that the drugs in which Snowy dealt were illicit drugs—opium, cocaine, morphine, heroin. He 'ran' drugs, he imported them, he exported them, all illicitly. London was a customer; he had secret agents there who were apprised of the date of arrival of a cargo. The waterproof silken envelopes, which the Thames River Police retrieved from the waters around the Docks had come from Snowy Freud.

This was the man in search of information about whom Dr. Manson, at ten o'clock in the morning, walked into the offices of the High Commissioner for Australia, and asked to see Mr. Fellowes.

"Snowy Freud?" echoed Mr. Fellowes. "Oh, lord, yes! I know all about Snowy. He introduced drugs into Melbourne, first among the Chinese, and then among the gay-livers. We figured that he made £100,000 a year from drugs. Got so bad, Chief-Inspector, that at last the C.I.D. began to clean the thing up."

"Any luck?"

"Not much, so far as the trade was concerned. The fellow was clever. We knew that a ship going to England had the stuff on board. We had evidence of where it had been collected and stored, and pretty nearly the hour of its arrival on board the outbound ship. But the police never once found a trace of it; and the ship always left with the drugs. The C.I.D. put an inspector on to him. Snowy was his sole duty. Leland was the inspector's name. He eventually cut out most of the traffic, but only because Snowy found his attentions so irksome that he shook the dust of Melbourne off his feet—and vanished, just as Leland decided that he had enough evidence to arrest him on a minor charge of being in possession of drugs."

"Where did he go?" Manson showed a lively interest in the story.

"Nobody knows. In fact, the police never found out how he went, or when. He just vanished. But with him gone, and the fear of him disposed of, members of the racket blew the gaff, so to speak."

"Would you know him if you saw him?"

"I never did see him, Chief-Inspector. I shouldn't know him from Adam."

"And he was never through police hands?"

"He was through them in the full sense of the word. Half a dozen times he was arrested, but no evidence could be found against him, though his flat was searched like a head of hair with a tooth-comb, and he could never be held more than long enough to conduct the search. We knew that he was a killer; two men, at least, who could have peached on him, and were going to do so, were found dead."

"Then there is no identifiable record of him—such as fingerprints?"

Mr. Fellowes grinned. "The police took them once," he rejoined. "But Snowy, discharged by a magistrate, demanded that they should be destroyed in front of his eyes—which they were. But Leland, by some means which only he knows, obtained a set of prints later, and they are in records."

"Did you ever hear of him as having come to England?"

"No. I think there is too much law and order here to suit Freud," was the reply.

Dr. Manson considered silently the interview for a moment or two. Then: "You use a beam telephone to Australia most days, do you not?" he asked.

Mr. Fellowes agreed that that was so.

"I wonder whether you would ask your people to pass over a message to the Melbourne C.I.D. Would you ask them to wireless me the code of Freud's prints?"

"I'll do that, Chief-Inspector, certainly," said Mr. Fellowes. He eyed the scientist curiously. "Do I gather that he *is* here?" he asked.

"That is what I want to find out," was the reply.

Superintendent Jones was pacing the laboratory like a cat on hot bricks when the scientist returned from his talk with Mr. Fellowes. Manson glanced at him in surprise. The superintendent seldom carried his bulk up the stairs to the top floor. "Hello, old fat man, what do *you* want?" he asked.

"Wapping . . . identified fellow in dope factory," he staccatoed.

"And who is he?"

"Chap . . . used to come up river in motor-boat pretty frequently, and moor at Old Stairs."

"Name?"

"Don't know. Boatmen never knew name. . . . Kept himself to himself. . . . Just said 'Goo' mornin',' and 'How do' . . . remained only a few minutes as a rule."

"Recognize the boat?"

"No. Only that it was a pleasure craft more than anythin' else."

"Then it doesn't help much, does it? What are you going to do about it?"

"Try with photographs up the river."

The scientist slapped him on his broad shoulders. "A brainwave, old fat man," he said. "Go to it."

Jones went.

Dr. Manson, after a moment's reflection, took from a table drawer his dossiers of the Thames Pagnall and the Wapping and Mews tragedies, and, dropping into an armchair, began reading through the entries and notes in them. He read slowly and meticulously, pausing now and again to go back to some sentence and digest it more thoroughly before passing on. The scientist had convinced himself that in some way, not yet apparent, the three cases were linked together; that the common denominator forming the link would, could it be found, give him the solution to all three, and also to the flood of drug addiction which was causing so great a concern, not only to Scotland Yard, but to the eminent person of the Home Secretary himself.

An hour passed, and still he was reading, and wondering, when a constable entered and handed him the radio reply to his request to the Melbourne C.I.D. For some moments he studied the words of the message. Then, humming softly the bars of a melody which the composer would never have recognized, he left the laboratory, walked downstairs and across to the Fingerprint Branch. Inspector Baxter's glance went from his visitor's face to the paper fluttering in his hand.

"Not another!" he protested.

"Another, Baxter," was the retort. "This, you may like to know, is the code of the fingers of a gentleman named Snowy Freud, by reason, you may conjecture, of his dealings." (Snow is the name by which cocaine, or heroin, is known in the dope traffic.)

"And you think we may know the rose by another name, Doctor?"

"I think we may, perhaps, recognize the scent, yes," the scientist agreed.

"We'll have a go," said Baxter, and took the proffered sheet. He bent over and studied the array of letters and figures which spell out to the expert the mysteries of arches, loops, whorls and ridges, as well as sweat ducts. Then, walking to one of the cabinets lining the room, he lifted a file from a drawer, and from it took a bundle of record slips. Rapidly, he began to turn over the slips, looking for the classification required. Within two minutes his search was ended. He looked at the description of the print and frowned. "I suppose it is all right, Doctor?" he queried, and handed over the card.

The scientist took it. "You know, Baxter, this department of yours savours more of mystery to me than all the magic of Devant, Maskelyne and Lyle put together. It is positively uncanny how you can produce an identification from a million prints in, at the outside, how long?"

"Say five minutes at the very outside, Doctor," chuckled Baxter. "There are three examples of the print here," he added. "And all nameless. One is that found on the deck-chair at Thames Pagnall, the other impressions from the cups in the Mews flat where a girl died—and the magic isn't mine but Sir Edward Henry's. He was the man who first developed the fingerprint classification."

"Well, you've got them identified, Baxter. You can now mark them with a name—that of Mr. William Freud, alias Snowy Freud, alias . . ." The scientist paused.

"Alias—whom?" asked Inspector Baxter.

"I'll tell you within a week," was the reply.

Back in the laboratory, the doctor resumed his study of the three dossiers. And an hour later, he was discussing them with Sergeant Merry. Together they went over their calculations of position and gunfire, but without finding variation of their previous answers. "It is vital that we can be certain of them, Jim," the scientist emphasized, "for it is the main prop of our conclusions. Now, supposing that in the printing of the photographs the light gun was not directly in front of the film, but was directed sideways at the printing-frame, would that have any effect on the shadows cast by the body in the picture?"

Merry, whose knowledge of photography bordered on that of the professional, cogitated over the problem. "I don't think so, Harry," he decided. "After all, there is no space between the film and the printing paper. They are clamped together tightly. I do not see that any difference of the shadow could possible occur wherever the light was projected on to the frame. But it is an interesting problem with which I have never experimented. It is quite easy of solution, however. Send for the actual film and we'll put it in our enlarging camera."

"But, of course, Jim. Why I did not think of that, I don't know. Get hold of Carruthers."

The Thames Pagnall inspector, spoken to over the telephone, announced that he still retained the film and would send it up to the Yard by a constable. He was as good as his word; and an hour later the doctor and Merry unwound it, and together examined the tiny images in negative. The film was the full roll usual in a 10 m.m. cine-camera. It presented a series of shots apparently taken over an interval of time. The first quarter of its length showed a landscape of country and river, with figures and a car in the foreground. Next, there were pictured groups of people taking tea in a garden. Then followed a dozen shots of a child in a perambulator, a number of cricketers walking in couples and, finally, those pictures for which the scientist and Merry were looking, and in which they were immediately concerned—the shots of the dead man in the chair.

Dr. Manson took, first, three of the shots from the left side of Leland. The film was masked and fitted into the enlarging lantern. This lantern, in the dark-room of Dr. Manson's laboratory, was made on a specially built 'table' sixteen feet long, with a permanently fixed easel and paper-holder at the other end. The lantern ran on tramlines, so that, when moved, it remained always square with the easel. A wheel was the entire motive force of the lantern movement. By it, actual sharpness could be obtained of any image thrown on to the paper-covered easel, no matter how many multiplications of enlargement were being made. A locking device held the camera in position, once focusing was decided.

With the arcs switched on, Merry manipulated the 'tram-lines', while Dr. Manson measured the enlargement thrown on to the screen until it agreed in size exactly with the figures in the photographic prints which had been the material of their previous calculations. The film, being a negative, the shadows appeared on the screen now, of course, as white bars, and were easy of measurement. With his micrometer gauge, Dr. Manson obtained the width of the body shadowline, and checked it with that recorded in their calculations. They were identical. Similar experiments with the other pictures gave a like result.

"Then, that settles it," said the doctor. "The confirming proof is there."

Merry released the film from the lantern. He was about to roll it up when Dr. Manson handed him a spool. "Wind it round this, Jim, and we'll run it through a projector," he said. "It may interest you."

The sergeant looked up in surprise, but said nothing. He threaded the end of the spooled film through the gate of the projector, and, switching on the light, focused the image on the screen. Slowly he turned the handle of the machine, while the two men watched the scenes unroll in front of them. At the end, Merry looked across at his chief with eyebrows raised, in inquiry.

"Not necessarily." The scientist answered the unspoken question. "But—we will have to go cautiously," he added. "Certainly not direct."

"I'll run down with an enlarged print of the kid in the pram," said Merry. "Carruthers can find out, I dare say."

"And tell Carruthers that we are holding a conference here at six o'clock, and he had better attend," was the doctor's parting shot. "I'll fix it up with the A.C."

"But why the urgency, Doctor?" asked Sir Edward Allen when the request for the conference was made. "And who do you want?"

"Urgent, because I shall be away for the next day or two, A.C.; and I'd like to have the reports of Jones, Kenway and Carruthers to chew the cud over while I *am* away."

"Away? Where?"

"I'll tell you when I get back."

The assistant commissioner sighed resignedly. "Have it your own way," he said.

Sergeant Merry was the last to arrive in the conference room. He sidled over to the doctor, and spoke in a whisper. "Kid belongs to people named Brightwell," he said. "The shots were taken, they say, Saturday, while they were out walking between ten and eleven o'clock." Dr. Manson nodded, and, after waiting for the sergeant to bring up another chair, explained his reasons for asking for the conference. "There are a number of points upon which I want to be clear," he said. "They are, at present, holding up the jigsaw pattern." He looked across at Inspector Kenway. "Are there any more developments in the Wapping business?" he inquired.

"None, Doctor," was the reply.

"Any news of Bickerstaffe or his company?"

"No communication has been made to the landlord of the premises. Nobody has been near the place, and Mr. Bickerstaffe cannot be traced."

"Has Wapping any description of Bickerstaffe?"

Kenway grinned, grimly. "Doctor, when I said that Bickerstaffe hadn't been seen, I meant just that. Neither Wapping nor I could find any man who had ever seen Bickerstaffe; and no one who would know him if they did see him. There is no evidence of the premises ever having been occupied during the day; and we assume from that, manufacture of the heroin was done during the night hours. Wapping is still keeping a watch."

"Tell them not to waste their time," said the doctor. "Nobody is likely to turn up there again. Now, what about the Mews inquiries?"

"There was a car in the Mews round about 4.45 a.m. that morning. Seen by Albert Bevis, a taxicab owner who lives in the Mews. He garages his car in one of the old stables and sleeps in a one-roomed flat over the garage. He had been out on a late West End job, and returned at a quarter to five. Garaged his cab, and as he was locking up, noticed the car in a corner of the yard."

"Did he recognize it?"

"He says he did not take any special notice of it. Just noted, casually, that it was there without lights, and went to bed. He says that it was nothing out of the way for a car to be in the yard. He'd seen one or more there most nights."

"Calling on Miss Malcolm?"

"Sometimes. But mostly he thinks that the owners dropped in there to use it as a park without paying any fees for an all-night garage. He's probably right. There's a lot of that kind of thing going on."

"Did he hear it go away?"

"Yes. About five minutes after he had gone inside. He said that the car drove out of the yard without lights. Had the lights been on, the shadows would have chased across his ceiling. They didn't."

"Did he hear any good nights called?"

"I asked him that. He said that he heard no voices at any time." Superintendent Jones broke into the questioning. "If I 'member rightly, Kenway, Catling took car out of garage at 4.25 . . . set off home. . . . Doctor said last night might'a gone Bayswater Road way . . . would land him at Mews 'bout 4.35. . . . She'd let him in . . . *fiancé* . . . if he doped coffee . . . put her to bed . . . came out . . . times'd match up."

"They could, Jones," agreed Dr. Manson. "How about your end, Carruthers?"

"Catling arrived home at 5.15, or thereabouts," was the reply. "Chauffeur heard him drive up to the garage. He had the toothache and that had kept him awake. The chauffeur, I mean."

"Anything unusual in that time?"

"Don't know, Doctor. Chauffeur only been there a couple of days. Doesn't know Catling's habits."

"Time fits in again . . . half-hour . . . Thames Pagnall," said Superintendent Jones. "Funny, too . . . got shuvver . . . and drives up to West End himself. What's he want shuvver for?"

"Nothing in that, Jones," commented the A.C. "The man would have to be hanging about the West End all night, with nothing to do. Lots of people prefer to drive and leave their cars in all-night garage."

"As a matter of fact, sir, the chauffeur was going to drive, but hadn't got through the job of painting Catling's houseboat and launch. Catling wanted it done in time for the regatta—and it'll take all the time. That's where I found the chauffeur this morning, up along the houseboat on the Hampton Court Reach, putting green and white paint on an oak launch. If that isn't sabotage, then I don't know what is."

"Did you make any inquiries into Miss Malcolm, Carruthers?" Dr. Manson resumed his questioning after the A.C.'s interruption.

"Yes, Doctor. Parents are furious. Say they are quite certain that she was not an addict. Never saw any signs of it. Saw her friends. They deny it, too."

"I saw the other people at the party, sir," added Kenway. "And they laughed at the suggestion. They describe it as a slander, and think the police must be crazy to suggest it. Nobody who knew her would credit it for a moment."

"You need not worry about that, Kenway, nor you, Carruthers. She wasn't."

"Well, the position, as I see it, is that there is considerable circumstantial suspicion against Catling," the assistant commissioner summed up. "This girl, according to Watson, saw clearly what he himself saw only dimly because he was without his spectacles—that Leland leaned forward on the green to see a man, and, later, that man was near him. She agrees to be interviewed by Carruthers, and a few hours before that interview was due to take place she is found dead from poisoning. One of the persons who knew the purport of the questioning, and the time for it, was Catling, her *fiancé*. He also put Carruthers off seeing her on the previous evening, saying that she was in town. Supposing the man she saw on the green was Catling. He might have thought that, unwittingly, and quite innocently, she would give him away. He could not, of course, coach her in what to say, because that would have aroused her suspicions.

"Now, on the night of her death, she left a party before it broke up—something she had never done before. She said she was dead tired—and she had never been dead tired at a party before. She goes home to her flat in a mews. At four-forty-five o'clock a car is seen standing, with lights off, in the Mews. It leaves about 4.50. At six o'clock she is dead. Catling leaves the 'Olive Grove' at 4.15. He picks up his car at a garage at 4.25. He could reach the mews, easily, by 4.35. He arrived home at Thames Pagnall at 5.15, which gives him time to have driven from the Mews to Thames Pagnall.

"In the flat are found two cups and a saucer on which are the fingerprints of a man not yet identified by us over here. The cups had been washed and dried, and then hung up in their accustomed places. The girl would have reached home well before four o'clock. To what man would a single girl of good character open her door at four o'clock in the morning? And when she was in her night-clothes. She might do it to her *fiancé*. And he is Mr. Catling. There is only one thing I can think of which may question this, and perhaps the doctor knows the answer." He looked across at Dr. Manson. "The doctor placed the time of death at six o'clock. Suppose the two-and-a-half grains of heroin had been administered, or given in coffee, at 4.35, would that be consistent with death at six o'clock, and why did she not raise the alarm?"

"It would be quite consistent, Sir Edward," was the reply. The effect of the drug in that quantity, combined with the fact that she had in all probability been previously drugged at the club, would be to throw her into a coma, and from the coma she would die from respiratory paralysis. As to giving the alarm, the drug would act very quickly on a person already sleepy and wakened, or on a person who had been doped earlier."

"Catling was with her all the evening, was he?" asked the assistant commissioner.

"No. Not until they met in the night club—at eleven o'clock," replied Kenway.

"Do you see any fault in those arguments, Doctor?"

"Only one thing, A.C.," was the reply. "You said just now that we had on the cups from the Mews flat the fingerprints of a man whom we had not identified. You were wrong. I *have* identified him." He produced the radio message from Melbourne.

"They are the same prints as these from the record office at Melbourne. And they are the fingerprints of Snowy Freud, the 'S.F.' of Leland's diary."

He looked round at the surprised faces of the company. "And they are, as you already know, the prints that were on the deck-chair on Thames Pagnall green. Get Mr. Catling's prints, and you have the answer. But I am interested in Mr. Catling." He turned to Inspector Carruthers. "Do you think that the chauffeur has completed that painting job of his?" he asked.

"He hadn't when I came here," replied the inspector. "And he was knocking off for the day. Why, Doctor?"

"Just an idea that I would like to see him, Carruthers. If anything comes of it, I will let you know. What is the man's name, by the way?"

"Traynor, Doctor."

"Doctor?" Sir Edward Allen, who had been deliberating for some moments, suddenly addressed the scientist. "Suppose the fingerprints of Catling do not coincide with those of Freud, and therefore with those on the cups and the deck-chair, does that seriously let out Catling? Suppose that he is an accomplice of Freud, and suppose that Freud is employed by him. I cannot get over the fact that Catling is the one person who had access to the girl in the night-club."

Dr. Manson smiled. "I wondered whether anyone would tumble on that line, Sir Edward," he said. "It would not, of course, exonerate Catling. If he did not actually do the deed, but connived or plotted with the actual perpetrator, he is concerned in committing a felony, and as the person involved died, he is chargeable with murder. That is the law, as you know.

"The first thing to do is to get his prints, Carruthers. I am sure you will find some way of achieving that without arousing in him any suspicion. If they coincide with those of Freud, and the deck-chair, well and good. If they do not, since the doctor thinks that the girl was probably drugged sufficiently in the club to make her tired, we shall have to find some connection between Catling in the club and some outside person, whose prints are those of Freud, under whatever name he is known over here."

Superintendent Jones leaned forward. "S'pose girl wasn't sleepy . . . only said so . . . to keep clan . . . clan, you know the word I mean, appointment?"

Dr. Manson laughed delightedly. "You *have* thrown a spanner in the cogs, Jones," he said. "Since when have you developed an imagination?" The superintendent's lack of imagination had long been a by-word at the Yard. His value lay in his ability to acquire facts; and he had never been known to let a fact get past him.

"Anything in that, Doctor?" The assistant commissioner looked across at the scientist.

"With a woman, A.C., all things are possible. Now, let me say a word. You have planned several avenues of exploration this evening. Carry them out, but will you leave the results at that until I return from a few days' wanderings? In other words, garner what you can—and hold it. If you put them into executive action you may sabotage my inquiries; and I think that when I return I may be able to give you a bigger haul than that of which you are at present thinking—that is, if my inquiries produce the results that I am expecting of them."

If the scientist expected to cause something of a sensation he was not disappointed. The A.C. let his monocle drop to the full length of its silken cord. Inspector Kenway scratched a puzzled head, but said nothing; and Carruthers sat staring, with eyes that were nearly popping out of his head. Curiously enough, only Superintendent Jones preserved an unconcerned air. "Knew he'd got 'old o' somethin'," he said. "Seen it all evenin'."

Sir Edward shook his surprise from himself, "Something we've said here this evening, Doctor?" he asked.

"Partly, A.C.," was the reply. He looked round the company. *"There are seven vital points which have emerged from the various talks we have had together, allied to certain lines of inquiry we have made. Six of those seven points are beyond doubt. The seventh I hope to make so within a few hours. Then . . ."*

The scientist stopped in the middle of the sentence. His fingers felt for, and extracted, a gold pencil from a waistcoat pocket, and with it he began a quiet tapping on the arm of his chair. Sir Edward, hearing and seeing it, stiffened. He had heard that sound a dozen or more times before in mystery cases. And he knew what it meant. He pointed an expressive finger at the scientist and jabbed it six times in emphasis as he spoke.

"You . . . know . . . who . . . we . . . want . . . Doctor," he said.

It was noticeable that there was no note of query in his voice. It was an assertion, not an inquiry. There was absolute conviction in its tones. He waited for the answer.

"I have known for some time, Sir Edward," was the quiet reply. "But I could not prove it to my own satisfaction. Nor can I now. But I think that I shall be able to prove it to the satisfaction of myself, you, and a judge and jury, within two or three days."

TO THE READER

The last two of Dr. Manson's seven points (clues to a detective writer and reader) are in this chapter. You should now have the solution in your hands.

CHAPTER FIFTEEN
WONDERINGS AND WANDERINGS

THE WANDERINGS of Chief-Detective-Inspector Dr. Manson took that scientist crime investigator exactly three days. For the sake of surprise—publishers of detective stories insist that the ending of the story shall be a surprise—these wanderings must be shrouded, as is occasionally the British Army, in a 'Security Silence'.

The observant and discerning reader with a good armchair training in detective work and an eye to detail may be able to pierce the smoke-cloud of dialogue, and follow Dr. Manson in his wanderings. He may even be ahead of him! There is no good reason why he should not so be able. As an extra guide, it may be said that a riverside walk began them; and that, subsequently, the doctor took in his stride a famous cathedral city, a place famous among schoolboys, and a well-known agricultural manufacturing centre. The journeyings ended in a visit to the Port of London Authority, and another to the Commissioners of Inland Revenue sitting at Somerset House, that sprawling building which has a gateway in the Strand and a long outlook over the River Thames between Waterloo and Blackfriars Bridges.

It was within five minutes of the ending of the conference in the room of the assistant commissioner that Dr. Manson began his itinerary. Back in his laboratory, he drew a telephone towards him and dialled a Wapping number. His demand to be put through to Inspector Lawrence, of the River Police, evoked a response from a booming voice, with a twang of salt water behind it. Inspector Lawrence, from years of hailing craft in the river, had developed a voice that rolled out in carrying waves.

"Dr. Manson here, Inspector," responded the scientist. "You remember . . ."

For a couple of minutes the scientist spoke into the receiver, while the inspector listened. The voice ceased at last with a final inquiry: "Can you manage that, Inspector?"

"Yes, quite easily, Doctor. I have a couple right at hand. Can see 'em from the window."

"Right, then, Inspector, I'll meet you on the bridge there, in—how long do you think?"

"Say an hour, Doctor."

"All right. . . . What? . . . No. I'll see to that."

Thus it was that, sixty-five minutes later, four men walked underneath a bridge soaked in history. A river craft was waiting, and in this they embarked.

With the sun sinking below the horizon on the starboard side the boat was pushed off, and its nose set upstream. With Inspector Lawrence at the wheel, it chugged a leisurely passage between high embankments, then past park and wooded land, past riverside bungalows, gay with flowers for the summer week-ending visitations, past houseboats with gangways on to plots of land which gave access to the floating homes.

During the journey, Dr. Manson had been keeping a sharp lookout along the left-hand bank. The trip had proceeded for some five or six minutes, when he called out "Dead slow". Inspector Lawrence throttled down the engine, and with only enough way to keep the bows pointing up-stream, the doctor, from their position in the centre of the stream, looked carefully at the objects nearer shore. "Yes, that, I think, is what we want," he decided. "Drop down a little lower and we'll turn back, nearer inshore, and get a closer view."

As the inspector opened up the boat's engines, the scientist turned to the two men who had been puffing at their pipes unconcernedly. He spoke in low tones for a minute. They nodded in reply. "Right," he rejoined, "then here we are approaching. Now, have a good look." As they approached the object of the scientist's interest, Inspector Lawrence again shut off the engine. The two men leaning over the starboard side, stared hard. The boat drifted down with the current, and passed.

"Well?" asked Dr. Manson.

"I reckon so," replied the elder of the two.

"And you?" The doctor turned to the second man.

"I suppose we couldn't see the other side, could we?" he asked.

Dr. Manson looked across at the inspector. "What do you say, Lawrence?" he asked. "I do not want to attract undue attention."

"There does not appear to be anyone about, Doctor, except a courting couple"—nodding towards the opposite bank. "I should say they are too busy with their canoodling to take any notice of us."

"Then we'll risk it."

The boat was put about, and steered this time close inshore. With engine again shut off, it drifted towards the object of Dr. Manson's interest. As they passed, the younger of the two men leaned over the side. An exclamation came from him. "That's what I wished to see, sir," he said, and pointed out a series of markings. "Yes, I reckons that's it," he concluded.

"You are quite sure of it?" insisted Dr. Manson.

Both men nodded emphatically.

The scientist caught the inspector's eye, and that officer once more put the boat about, and opened up the throttle. Running full out, a quick return was made to the starting point of the adventure.

The two men were returned to their homes in a police car with strict instructions to make no mention of the incident. Dr. Manson, driving the inspector back, held a short confabulation with him. "It should be shadowed, Lawrence," he maintained. "I think that is the way it is done. But for heaven's sake don't arouse any suspicions, or we are sunk. It will only be for three or four days at the outside. These men won't talk, will they?"

"No, Doctor. They depend upon us for their licence. They won't talk, after what I said to them before we started."

Next morning the scientist began those wanderings which were to provide the evidence needed to bring the Thames Pagnall village green tragedy to a solution. In the long Oldsmobile, which was usually the link between him and his fishing waters in far distant Cornwall, he drove, first to the famous city set amid lovely countryside, and with the river running past its meadow-lands and parks. Turning through a gateway, he sidled a lawn and pulled up at an oaken door.

"Good heavens, what are *you* doing in this emporium," came a voice from the doorway. A burly figure emerged with outstretched hand.

"I've come to see you, Bill," was the reply.

"Then you probably want something, Harry."

The two entered a library, and it was an hour before they emerged. Thrice a bell had been rung, and visitors had been ushered into the library, and left again. His host accompanied Dr. Manson to the car. "Well, *au revoir*, Harry. And good luck. On my soul, if it is as you believe, it's extraordinary. Never heard of anything like it being done before."

"Mind, Bill, not a word to anybody," warned Manson.

"Not a word, Harry."

Turning the facts he had accumulated over in his mind as he drove back towards London, the scientist felt that he had good grounds for satisfaction. He had, in his opinion, acquired the modicum of background which, before embarking on his tour, he had decided was required from the first point of call, if the other destinations were to be taken in. He was satisfied that such background was that which he had, days before, visualized.

His next visit was more or less a chance shot, which might shorten his touring. If nothing came of it, it would not matter particularly. His mental preoccupation over his problems almost led him to stray from his route. It was not until he had passed a secondary arterial road, and a gaunt building suddenly confronted him, that he realized that he should have turned down the road a few hundred yards back. Hastily he braked, and swung his car round, turning right at the crossroads. "Now, I must put the thing out of my mind until I reach the next stage," he abjured himself.

It was a glorious afternoon, with the sun pouring down from a deep, cloudless blue sky. A light breeze circulating kept the heat within comfortable bounds. As he pursued his course, almost alone, through the Surrey country lanes, and across bracken-buried heath-land, he soliloquized that nowhere in the world was the countryside more pleasant than in England in the summer months, with its cool, green grass and rippling streams, its vari-green trees reaching up to the dome of heaven. The scientist had travelled in many countries, from the arid wastes of the deserts beyond Cairo, the hard heat of Australia, where pasture is burnt by the rays of the sun and for lack of water during years of drought; the heated moisture of New Zealand, where the hot geyser springs give the countryside the appearance of giant Turkish baths.

"And I think that of all England, nowhere is more lovely than a Surrey lane," he communed. For no reason at all, he recalled a drive in the same car a year before, along a road in the south of France. The green of the hedges had been completely hidden by the thickness of the white dust which covered it; dust which, if the hedge was shaken, came out in choking, enveloping clouds. Alongside the hedge had been a three-feet deep sunken track, winding in its shade. That should have been a stream, rippling on its way to the Mediterranean. It was bone dry, and had been so for months. In the winter it would become, again, a raging torrent. The hedges of this Surrey lane were verdant, the stream which flowed alongside it was no higher and no lower than it had been in winter. There was a balance between winter and summer here, the scientist said to himself, which, however uncomfortable it might be in certain periods, was more to be desired than the drastic contrasts of the winter Playground of the Wealthy.

The car ran out of the lane on to a concrete-based highway. Dr. Manson pulled himself together. He was approaching his second destination of the day. A toot on the horn, and two large gates were thrown open. Once again he drove up a long drive and to a door, this time at the head of a flight of broad stone steps. Once again he was shown into a library; and, as before, there were comings and goings. It was less than an hour when he re-entered his car and departed in the direction of his third destination. A mile on his way, and at a cross-roads, he pulled into the side and consulted a road map, running a map measurer over the route he was following.

"H'm! No need to hurry," he said to himself. "I'll not be able to do anything tonight. Might as well trundle along slowly, have a cup of tea and arrive in time for a dinner and a music-hall, or something." He proceeded to put the plan into operation. As a church clock struck 6 p.m. he arrived in an Essex town.

Ten o'clock next morning saw him setting out on a walking tour that was to take him up to the luncheon hour. In all, he made some half a dozen calls, and if variety is the spice of life the scientist spent a lively morning, for the people to whom he paid visits included two parsons, a solicitor, two aged women who in their heyday had been domestic servants to members of what they themselves referred to as 'gentry families', a prosperous estate agent, and a pedagogue. After each visit, he made brief entries in his note-book. Only once did he evince more than a polite interest in the answers he received. That was after a remark made by the second of the clergymen.

"What!" he said, and looked in surprise at the vicar. "Are you sure of that?"

"Well, sir," was the reply, "I do not know of my own knowledge, but it was given to me by a brother priest in whose word I have complete confidence. Does the fact so much surprise you?"

"I ought not, in my profession, to be surprised at anything, Padre," the scientist replied. "But I must confess that this was most unexpected. Thank you for your courtesy and patience."

The doctor ate lunch in thoughtful silence, and as soon as it was over collected his car and drove to the little village of Dewsley, some five miles out of the town. The car he left parked alongside the pond which stood at one end of the village green. He himself made his way in the direction of the village church, the tower of which stood high above the tops of the thatched cottages and the trees.

A man cutting the grass with the long, sweeping rhythm of the scythe looked up, and stopped his swinging. He laid the scythe against a gravestone, and came forward. "Be yiew a-wanting to see t'old church, sir?" he asked.

"Will you be the sexton here?" Manson countered.

"Man and boy this fifty-five years, sir," the man replied. "And will be come many more years, God willing."

The scientist spoke a few words quietly. The sexton nodded. He led the way to a corner of the churchyard, pointed. Dr. Manson looked. He copied a few words into his note-book.

"You remember?" he asked the man beside him.

"Aye, sir. I 'members very well."

A coin changed hands. The scientist left the yard and walked back to his car. He let in the clutch, accelerated, and retraced his wheel-tracks. Nor did he stop again or slacken until he reached the entrance to his flat in London.

It was the evening of the second day.

The morning of the third day found him in the offices of the Port of London Authority. His visit lasted no more than a quarter of an hour, and left him with a foolscap sheet of paper full of figures. Another hour, and he was closeted with an official of Somerset House. His errand explained, the official produced two forms. "The alpha and the omega," he chuckled.

Dr. Manson, too, chuckled in reply. But the chuckle was a grim one. "It is omega, I think," he said; and smiled at the puzzled look in the eyes of the official.

One more visit remained—to another part of Somerset House which is a little nearer the river and Waterloo Bridge. There, ledgers were laid open for him; from them he copied out a number of entries. Then, after inspecting several bundles of forms, he took up his hat, and, with a word of thanks, walked down the steps to the Embankment below, and, turning left, strode Westminster way—and so on to Scotland Yard, and up to his laboratory.

Save for Wilkins, the assistant, the laboratory was empty. The doctor slipped off his dustcoat and dropped it on the table. He laid his hat on top of it. He lifted the telephone receiver and dialled a number. "Inspector Lawrence, urgently," he demanded.

The inspector's voice came booming back. "Lawrence here . . . oh, is that you, Doctor?"

"Any news, Lawrence?"

"Two trips, Doctor. The evening after, and again this afternoon."

"Where?"

"Kew. You know where the river runs to the ferry entrance to the Gardens? Couldn't do much the first time, you understand. We had to track. But had a man waiting inside the Gardens after that, on the off-chance. They had gone into the Gardens on the first occasion, and we couldn't follow. This time he walked into the Gardens and met a man by the railings which look over the river at the bottom. They talked. He handed something over and walked back to the ferry. He went straight back."

"Good man! Have a second man there, and let him follow. Get him when he leaves the Gardens. Make any excuse, but get him to a station and search him. Your man will have to watch him pretty closely, you understand. And listen, Lawrence. Bring a boat up to Westminster tonight, about ten o'clock. We are going up the river—you and I and Kenway, and one other. I want nobody else. Is that clear? Tie up at the station and come up to the laboratory."

One more telephone call the doctor made before he went in search of the assistant commissioner. Inspector Carruthers an swered the ring in person. "Manson here, Carruthers. Did you make that particular inquiry for which I asked?"

"Yes, Doctor. He did not give notice. Just left. And—"

"No more now, Carruthers. Come along here tomorrow morning at ten o'clock, and I'll tell you all you want to know. Thanks for the trouble." And he rang off.

The assistant commissioner looked up as the door of his room opened. "Hallo, Harry, didn't know you were back." He greeted the appearance of Manson with surprise.

"What luck?" he asked, anxiously.

"The best, Edward. I've got them."

"Them, Harry?"

"That is what I said." He leaned forward and spoke a few words.

"Good heavens!" The monocle fell from the left eye of the assistant commissioner with the ejaculation. "Who are they?"

"All in good time, Edward. There is one more knot to untie. Leave it until tomorrow. But first, I want your authority to do something not in accordance with police etiquette in this country. I would not ask it if it were not imperative and if there was any other way of doing it. Listen."

He spoke rapidly for five minutes. He spoke earnestly, marking off on his long, restless fingers the points of his argument. At the end he sat back and waited the verdict.

The assistant commissioner's face wore a worried and grave expression. He pressed the fingers of his hands together. He pursed his lips, and looked long at the scientist.

"I don't like it, Harry. I don't like it. If it does not come off they'll have the coats off our backs. At the best it is legal trespass. At the worst, it is breaking and entering."

"It *will* come off, Edward. Of that I have not the least doubt. But suppose it does not. Who is to know? If things turn out as I expect, we can get a search warrant and do the thing over again, all nice and legal. The game is worth the risk."

"Who do you propose to take with you?"

"Lawrence, Kenway and Sergeant Billington—the latter for obvious reasons."

"Very well, I'll sanction it. Against my better judgment, mind you."

"Fine! And we will meet tomorrow at ten o'clock, when I will tell you the whole story."

* * * * *

The police launch cast off from the pier at Westminster, and, with navigation lights burning, pushed its way in the moonlight, upstream. Its four occupants sat in the glass-screened cockpit, sheltering from the cool night breeze blowing down the river. For nearly an hour the launch sped its swift way, under Hammersmith Bridge, past Kew, through Richmond and Kingston. Presently, the shape of another bridge loomed up. Dr. Manson leaned over towards the inspector. "There is hardly likely to be any traffic about, is there?" he asked.

"Shouldn't think so, Doctor," was the reply.

"Then as soon as we have shot the bridge I think it would be wise to put out all lights. We do not want any witnesses if we can help it. And I think we might hug the shade of the shore, too."

Inspector Lawrence switched off the lights and steered across to the shore. "You know the bearings, Doctor. Then you had better tell me when to shut off," he said.

The scientist peered ahead up the river. "Steady," he whispered; and after a minute or two, "Now!"

The engine died out. The launch continued, silently, on its way. Its pace grew slowly less, and it was hardly moving when a house-boat loomed up in the near distance.

"Get astern, Kenway, and be prepared to hold her off," whispered Dr. Manson. "And you do the same thing forward, Billington. We must not make a sound for the time being."

The launch drifted, inch by inch, towards the house-boat, until, when it drew level, Kenway and Billington clutched the dwelling's protecting fenders, and held the two vessels close together. Not even the suspicion of a bump had happened.

The doctor and Inspector Lawrence surveyed the house-boat. There was no sign of life aboard. The windows were fitted with heavy wooden covers to prevent unauthorized people from gaining entrance, and the door in the centre of the 100 feet long vessel was securely padlocked through staples which penetrated the door and were bolted on the inside. Without a sound, Dr. Manson, after slipping on a pair of rubber shoes, stepped on to the platform, and cautiously walked round the verandah. He reappeared from the opposite side, and knelt down. "I do not think there is anyone here, Lawrence," he announced. "There is no boat, and the only way to get aboard is by boat. There is no communication from the land. I think we will risk it. Tie up fore and aft, you three, and come aboard."

A moment later the four men were on the deck of the houseboat. Sergeant Billington stepped up to the padlocked door and examined it. "Any other entrance, Doctor?" he asked.

"Yes, Sergeant—a door in the side." The men walked round to it. "That's better, Doctor," announced the sergeant, with satisfaction. "There is more shade here, too." He felt in a pocket and brought out a number of instruments. It became evident now why the scientist had asked for the services of Billington. The sergeant was the Yard's lock expert. He selected, by touch, one of his selection of tools and inserted it in the keyhole. A few seconds of operation, and it was withdrawn. A second attempt fared no better. "Sorry, Doctor, but I daren't show a light to inspect the lock. I'll have to try them one by one."

The next tool, however, did the trick. After a few gentle probings, a click sounded. The sergeant turned the handle and the door opened. "Leave it in the lock, Sergeant," warned Manson.

With the door closed behind them, Inspector Lawrence switched on his torch, and the four men began an inspection of the interior of the houseboat. From the square lobby in which they stood three doors led off. All were locked. Sergeant Billington shone his torch at the keyholes. "Chicken-feed," he said. "Any skeleton key will open them."

He selected a key from his bunch, slipped it into the lock and turned it. The door opened. "The lounge and dining-room," decided Manson. "Keep your torches away from the windows," he warned. "There may be chinks in those shutters. Let's try the next room." This, however, proved no more than a bedroom.

The third room was a small one, also, apparently, used as an occasional bedroom. At the end of it a narrow door opened on to a companionway.

"The way to the top-deck, Doctor," said Kenway. "We can't go up there with the lights."

"What now, Doctor?" asked Lawrence.

For answer, Manson led the way back to the large room which they had first entered. From it another narrow door gave entrance to the kitchen, or galley. An electric stove occupied one corner. Crockery and kitchen utensils were accommodated in a cupboard in another corner. There remained still another door in the room. It, too, was locked. Sergeant Billington inserted a skeleton key, turned, looked puzzled, and withdrew it. He shot the rays of his pencil torch into the keyhole, and muttered.

"Why the devil do they want a lock like this on a kitchen door?" he protested. "It can't lead on to the deck, because this was the part where there was only a narrow slip." He examined his collection of tools, and after another glance into the lock selected one. A few moments' tinkering and the lock turned. The door opened inwards. It guarded no more than a square, cupboard-like space.

"I'll be damned! A blessed storeroom!" said Kenway.

Dr. Manson joined the light of his torch to that from the batteries of Inspectors Lawrence and Kenway. The lights were passed over the wooden sides, along which, high up, a shelf ran and over the hooks intended for the hanging of articles.

"Doesn't make sense," he said. He let his light wander lower until it shone along the floor. "What's the trap-door?" he asked

"Down to the bilge, I expect, Doctor. All these boats have one, you know," replied Lawrence.

Together, the two men lifted the trap. A short ladder led into the darkness below. "May as well go down, I think," the doctor decided; and the four men descended. The bottom was bone dry

"That's pretty good for a boat of this size," Lawrence opined "But why the partition across the bulkhead? Bless me, another door!" he added, as their lights explored the boarding.

"The one we want, I should think," retorted the doctor. "Open it, Billington."

The lock was a simple one. A couple of seconds and the sergeant threw open the door. The torches of the men lighted the interior.

"There you are, Lawrence." The scientist's voice held a note of exulting satisfaction.

In front of the four men was a miniature laboratory. On a bench were set beakers and test tubes, and an electric Bunsen burner.

Chemists' jars of ether, chloroform, and other drug-refining requirements were housed in glass-fronted shelves.

Dr. Manson pointed to two sets of apparatus. "This one is for extracting morphine from the raw opium," he announced; "and this," pointing to the second of them, "for manufacturing heroin from the morphine. It is a replica of the place in Wapping."

"Don't touch a thing," he warned. "Lock the door again, Billington." The sergeant did so, and the men ascended the ladder. Each door in turn was relocked as they passed through, after careful examination had been made to ensure that no sign of their intrusion was left behind. Finally, the intricate lock of the deck-door was refastened; and the men re-entered the police launch.

"Push off, Lawrence, and let her drift a little way before you start the engines," said the scientist.

They were carried by the current, then the engine sprang to life. The boat was turned, and the journey back to Westminster began.

CHAPTER SIXTEEN
ARREST

SIX MEN SAT in a semi-circle round the desk of the assistant commissioner in his room at Scotland Yard. At the desk, Sir Edward Allen sat with Dr. Manson beside him.

"Before we listen to the doctor, gentlemen, I will tell you what I have already put into operation," said the A.C.

"A warrant has been issued for the arrest of Catling on a charge under the Dangerous Drugs Act, and a search warrant has been given to Inspector Lawrence for Catling's houseboat on the Hampton Court reach of the river."

"He has been given no intimation, Sir Edward?" asked Dr. Manson.

"None, Doctor. He is coming up to the Yard at our invitation at twelve o'clock. To allay any suspicion we suggested that Mr. Bosanquet might, if he liked, accompany him. Our excuse is that we hope to be able to learn something of the drug traffic from the fact that Miss Malcolm, his *fiancée*, was an addict. He will then be arrested. The doctor seems to have given into our hands the head of the drug crowd—"

"One of the heads, Sir Edward," interrupted Manson. "I have a second for you yet."

". . . And, more, he has promised to tell us the name of the murderer on the green at Thames Pagnall—and give us proof," added the A.C. "I must say that I know no more of the identity of the person than you do. Now, Doctor, you take over."

"Just a word, first," said Manson, "Have you that list of cricketers for which I asked, Carruthers?" he demanded. The inspector handed over a piece of paper, and the scientist glanced through the list. He smiled slightly, and laid it on the table. He cleared his throat, and began his analysis of the case . . . or cases.

"Now the seeds of the murder at the match were germinated a long time before we knew anything about it," he began. "I shall have to take you to Australia for the start. There, in Melbourne, in 1926, were three gangster leaders. One was a person named Squizzy Morgan, who specialized in robberies on both a grand and small scale, in that he would as soon lift your cycle tyres as your £1000 motor-car or a bank's balance. He was a gunman, too. The second does not matter. But the third was a fellow of less likable habits—for Squizzy was good company and a good fellow, except for his gangster habit. The name of the third man was William Freud—he was mixed up with both the others, and his line of business was sending people to death, or madness, by means of drugs. He created addicts, and sold them the cocaine, the heroin, or the morphine to continue the habit. He did a great business in smuggling drugs to this country. He had agents here, and there was a pretty continuous traffic, as Inspector Lawrence here knows.

"Then, suddenly, it came to an end. Bad blood broke out between Squizzy Morgan and the second gangster. Whether Freud had a hand in it we do not know, but Morgan was shot dead m his bed. His gang started after 'Snowy', a vendetta which can well be understood, since it is usually a rival gangster who does the blotting-out in such circumstances. Freud vanished.

"Now, in spite of all his activities, the Melbourne police had never been able to apprehend Freud on any charge. His nefarious business was well known, but so carefully had he safeguarded himself that the goods were never found on him, nor ever traced to him. However, just before the death of Morgan, Inspector Leland, of the Melbourne C.I.D., had been given charge of the dope investigations; and I think it was partly the probings of Leland, as well as the fear of Morgan's gang, that decided Freud that things were getting too hot for him. He vanished. He was never seen again in Melbourne, or in any other part of Australia; and nobody knew where he had gone. It was supposed, however, that he had migrated to that mecca of gangsters—America."

Dr. Manson paused, and relit his cigarette. Then: "He had not gone to America. He had come to England. You will understand that all this has taken some discovering. The part we knew was when there started up again a traffic in dope in the West End of London. We knew nothing of Freud, you understand. What we *did* know was that, for some reason, the dope-smuggling from the East to us was in full swing again, and thousands of people were becoming addicts. It was on this problem that I was working when the Thames Pagnall murder was committed.

"Now, between these times, Inspector Leland had completed his term of service with the Melbourne Police, and had retired. He apparently decided to carry out what had been a long-cherished idea of his—to spend a long holiday in England. He reached here about the end of March, and began his tour of the country. On June 13 a queer chance took him to Thames

Pagnall—on a Saturday, when a cricket match was in progress on the village green. I suppose most Australians are interested in cricket, more than we are in this country. Leland stopped to watch the play. And there, he saw, it must have been to his amazement, Snowy Freud. That night he entered in his diary the note:

"*Saw S.F. to-day. Strange. Must look into it. May be interesting.*

"Why he did not stop, there and then, and look into it, we are not likely ever to know. Possibly he may have had some other appointment, or was dependent on some mode of transport. But he must have inquired about the cricket, because he had made another note in his diary at the same time for June 21—that was the following Saturday—'*T.P. Saturday*', and the following Saturday found him again at Thames Pagnall, and again watching the cricket. He died there. We know all this now. But you will bear in mind that, on that day, we knew no more than that a man we could not identify had been shot dead by somebody we didn't know.

"I told you three days ago that I had seven vital points in my investigations. Those seven points spelt out the entire story if I could prove them. The first of the seven came at this present stage of which I am speaking. I was quite certain that the man had been shot, not accidentally, but deliberately. Inspector Carruthers, telling me of the complete lack of identifiable matter, detailed the things found on this tourist. Most of you are now familiar with this first point, but for the benefit of Kenway and Lawrence, I may explain that this man, touring round the country, had only a few shillings on him, no ticket, no letters to identify him, no cheque-book—in fact nothing at all which any man going round the country would have in his possession. He did, however, have a letter inviting him to spend a week-end with a family named Smith. This was of little help, however, for the address had been neatly cut off—to put away for safety, of course. All this convinced me that the means of identity had been taken away from the body. And, since a man usually keeps his money, letters, and so on, in a wallet, the robbery seemed to me to have been of a wallet. That, obviously, meant that the man had been murdered, since only the murderer would have any interest in taking away all the proofs of identity. So we now had the murder of an unknown man, by an equally unknown man; and all the usual police channels to trace the identity of the dead man had failed.

"Up to now I had only had Inspector Carruthers' description of the entries in the diary. He had merely said that they showed that the man had been in Yorkshire, Nottingham and Kingston areas. But while with the inspector, the following day, I seized the opportunity to see the actual entries. I also had an opportunity of examining the man's clothes. Now, the atmospheric contents of a man's clothes are, as often as not, an open book to his surroundings. In the hands of science, they tell the story of his habits, his work, his play, and many other things. Sergeant Merry and I went thoroughly through the diary and the clothes; and we found one or two curious things. So much so that I at once wirelessed a message to the Melbourne C.I.D. in these words:

"Wanted, name of man beginning with L who sailed for England probably March. Habitually carried revolver. Resident in Melbourne. Here on holiday."

Inspector Carruthers, who had been listening with a marked personal interest, now interrupted. "But why, Doctor?" he asked. "What were the facts which made you radio Melbourne?"

The scientist looked across at Merry, and from him to the inspector, and smiled. "Let us leave that for the present, Carruthers," he said. "I will explain it later. It is, in matter of fact, *POINT TWO.*

"The answer from Melbourne soon reached me. 'L' was probably Leland, a former C.I.D. officer there, it said. I wirelessed again, and received in answer the fingerprints of Leland. We now knew who was the dead man. But we still had not the slightest clue to the murderer. There was, however, a guide. If Leland was surprised to see S.F., and thought it strange, and likely to prove interesting, it seemed to me that S.F. must be an Australian, also. It might be, of course, that Leland had met someone in England, and suddenly come across him again. But I could not see how that could be regarded as strange. On the other hand, to see on the cricket pitch, in an English village, someone last seen in Australia, was certainly strange. Moreover, I could think of only one reason for 'may be interesting' being used by a detective officer—I concluded that it meant that S.F. was a member of the criminal class. This was quickly confirmed by Melbourne, who said that the only S.F. they knew was Snowy Freud, head of a dope gang, and that Leland was in charge of dope investigations.

"This came as a complete, though welcome, surprise to me. You have already heard that before Thames Pagnall I was searching into dope addiction and supplies. Now I had a man murdered in a village, and a man known to be a dope gangster in Australia involved, somehow or other, in same. In other words, the dope gangster was in England.

"Now, why should Snowy Freud murder Leland at the match? Bear in mind that nothing had ever been proved against Freud in Australia. He had never been in the hands of the police, in the true meaning of the phrase, and nothing had ever been found to connect him with dope, although everyone knew quite well that he was the leader of the dope gang. *Therefore, he had no need to murder Leland to avoid being arrested and sent to Australia. Leland had nothing on him from the past.*

"Why, then, did he kill Leland, who could not harm him?"

The assistant commissioner coughed. "If I had to hazard an opinion, Doctor, I should say that Freud was engaged in the drug traffic over here, but was masquerading under another name, and in an innocent guise. The one person whose inquiries could expose him, and ruin his business, was Leland—alive."

The scientist nodded. "That was the way I reasoned it myself, A.C.," he agreed. "And it was the first glimmering I had that Thames Pagnall and the West End drug trade were associated. I was investigating not two mysteries, but one. We have, however, somewhat over-run ourselves. Before we had identified S.F. as Freud we were looking for S.F. in Thames Pagnall.

"We knew from the missing wallet that S.F. must have been in the village. We knew that Leland had seen him there one Saturday and had returned there on the following Saturday to check him up. And we knew, by inference, that the cricket had something to do with it. So we checked up all the cricketers with 'F' in their name. None of them was implicated. The inquest gave us no assistance at all. I decided on the experiment of reconstructing the murder at the scene of the shooting. I need not worry you with the full details, but merely say that by taking the angles of the wound in the back, I decided that the firing point had been from a height of eight feet at a point some forty feet to the left of the bungalow of Mr. Bosanquet. Now, that spot was open road, and two explosions had come from somewhere down that road. Except for the eight feet height, I should have accepted those explosions as shots from a car. The measurements were open to question in my mind, for they were made with Constable Lambert lying squarely on his back in the deck-chair. Few men lie dead flat on their backs. Merry and I secured the photographs so excellently, and so kindly, taken by Mr. Bosanquet on behalf of the police. We examined them.

"It will be well known to you, of course, that the depth of a man's body, when photographed from an angle, in brilliant sunshine, against a background, must throw a shadow on to that background. The lower the sun in the sky, the greater will be the width of the shadow on the shady side. Merry and I computed the angle of the sun's striking on the chair, and we took those excellent photographs, snapped from either side of the chair, and measured, microscopically, the shadows. At once we were conscious of a queer contradiction.

"Measured in conjunction with the photographs from directly in front of the man, the two side views demonstrated the shadows *to be widest on the wrong side of the body, in association with the direction of the sun.* The only explanation to fit that fact could be that the man was leaning to one side. That, of course, altered the direction of the firing point at which we had arrived. Merry and I settled down to work out the new position, taking the relative widths of the shadow line. It left the height still at between eight and nine feet, but altered the width between shot and firing point by not less than thirty-three feet and not more than forty feet, allowing a small margin for error."

The Chief Constable suddenly sat upright. "But surely, Doctor, that puts it slap bang in the middle of the bungalow garden of Mr. Bosanquet."

"It certainly did, Colonel. And now you see the impossibility of the thing. There were five people in that garden. They were there from the time the match started until it finished. Not one of them left. They were, and still are, an absolute alibi for each other. How could one of them fire a shot without the others, or one of the others, knowing? One of them was Mr. Catling. Another was Miss Malcolm. I put Carruthers to cross-examine them all, thoroughly. Note the sequel. Mr. Watkins remembers, ultimately, that he saw Leland lean forward as the cricketers came out of the tents, and thought that he also saw a man near him. He was not sure, because he had not his glasses, but thinks that Miss Malcolm saw the incident.

"Carruthers tells Catling this, and says that he is asking Miss Malcolm if she remembers it, and if she can identify the person at whom Leland was looking, since she was watching the field from the side of Mr. Watkins. That night Catling takes Miss Malcolm to a night-club and next morning, a few hours before she was to see Carruthers, she is dead—poisoned by heroin. Catling, we know, lied in saying that she was a drug addict, and had been one for some time. And on the cups in her flat was a fingerprint identical with the one which had been left on the deck-chair in which Leland died. Prior to this we had been presented with a heroin-distilling plant, with a dead man beside it, in Wapping. The man was identified as one who had been seen frequently to run up to the Wapping Stairs, near the warehouse, with a motor-boat.

"Days later, after we had failed to trace the boat, Miss Malcolm dies. The point arose whether Catling could have called at her flat, poisoned her, and then driven home to Thames Pagnall. It was good circumstantial evidence, in view of his lying about her alleged drug habit. Carruthers' inquiries as to whether Catling's car had reached Thames Pagnall at such an hour as would make the times agree with our hypothesis did, in fact, do so. The chauffeur gave the time he heard Catling return as 5.15 a.m. Was it unusual for him to return at that time? The chauffeur did not know. He had been in the job only a couple of days. He had been going to drive Catling to the club, but hadn't finished a job which Catling had particularly wanted done: he was painting a houseboat and a launch. Sacrilege, Carruthers called it, to paint over good oak. That night, Inspector Lawrence collected a couple of boatmen who had regularly seen the motor-boat which came to Wapping Stairs. Together, we went to the river stretch on which Catling's houseboat is moored, and the men identified the boat, still only half-painted. You now know what happened when subsequently we searched the houseboat itself.

"So now we knew that Catling was linked up with the drug traffic. We knew, also, that something Miss Malcolm *might* have seen was such that she had to be put out of all reach of questioning. We knew that Catling was concerned in her death, because he had lied about her drugging. He had to lie, because some reason had to be advanced for her being found poisoned by heroin. We knew that Snowy Freud was in it, because we had his fingerprints on the deck-chair and on the girl's cups. You see how the cases were now falling together. Yes. Carruthers?"

For some minutes Inspector Carruthers had been nearly bursting with impatience to get in a word. Twice he had opened his mouth to speak, only to find no pause in the doctor's even tones into which to break. Now Dr. Manson waited his comment.

"You are going wrong somewhere, Doctor," he announced.

The Scotland Yard men looked up, startled. It was something new to them to hear Dr. Manson told that he was off his track when he was outlining a case against his suspect. They had been so often disconcerted in their attempts to find a fault in his reasoning that they had long given up the attempt as impossible of achievement. Only too well they knew that the scientist never talked until he was cast-iron sure.

"And where am I wrong, Carruthers?" asked the doctor, quietly.

"It wasn't Catling, Doctor. His fingerprints are not the same as the other two, and not the same as those we know to be Freud's. I've tested them."

Dr. Manson eyed the triumphant inspector, a twinkle in his eyes. "And when, Carruthers, did I say that Catling is the man? I am, perhaps, a little to blame; I have not kept to chronological order, because to do so would make the story a little more involved. I have gone past the stages of my investigation in order that we might conclude Mr. Catling's first-hand connection with Thames Pagnall. Inspector Carruthers, remembering that I am placing the murder on the head of Snowy Freud, says that Catling is not Freud because his prints do not match up. And Carruthers is correct. Catling is not Snowy Freud. But, again, I point out that he shared, or connived, in the murder of the girl.

"Even so, we still have the proved fact—by fingerprint—that Freud was on that cricket green. Then who is Freud? Of the people on the lawn of the bungalow, from where, if our scientific calculations were correct, the shot was fired, we have now disposed of Mr. Catling. You have also exonerated Mr. Bosanquet of being Freud. He produced his birth certificate. He was at Oxford as long as ten years ago. Sergeant Willoughby was at Oxford; he had a friend, one 'Stinky', who had been up at Wadham during the same term as Bosanquet. Stinky recollects Bossy, as he calls him, perfectly; in fact Bossy had nearly got Stinky sent down— he couldn't fail to remember a man who had done that. Not only did he know Bosanquet, but he knew, through his aunt, Bosanquet's mother. Ten years ago Snowy Freud was in Australia, and had not, up to then, ever been out of Australia. So that, on the very face of it, ruled out Bosanquet.

"Now, I do not, as a general habit, accept statements of that kind without some confirmation. I hope that neither of you here, nor Sergeant Willoughby, will ever do so. Hearsay is like what the soldier told the girl—it is not evidence. I spent three days on a trip round various places. I went to my old friend the Dean of Wadham College. Certainly, he said, Bosanquet was up there. He was, in fact, a nuisance about the place. We called in the Master. He, too, confirmed Bosanquet's three years at he college. From there I went to Godalming, to Charterhouse School. Bosanquet, as Willoughby had said, had been there too. They also recollected him perfectly, and were very glad when he went up to Oxford. I went on to Chelmsford, where the family had lived—actually to Dewsley, a village a few miles out of town. Yes, I found that ten years ago he was living there; he was living here twenty years ago, when Freud was still in Australia.

"I am telling you this in order that you may see the advantage of testing, thoroughly, every bit of information you are told by word of mouth.

"Now, let me hark back to the point at which I learned the identity of Snowy Freud—knew it, without any shadow of doubt; the identity, therefore, of the murderer on the green. It was that day in this very room, when Inspector Carruthers gave us, almost verbatim, his interviews with four of the five people who had been at the bungalow. Think it out while I have a rest from talking and light up a cigar."

He busied himself with a cigar-cutter, for the scientist was a connoisseur in cigars, and lighted none until judicious and accurate opening of the end allowed it to draw evenly and slowly. From time to time he glanced at his colleagues. A little smile flickered round his lips but never in the eyes of him, those eyes in which was the hard light, like the glint off steel when the sun strikes it.

"Something that I said, Doctor?" asked Carruthers, ingenuously.

"Something that you *said* was said," replied Manson. "Incidentally, there were two somethings, and they made numbers three and four in the seven vital points."

Superintendent Jones heaved his bulk upright in his chair. He chuckled. "Hoist Doctor . . . own petard," he rumbled. " 'Limination . . . only way . . . doctor says so. . . . Let's 'liminate 'em one by one. . . . Then that's the answer."

A ripple of laughter ran round the Yard men, and came, also, from the Chief Constable of Surrey, to whom the elimination theory of Dr. Manson was equally a legend in detection.

"Right," said the assistant commissioner; but there was a Doubting Thomas inflexion in his voice. "We'll do it; but it sounds too easy to me! Who is the first to go?"

"Miss Malcolm," put in Inspector Carruthers, promptly. "Because I never interviewed her at all, and therefore she could not have said anything."

"I'll take out Mrs. Bosanquet, because she can't be Freud, she being a woman," decided the assistant commissioner. "What about you, Merry?"

The deputy scientist laughed. "Count me out," he said, "because I know the answer."

"Then there is Mr. Bosanquet, who has lived in this country man and boy, so can't be Freud of Australia," put in Carruthers as a second shot. "Then there is only one left—"

"Old Mr. Watkins, by heaven!" roared the chief constable. "Well, gol' darn it, I'd never have believed it! . . ."

He paused, and a look of comical astonishment spread over his face. His bottom jaw dropped open. "But, dammit," he said, "I've known him since he was a boy. Can't be him."

"But . . . but . . ." The assistant commissioner looked round. "We've eliminated the whole ruddy lot." He slipped his monocle into a perfectly good left eye and stared hard at the scientist. "There's nobody left," he challenged.

Dr. Manson looked up at last. The smile had gone from his lips. The steel in his eyes was even more chilly than before. He addressed the assistant commissioner. "What time do you make it, Sir Edward?" he asked.

"Time?" The A.C. stared. "Eleven forty-two," he replied.

"And we are going to arrest Catling at twelve o'clock . . . ah well . . . the comedy is ended."

He turned to Superintendent Jones.

"Have you that blank warrant for which I asked, Jones?" he said.

The superintendent nodded, and produced it from a pocket. He spread it out on the table in front of him.

"Then you may as well fill in the name."

Jones drew a fountain-pen from his pocket, unscrewed the cap, put it on the other end of the pen, and bent over the warrant.

Four men waited in expectant silence.

"The name, Doctor?" asked the superintendent.

"Alfred Bosanquet," replied the doctor, quietly.

There was a stunned silence. Four men sat as motionless as though they had been turned suddenly to stone. Outside, the muted sound of a clerk, tapping on a typewriter in an adjoining room, could be heard. For full thirty seconds there was no movement. Superintendent Jones sat, the pen in his hand still hovering over the face of the warrant beneath. The assistant commissioner was the first to find his voice.

"B—B—Bosanquet, Doctor?" he queried. "B—but surely, we've . . . I mean to say, Charterhouse and Oxford."

"Alfred Bosanquet."

The scientist said the name again, each letter articulated as clearly as though it had been cut off from the others with a knife.

He paused.

"The last visit I paid in the village of Dewsley was to a churchyard—*to the grave in which Alfred Bosanquet, of Charterhouse and Oxford, was buried seven years ago,*" he said, and the chill in the voice of him made the assistant commissioner shiver, as though with cold.

* * * * *

The time was five hours later. The same company were assembled again in the room of the assistant commissioner. That chief passed a box of cigars round, and the men lit up. He waited until the smoke was rising in six spiral curls. Then . . .

"Did you find the rifle, Doctor?"

"Yes, Sir Edward. Where I expected—under a floorboard in the room behind the dormer window in the roof of the bungalow. I knew that the shot had been fired from there. The calculations of Merry and myself were accurate to a foot."

"Silencer, of course?"

A nod from the scientist.

"But how did you break the alibi, Doctor? Everyone said he never left them." The chief constable asked the question.

"Did you ever read Poe's *The Murders in the Rue Morgue*, Colonel? The situation turned on whether anyone had gone into the building. Everybody, you will remember, agreed that nobody had gone in. Poe argued that someone *must* have done so; and if he had not been noticed, it must be because it was someone *who would be expected to enter*, and of whose entrance no notice would, therefore, be taken. The hypothesis, as you know, was correct. It was a postman. Nobody would take any notice of a postman, who went into the building as a right, two or three times a day. The same argument was in my mind. A man had been shot from there. I *knew* he had been shot from there. Ergo, somebody there had shot him. Somebody must have left the lawn to shoot him. If that someone had not been missed, then it was because he was engaged in some necessary duty which would not be counted as absence, in the meaning of the word. Bosanquet, it seems now, had a few moments' trouble with his stomach—at the time that the shot killing Leland was fired.

"He has admitted taking the chair and placing it for Leland, after Leland had recognized and spoken to him that afternoon; and, at a suitable opportunity, had slipped upstairs and shot. He was, by the way, a crack shot with a rifle."

"But what first made you suspect him?" asked the assistant commissioner.

"When he said that he heard only one backfire—for the explosions *were* backfires. Everyone else heard two. Yet they were said to be all together. I asked myself why should Bosanquet be the only one to hear a *single* explosion? The answer was simple deduction—because he was inside the house at the time—and well inside."

"Doctor!" Inspector Carruthers leaned forward towards the scientist. "You said this morning that something which I said was said in my interviews with the four people at the bungalow gave you the identity of the murderer without a shadow of a doubt. What was it?"

"Carruthers, there were two things said which gave me the name. They made points three and four of the seven. Give me your note-book."

The inspector handed it over, and Dr. Manson searched through it. He read two sentences. "Take nothing for granted at any time, gentlemen," he warned. "That is how I found the stolen identity of Alfred Bosanquet, alias William Freud. The man was brilliantly clever. He knew that if he came here he must have a cast-iron identity in case of trouble. I do not know how he came to pick on poor Alfred Bosanquet. He must either have lived near there at some time, or gone very carefully into the family, because he knew all the family history. He wrote to Somerset House for the birth certificate, gave an excellently forged excuse, paid the fee, and, of course, he got it. And there are, altogether, nearly a thousand Bosanquets in the country. Who was going to check up on the name, when the man has his birth certificate in his hands and his scholastic record, letter for letter?"

"And Miss Malcolm, what did she see?"

"She saw Bosanquet with Leland on the green. When Bosanquet heard from Catling what Watkins had said, he knew that there was grave danger that Miss Malcolm might, quite innocently, give him away. And, since he was the chemist who prepared heroin with Catling—they were partners in the drug racket—the whole of the drug business was likely either to come out or be broken up.

"That would have been the ruin of Bosanquet. My visits to the dock people showed that the importing business was no more than a cloak for the drug business. The income tax which he paid, according to the tax people, did not show sufficient income to allow him to live in the state he kept up. So Catling had to agree to the plot to get rid of the girl. He drugged her coffee at the 'Olive Grove', to cause her to go home. He put her in the taxi, to make sure she went. Bosanquet went, at the time arranged, to the girl's flat."

"There is only one other point, Doctor," said the A.C. "You knew from Watkins that Miss Malcolm had seen someone with

Leland that morning. But how did you know that it was Bosanquet he was with?"

"That was point six," replied Manson; and explained it.

"Well, all's well that ends well." The assistant commissioner rose, and in doing so wrote off the murder and the drug cases. "It's another feather in the cap of science," he said.

L'ENVOI
THE SEVEN POINTS

AUTHORS' NOTE: It has been our practice in the "Manson Books" to present the reader with an opportunity to solve the riddle of deduction. We have never, at any time, 'pulled anything out of the bag' at the last minute—a fact upon which three distinguished reviewers of books have most kindly commented; and have commended.

In *Murder Isn't Cricket* there were, as has been emphasized, seven vital points—in detection-writing jargon, clues. For those who did not succeed in deciphering them, we append the seven.

Clue No. 1
This was the proof to Dr. Manson that the death of Leland was murder; and was subsequently revealed in Chapter Five.

Clue No. 2
This appeared in Chapter Two. Dr. Manson, after reading the entries in the dead man's diary, and examining, scientifically, his clothes, wirelessed Melbourne for the name of any man beginning with the letter L who had sailed for England. The entries read:

"B. told me that I would find the Yorkshire Moors as adventurous as I should like. Too right he was," etc.,

and:

"Kingston—King's Stone. H.C. again. Fair bonza."

Now, the expression 'too right' is essentially the Australian equivalent of the American 'You're telling me'; and 'bonza' is even more Australian. One can hardly chat to an Aussie soldier, today, who doesn't think that London is either 'bonza' or is 'dinkum'. From the language, therefore, Dr. Manson was certain that Leland had come from Australia. Hence his radio. Chapter Seven.

In the examination of the clothes of the dead man, Dr. Manson found dust crystals which, when water was added to them and stirred, produced a red liquid—Chapter Seven. He had decided, already, that the man was an Australian. He accordingly consulted a book on geology. The 'red rain' of the city of Melbourne is due to the red dust from the interior at certain seasons, and is a well-known freak of weather.

Clues Nos. 3 and 4

These, as Dr. Manson stated in his explanation in Chapter Sixteen gave him the identity of the murderer without any shadow of doubt.

Bosanquet, interviewed by Inspector Carruthers, said in Chapter Twelve that he did not think he could help any further. He had already told the police and the coroner all that he could tell. He realized that he had placed himself in an unfortunate position, since he had been alone with the dead man for some minutes. (Clue No. 3.)

Since the man had been dead an hour or more before the arrival of Bosanquet, how could Bosanquet's being alone with the body place him 'in an unfortunate position'? He did not know that the police were aware that the body had been robbed of a wallet. Only a man with guilty knowledge, trying to hedge himself round in security, the scientist argued, would have made such a statement.

But the more important, and fatal, slip was made by him in the same interview when, in Chapter Twelve, he said, for Clue No. 4:

"And as for Crombie killing him, I don't reckon old George knows anything about guns. No, I still think Leland was shot from the road by accident."

At this stage of the investigation only the police actually engaged in the case were aware that the dead man *HAD BEEN IDENTIFIED AS LELAND*. Bosanquet's use of the name could only have been due to guilty knowledge.

Clue No. 5

In working out anew (after tests from the photographs of the dead man in the chair) the angles obtained from the reconstruction of the crime, Dr. Manson and Merry made the difference, due to the leaning position of Leland, 'not less than 33 feet and not more than 40 feet'. The previous angles had placed the firing point at 40 feet from the left-hand side of the Bosanquet bungalow.

The new figures put the firing point in the centre, or slightly to the left of the centre, of the bungalow. That, in the eyes of the doctor, was scientific, and incontrovertible evidence. Chapter Twelve.

Clue No. 6

This was the point which made it clear to Dr. Manson that Bosanquet had been on the green when the match started, and had obviously seen, and been seen by, Leland, and must have arranged or noted Leland's position.

Inspector Carruthers had sent, at the doctor's request, the actual negative of the film taken by Bosanquet of the dead man in the chair. In examining it—(Chapter Fourteen)—the scientist noted that the 'shots' of Leland were preceded by the following pictures, taken over an interval:

1. Landscape of river and country, with figures and a car in the foreground.

2. Groups of people having tea in a garden.

3. A dozen 'shots' of a child in a pram.

4. Cricketers walking in couples.

5. The dead man's pictures, taken for the police.

Carruthers, in reply to a question, stated in Chapter Fourteen that the child in the pram belonged to people named Brightwell and the pictures had been taken between ten and eleven o'clock on Saturday morning.

Therefore, the shots of the cricketers walking out must have been taken by Bosanquet on the Saturday, and he must have been on the green to do so.

Dr. Manson realized, later, that the man who was seen by Watkins and Miss Malcolm with Leland must, therefore, have been Bosanquet. He also realized that Leland's presence at the match must have been because he had seen Bosanquet there on the previous Saturday. Carruthers, asked for a list of the men who had been playing the previous week, produced it—(Chapter Sixteen). Bosanquet had been one of the players.

Clue No. 7

This was the clue that led up to the arrest of Catling, and showed his association with Bosanquet. Wapping police had identified the dead man in the burned warehouse as the chauffeur of a motor-boat who used to call at the wharf near the warehouse.

Some days later, Carruthers, reporting on Catling's arrival home on the night of the murder of Miss Malcolm, stated that Catling's chauffeur did not know the customary hours of Catling's homecoming, *because he had been in the job only two days*. He did not drive Catling to the club because he was engaged on an urgent job of painting a houseboat and a motor-launch. Inspector Carruthers thought it sacrilege that any man should paint an oak-wooded boat—(Chapter Fourteen). Dr. Manson took the view that the only reason such a painting was being done *was to disguise the craft*. Hence the taking of the two boatmen to the scene, one evening, when they recognized the boat as the one which customarily called at the wharf.

Suspicion became certainty when it was revealed that the previous chauffeur of Catling had not given notice, but 'had just left'—(Chapter Fifteen).

THE END

Printed in Great Britain
by Amazon